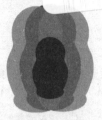

# THE STORY OF US

Dispute it April 22.
Dept - 800 - 564 - 0716

ALSO BY CATHERINE HERNANDEZ

*Crosshairs*
*Scarborough*

CHILDREN'S BOOKS
*Where Do Your Feelings Live?*
(illustrated by Myriam Chery)

*I Promise* (illustrated by Syrus Marcus Ware)

*M Is for Mustache* (illustrated by Marisa Firebaugh)

# THE STORY OF US

## CATHERINE HERNANDEZ

HARPER**AVENUE**

Published by Harper Avenue, an imprint of HarperCollins Publishers Ltd

First edition

HarperCollins Publishers Ltd
Bay Adelaide Centre, East Tower
22 Adelaide Street West, 41st Floor
Toronto, Ontario, Canada
M5H 4E3

*www.harpercollins.ca*

Library and Archives Canada Cataloguing in Publication

Title: The story of us / Catherine Hernandez.
Names: Hernandez, Catherine, 1977- author.
Identifiers: Canadiana (print) 20220405220 | Canadiana (ebook) 20220405239
ISBN 9781443459754 (softcover) | ISBN 9781443459761 (EPUB)
Classification: LCC PS8615.E75 S76 2023 | DDC C813/.6—dc23

Printed and bound in the United States of America
22 23 24 25 26 LBC 5 4 3 2 1

*To my ates, documented and undocumented,*
*who have cared for our children and elders.*

*To my queer and Trans elders who have paved a path*
*for me and my family.*

*This book is for you.*

# AUTHOR'S NOTE

Depicted in this book are ways in which we hurt each other that may hurt you while you're reading it. Please take care of yourself the best way you know how.

# 1

Hello? Hi. Liz? Can you hear me? Can you see me if you look into my eyes? See the spirit in this infant body? I know you're distracted by my sweet smell and the plump of my cheeks. If I wasn't swaddled this tightly I would try and wave. Get your attention. Or . . . maybe that would make things worse. Then you might be distracted by my advanced motor skills. Ugh! I want to sigh in frustration, but even sighing has made you all coo at me before, and really, what I need from you is your focus. You, more than anyone.

What I'm saying isn't out of the blue. I think you've known it all along, but too many have pushed the idea to the fringes of folklore and myth. All that nonsense about babies and past lives.

Maybe, while doting over the miniature edges of my fingernails, you caught a glimpse of me, the true me, the past me. Maybe you watched me sleep in my first twenty-four hours and you wondered at my expressions, the frowns, the smiles, the knitting brow, wondered how I could be anxious when surely I had never experienced anything but my mother's heartbeat and the warmth of her womb. Maybe you had a sense there was more that I knew. But as days pass, you've noticed this less. That is why I need you to listen. The former me, the real me, is fading by the second and there are things I remember, at this very moment and never will again, that I need to share with you.

Yes, this is a lot to take in. But we're in a sweet spot, you and me. I'm leaving this in-between world, once housed by the shell of my mother and her body memories, and you . . . you are leaving your memories behind too. That's why my mother is here taking care of you. I know you're leaving the world of order for one that rarely makes any sense at all and my mother's purpose in your life is to keep you safe during this transition.

I did mention limited time. I should be more clear. I'm talking days, not years, okay? And then there's the interruptions of diaper changes, bothersome visitors, bath time and my own hunger—not to mention all that burping business—so we should get started.

I think it's best we map out the body of my mother first. To you, it may seem pretty simple. Like . . . there's her head. Those are her arms, her legs. Whatever. But in my in-between world, the map is more like this:

*The back of her skull.* This is what touched the tailbone of her mother, my Lola, with every contraction, during a lengthy and difficult birth at the humble district hospital. The nurse encouraged Lola to pace the hallways. She did hip circles. She squatted over the toilet. Nothing was working. Ma was showing all the signs of being a posterior-facing baby. Head down but facing the wrong way. What finally helped the labour progress was the nurse standing Lola upright and presenting her with a stepping stool.

"Put your leg here. Here. On top. The other leg back in a lunge. Yes. Okay. When you feel the contraction, I want you to lean forward for me." Lola moaned in pain at the nurse's suggestion. "Sige na. I know it will be painful, but it's this or surgery." She was right. The lunges helped to contort the shape of Lola's uterus, allowing my mother to corkscrew into position and crown. No surgery needed.

If you're wondering how I know all of this, let me explain. I am small, but I have lived an enormous life well before this year of my birth, 2001. In fact, I have lived for years as a seed in the ovaries of my mother while my mother gestated in the body of my Lola Daning. I was a dream of a dream back then, a nesting doll of possibility. Before I had my own organs, I listened to the simultaneous beating of my grandmother's heart (bass heavy, slow, sure) and my mother's heart (quick, excited) in an odd mismatch of a song. When my mother emerged into the cold air of the world, the year was 1972 in San Marcelino, in the province of Zambales, Philippines. The nurse placed my tightly wrapped mother into the arms of Lola Daning and Lola said, "Happy birthday, Mary Grace."

Mary Grace, I thought to myself back then. I like that. Of course, since she was Filipina, this name was rarely used unless there was paperwork to be filled out. She was destined to be called a combination of Mare, Gracey and, more commonly, MG.

MG's father, my Lolo Ruben, was not present. He was working the oil fields in Saudi Arabia, eagerly awaiting word of MG's birth. That is why, once Lola Daning was well enough to brush her hair back into a ponytail and rub on a bit of pink lipstick, the nurse snapped a Polaroid of her with the newborn baby. While the nurse checked on MG's latch onto Lola's breast, the Polaroid sat on the night table next to the bed and processed into full colour. In the photo, my grandmother wore a weary smile. In her arms was my mother with her face swollen and her eyes shiny from ointment. You couldn't see me, but I was there too. I tried to smile for the picture. I think I blinked.

Lolo Ruben received the photo one month later, along with a series of other letters meant for him. They were bound together by a rubber band and held in the foreman's office, where all correspondence was kept until the monthly mail pickup. Each bundle contained letters my Lola wrote him detailing what was happening back in San Marcelino. Thin paper. Felt tip pen. Some of the ink pooled where Lola's pen lingered too long over what details to include and not include. How the three older children were doing in school. How excited they were for the new baby's arrival (even their youngest child, who they assumed would take it hard). Pictures of Lola Daning showing off her pregnant belly. Pictures of my Tito Onofre's first communion. A charcoal sketch of the Rizal monument by my Tita Fay, which earned her the Outstanding Visual Artist award. The outline of my Tito Mike's tiny hand on a heart-shaped piece of construction paper. And finally, in the whitest, least tattered envelope, the Polaroid of Lola and MG in the hospital.

There are details about how Lolo Ruben received these letters, how he lived his life in Saudi Arabia, that my mother does not know. Will never know. Those places people go to be a hero, to be an Overseas Filipino Worker, are all places constructed only through the imagination. These imagined places are the places our loved ones go for months, even years at a time. What Ma did know is that each time her father, like all OFWs, returned home—if he returned at all—he looked a little more worn down, a little older, a little more like a mystery.

This is why my mother pieces together dreams of her father each time she brushes her hair. This is why each time the bristles caress the back of her skull, she adds those dreams to the real memory of seeing Lolo Ruben arriving at the doorstep of their sari sari store and wondering, *Who is this stranger?*

*Her hands.* There are countless sensations MG remembers through the touch of her hands.

Age two. The family apartment sat above the sari sari store. Front window, with one green curtain (pattern: faint gold outline of peacocks facing one another, or was it more like the peacocks were facing away from one another?) to block out the hustle and bustle from Olongapo Road below. Tricycle. Tricycle. Jeepney. Jeepney. Jeepney. Bus. Truck. Back window, with white lace curtain (one tiny corner stained by ketchup? spaghetti sauce?) just above a small metal sink. In the corner beside the kitchen sink, there was a Tower of Things. Random things. Things that needed tending to but became even more random and grew in number and height the more tired and exhausted Lola was from raising four children on her own and running the shop downstairs. One day, when Lola was busy washing the birch flowers for that night's laing with rice, the Tower of Things fell to the ground. Lola stood still for a moment and closed her eyes.

One long breath, in and out.

The silence was broken by the sound of Ma dragging a chair to the counter to begin rebuilding the Tower of Things. MG rebuilt the tower to the same exact specifications. At the base was the blue plate that was not fit to eat off (the tiniest crack in the porcelain that threatened to break at any second). Then there was another blue plate (same make, slightly smaller) that was fit to eat off but hadn't been washed. Then a stainless-steel mixing bowl. A series of red plastic cups from Jollibee. Empty box of SkyFlakes crackers. Half-empty box of SkyFlakes crackers. Serving dish that was clean. Empty tin of instant coffee. Empty bottle of powdered milk. Ma even put the bottle on its side, exactly how she remembered it. Using the tips of her toddler fingers she pushed each object slightly to give the tower its wonky balance.

"Ay, my goodness!" Lola chuckled, delighting in Ma's eagerness to help, before pressing her lips into Ma's toddler face. Lola and Ma had a game, where Lola would blow up her cheeks and let Ma pop them like a balloon. The sound of Lola's cheeks deflating made Ma giggle uncontrollably. But this time, when Ma did it, her palm could feel a strange tremor in Lola's jaw. This tremor—a symptom of early-onset Parkinson's disease—would grow in intensity and frequency, spreading throughout Lola's body over the rest of Lola's life.

Age five. Ma liked to visit her uncle whose work shed shared a yard with the sari sari shop. Tito Crisanto was a sculptor. His specialty was the creation of religious icons for church celebrations. In his work shed stood no fewer than a dozen Mother Marys and Jesuses in various stages of development and tableaus. Some were missing ears. Some were still undressed. Some were crying to the heavens. Some reached out their arms at a perfect angle for devout worshippers to place a strand of sampaguita flowers on after a church service. When each sculpture was completed, Ma would admire their complex detail. Realistic tears pooled at the ducts of glass eyes. Graceful tapestry draped over their shoulders. Even their palms were imprinted with creases and lifelines.

"MG." Tito Crisanto gestured with a downward wave at Ma standing by the door of his shed. "Stand here and don't touch anything." Ma came closer to his workbench, willing her lanky arms to stay still despite her curiosity. Tito Crisanto cleared the surface of all wires, knives and eyeballs before placing a cloth bundle on it. Inside the bundle were several other bundles, each containing hair of different colours, textures and lengths.

"Is this real hair?" Ma asked.

Tito tilted his bottle-cap glasses downward to regard the young girl. "Yes. I collect it from the barber. Now open your hand." He took fine hair from one of the bundles and cut the strands to half an inch before placing them in Ma's palm. The hair was so fine she had to hold her breath, in case the gentle wisps would fly away. Maybe the hair had belonged to a child, or even a toddler. Maybe it was their first haircut. She imagined them, sitting on a plastic stool by the edge of the road while the barber went to work on their head, jeepneys whizzing by just inches away.

Tito applied a line of sweet-smelling glue along the eyes of a stout Santo Niño statue. He gestured for Ma to come closer and she did, ever so slowly, with the tresses threatening to take flight. Using a tweezer, Tito took each strand and adhered it to the eyes to make lashes.

At the last strand, Tito pointed the tweezers towards Ma. "Do you want to try?" At first, she shook her head no, worried she would ruin his masterpiece. But he took her hand and guided her in the process. Once the eyes were finished Ma clapped her hands together and squealed.

"Shhh, anak," Tito Crisanto whispered playfully, his finger to his lip. "Now that he is complete, he doesn't like loud noises."

Maybe Tito was right and the statue had come to life. It looked so real, Ma was convinced the Santo Niño would wink at her at any moment.

Age seven. Beside the sari sari store was a bowling alley. After school, teens would often come to the shop to purchase bags of shrimp chips and bottles of Sarsi cola before heading to the bowling alley to play a few games. When she was done restocking shelves and taking inventory, MG liked to peek through the Florida windows next door at the action inside. Three small boys took turns putting the five pins in place before one of the teens would knock them down.

"Come help," said one of the boys, seeing her at the windows. His name was Ale, short for Alejandro. Although he was dressed like a boy, he smoked like a man, with one cigarette tucked above his ear. MG followed Ale to the back entrance. He showed her how to reset the frame of pins by pressing a foot lever, which made steel joints emerge from the wooden lane. MG wrapped her small hands around each pin and placed them on top of the joints to make a perfect triangle. Ma's favourite part was using the ball return and watching the black sphere make its way back to the player.

"Faster, MG! Come on! Faster!" Ale would shout while Ma laughed and scrambled to keep up. Pins on joints. Ball back to player. Pick up pins. Repeat.

Age nineteen. She remembers the sensation of rubbing Lola's back as her ailing mother struggled with her bowels. It wasn't a blockage. Lola's body was starting to forget how to function. That's why she needed Ma's help rubbing her back, pressing acupressure points at the dimples of her buttocks, as Dr. Jimenez instructed. On this sixth day of coaxing, Lola finally defecated.

"Do you feel better?" Ma stood up from the bathroom floor and flexed her spine with a groan. It had been hours. Now it was time to clean her. Ma reached for the tabo container, which swam in the large plastic drum that collected water from the leaky shower tap. Just as Ma was about to dip the tabo into the pool of collected water, the bin wobbled. Ma was able to embrace it with her arms to steady it back to centre.

"What was that?" Lola asked, her voice weary and raspy.

"I don't know . . . I think—" The drum of water wobbled again, but this time it toppled over, spilling water all over the bathroom floor. "Mommy. Stay here," she told Lola, who sat fearfully on the toilet with her duster nightdress still bunched above her waist and her underwear still gathered around her ankles.

Ma tiptoed through the puddle, her tsinelas splashing water across the floor, towards the bedroom. The digital clock by Lola's bedstand was dead. The power was out. *Why is it so dark outside?* Ma wondered as she made her way to the open window.

A sonic boom was followed by a thick cloud of white ash bursting through the window's intricate iron bars. Ma's body was flung backwards like a rag doll. A ringing in her ears tapered off to the sounds of dogs barking. A car's jammed horn. A crying baby.

"MG? MG?" Lola called out. Ma tried to wipe the mysterious white powder from her face. *What is this?* A milky residue filmed the surface of her eyes, so she had to palm her way back to the washroom, back to her crying mother. Broken vase. Open book. Foot of bed. Threshold.

"I'm here. I found you." The tears in Ma's eyes washed enough of the silt away so that she could see Lola had fallen on her side. Ma clumsily re-dressed her, helped her up to standing. The smell of Ben-Gay cream in the crease of Lola's neck where Ma had last massaged her. "Come. Hurry, po." She coughed. The powder was everywhere, entering her mouth and lungs. When Lola joined in on the coughing, Ma began to search the upended apartment for some clean fabric. Inside Lola's wardrobe, she found two long-sleeve shirts that had been gifted to them by her Kuya Enofre, who had become an OFW in the United States. Ma covered each of their faces with the shirts. The words "San Diego" draped over Lola's face and the words "California Dreaming" over Ma's.

She found Lola's church shoes (size six black leather penny loafers) and emptied them of the powder inside. "Put them on, Mommy," Ma insisted with an urgency muffled by the T-shirt. Lola obeyed as fast as she could, wincing at the strange sensation.

They emerged onto the street below. Through the cloud of white ash, their neighbours ran in random directions, fearing for their lives. A jeepney stopped within inches of Lola's hip, its wipers struggling to push heavy wet sand off the windshield, and then its wheels spun in place as it tried to drive away. When Ma and Lola stepped off the road, the jeepney's wheels finally caught the rough of the asphalt and sped off, only to crash into an overturned fruit stand.

"Daaaaddyyyyy!" a tiny voice cried from somewhere close by. Out of the haze a little girl, no older than a toddler, came running towards Ma. She wrapped her mucky arms tightly around Ma's legs, relieved to have been found. When her frosted eyelashes looked up and realized it wasn't her father she screamed, "Daddy! Where's my daddy?!" over and over again.

Ma braced Lola with one arm and held the girl's small biceps with the other. "Do you need help? Are you alone?" Ma shouted, thinking the volume would make her vision clearer. From behind her, a man emerged from the smog.

"Tess? Anak?" he cried from his muddy circle of a mouth.

"Daddy!" the little girl confirmed. She jumped into his arms before they both ran back towards the smoke.

"Sir? What happened?"

As father and child began to disappear from view, he called out, "The volcano! Mount Pinatubo just erupted! We need to evacuate." Ma looked in every direction. Nothing but white.

"I can't . . . I can't see." Lola clung to her spot, too scared to step forward.

"I'm right here. I won't leave you," Ma insisted, trying to

sound confident despite not being able to see six feet in front of her.

A pack of four dogs ran by them, wind whooshing as they passed. For a brief moment, for a split second, Ma met eyes with the mid-size mutt at the front of the pack. Eyelashes and coat covered in soot. The four of them looked magical galloping from the cloud and back into obscurity. The soft pitter-patter of their paws.

Mount Pinatubo had erupted after six hundred years of being dormant. And, not an hour later, Lolo and Lola's apartment and their sari sari store collapsed under the weight of volcanic ash after twenty-two years of business.

Half a year into living with Lola's sister in Manila (cinderblock home overlooking a muddy river on one side, a crowded cemetery on the other), Ma's distant cousin Jojo paid them a visit. He was one of the few who remained back in San Marcelino, joining the efforts to rebuild their small town. He reported that the area had been devastated, its residents draping their mouths with rags because of the continously falling ash, their outstretched hands begging for alms.

He unzipped his backpack, reached inside and presented Lola with a clothbound parcel. Ma helped to unfurl the bundle. Inside were the few things Jojo had been able to pull from the wreckage of their former home. An old Romana Peanut Brittle jar full of pesos Ma had saved, which she once kept beside her bed. Lola's antique Spanish silver rosary, which she had placed on her altar beside an illustration of Mother Mary and child. A small, framed photo of Lolo Ruben, which used to be on display near the kitchen table, under the print of Jesus's last supper. Using her thumb, Ma rubbed the ash from the image of her late father and the pewter frame until his half smile was revealed.

If you go into Ma's purse, you can still find this framed photo, in the pocket where she keeps her keys. It is small enough to fit in the palm of her hand.

*Her breasts.* Where do I even start? Breasts carry a lot of memory. Ma's breasts are no exception. That's why she protects them with the cross of her arms. Although, there is very little she can do to protect them these days. Now that I've arrived and am feeding often, they rarely feel like hers. (Which reminds me . . . I'm almost hungry, but not quite.)

Her right breast holds the memory of standing in front of her bedroom mirror. With thumb and forefinger, Ma felt the tender beginnings of breasts behind her inverted nipples. It was bothersome, whatever this lumpy thing was. The edges of her school desk kept poking into her growing chest, as did the straps of her school bag and the elbows of her classmates. What bothered her most, though, were the intrusive looks of men. None of them had mastered the art of discretion. Some of them made it obvious when they were looking, as if there was pleasure in seeing something they weren't supposed to see, pleasure in making her feel ashamed. A game of peeka-boo with her chest.

"Ks, ks, ks." A passing jeepney driver's lips smacked at Ma's prepubescent body.

"Sssssut. Sssssut." The streetside barber acknowledged Ma with a jut of his chin before continuing the fade on his customer.

It wasn't until Lola Daning caught Father Paul staring

at Ma while placing a communion wafer on her tongue that she rushed her to the nearest Shoe Mart mall to buy a set of training bras. The Easter-egg-coloured lingerie was not made for fashion. The bras did not resemble the ones worn by the beige-skinned models that graced the ads in Lola's copies of *Liwayway* magazine. They looked more like two triangles of tightly woven cotton meant to cease and desist all signs of puberty.

That is why Ma stood in front of the bedroom mirror, trying to figure out how to get rid of her breasts. She tried squeezing. She had seen her Manong Mike do that to his pimples. Surely it would be just as easy.

"Hoy, MG! Hurry up! You'll be late for school," Lola screamed from the kitchen below.

"Sorry, po."

No luck. Instead, her right breast became enlarged for several days. Once the inflammation subsided, Ma made a habit of crossing her arms, especially under the watchful eyes of Father Paul.

*Her feet.* In her left foot, she carries the memory of coconut husk against her big toe.

Ma's maternal grandmother, Lola Edith, lived a bumpy twenty-minute tricycle-taxi ride away. The home was a typical rural provincial bungalow, with its cinder-block structure surrounded by lush palms that creaked like rusty doors in the wind. Everything was alive in this sprawling home, including the dead. Just outside the front door lay a rotten teak log with several orchid roots twisting and feeding on its decaying fibres. Inside the house, translucent green forest monitors played musical chairs between the picture frames.

Pitter-patter, pitter-patter. Pitter-patter, pitter-patter. Back and forth. The skittish creatures took turns hiding behind eerie black-and-white photos of relatives long departed from this world. The way the lizards' tiny bodies animated Ma's ancestors from behind the frames made the hair on her arms stand on end. The most chilling image was the painting of her great-grandparents, Lolo Rolando and Lola Manuela, which was hung in the centre of the home, always watching, always present. In it, the pair stood side by side, as close as Lola's crisp butterfly sleeves would allow. Lolo Rolando's barong tagalog shirt was as stiff as his face was sullen. It seemed as though they were staring right at Ma as she walked past. Just like the forest monitors, Ma would scamper from bathroom to kitchen, kitchen to front door, hiding from her great-grandparents' gaze. It was here in this home where she first met Rhea, a girl her age who worked in her grandmother's home. Rhea's father had dropped her off at Lola Edith's hoping the old widow would trade mah-jong money in exchange for his dutiful daughter. She was only six at the time. In the hopes she would have a future trade, Rhea was trained by Lola Edith to become a domestic worker. *This is how you clean a toilet. This is how you hang laundry. This is how you cook food.*

Ma and Rhea delighted in the times the adults were away and they could play as two children, instead of master and servant. Hide-and-go-seek. Jacks. Clapping games.

"Stand like this, MG," Rhea showed Ma one afternoon. Rhea demonstrated by placing her feet on top of half a coconut husk and twisting her hips back and forth to polish the mahogany floors. Then it was Ma's turn. She tried to balance, but her toes were not as long or as dexterous as Rhea's to grasp the straw-like texture.

"I can't! I'm going to fall!" Ma giggled. It took a few times, but eventually she got the hang of it. Ma shuffled back and forth along the floors, trying her hand at being a maid. Meanwhile, Rhea lounged on the sofa and read a magazine, trying her hand at being a woman of leisure.

In Ma's right foot she holds the memory of dancing. If there is one thing she loves, it's dancing. She loves it enough to have recurring plantar fasciitis on her right foot. A painful swelling from her arch to her heel. She has been advised countless times to never dance barefoot but has never listened. She never will. It feels too good to cut a rug, so she risks cutting herself on broken glass left behind on the dance floor. She has never been to a club or a lounge. But at every wedding she has attended, she has been in the centre of it all, painting the air with her arms, making a picture of the music with her body. And in between family gatherings and big social events she would just dance in her room or the kitchen or even listen to music and dance in her head. Her favourite dancing moments include (in no particular order):

- Her sister Fay's wedding. Disco moves, twirling lights and fog-machine magic.

- Her cousin Rolly's wedding. First line-dancing experience. A bit complicated, a bit corny, but worth the trouble.

It was at Rolly's wedding where her dancing caught my father's attention. Partly because she looked beautiful dancing in a bleached cotton dress. Partly because he recognized her.

"MG? Do you remember me?" my father said to her over the loud music. Ma squinted her eyes, trying to place his face. His stubble and wide shoulders were unfamiliar. But when she saw the cigarette tucked at the top of his ear, she knew. He nervously continued, "I was one of the pin setters at Roque's Bowlerama. It's me, Ale."

He filled her in on all the goings-on back in San Marcelino. The school had been rebuilt. The bowling alley had been replaced by a karaoke bar where he had worked for a while. The volcanic ash had become the community's biggest win, making the soil rich for farming, although he had bigger dreams and had recently relocated to Manila. Ale laughed nervously and averted his eyes, taking a swig from a bottle of San Miguel beer. Was he flirting with her? Ma was not accustomed to attention from suitors. That was the kind of thing that happened to other women. And that's because of . . .

*Her teeth.* Ma's teeth hold the memory of dodged school portraits and family photos. It all started at six years old, when she lost her canine tooth on the right side.

"It won't always be this way, anak," Lola Daning said to Ma's reflection as she tongued the empty space in her gums in the mirror. "An adult tooth will grow in soon."

The adult tooth did not grow in the same space as the baby one. Instead, it poked through the upper gums, outwards towards her cheek like a Chiclet she had chewed and saved in her jowls for later. The other baby teeth were replaced by adult teeth growing in random directions, making it next to impossible to chew properly.

Lola Daning sent Ma to a dentist to assess the situation.

"The problem, ma'am," the dentist explained, "is that your daughter's maternal family's small jaws and paternal family's large teeth has created an abnormal smile." Unless teeth were pulled and braces were used, Ma's mouth would be deformed.

Lola and Ma left the dentist's office and never spoke of her teeth again. This was not a choice Lola could even entertain. Lolo Ruben's remittance was to be used for food, shelter and school. Certainly not on vanities.

That is why Ma added the tight press of her lips to her bodily habits. Hiding her malformed teeth required a lot of coordination (hand covering the mouth when she couldn't help but laugh; a dip in the head to divert attention from the odd purse of her lips) and commitment (either close her mouth or risk people jolting at the sight of her smile) until it became as natural as crossing her arms over her breasts.

*Her tongue.* My mother is the kind of person who will remember the taste of a particular chef's broth from years ago or can identify which of her titas made which lumpia, which ginataan, which asado. She has an extensive collection of gastronomical sensations stored in her tongue. This includes (in no particular order):

- Dining on lato seaweed at her grandparents' home. A rainstorm had disconnected their electrical power, so they devoured each green jellied tendril in candlelight. She remembers the satisfying pop

18

in her mouth. A burst of the salty ocean in every bite.

- Any and all lechons served at family get-togethers. First, there is the initial crunch of the balat, the pig's crispy skin crackling against the teeth. Then there is the buttery texture of fat before the animal's soft salty flesh. To Ma, lechon is an out-of-body experience. It's the reason why she turns her face away from everyone so that she can roll her eyes in pleasure without being judged by her cousins.

- Mais con hielo under the hot sun. She loved holding a pocket of the sweet corn sherbet on her tongue, waiting for the ice to defrost into evaporated milk once again. It was like air conditioning— but from the inside of the body. The cold sensation would travel from her molars to the nape of her neck to her temples, making her grimace from the brain freeze.

Other than food memory, her tongue holds other things. If you look way in the back, close to its root, you will see a bumpy texture. Scientists have fancy names for these things. Whatever they are called, and whatever they do, I am here to tell you that in Ma these bumps are more like . . . how can I describe it? They're more like a filing cabinet. Yes. That's it. This is where she keeps words or thoughts that she cannot express. You see, she has become accustomed to a way of expressing herself that makes her appear to be agreeable.

Pleasant. Tolerable. When she needs something, she must begin a request with phrases like "If only someone can help me" and end the request with phrases like "if it's not too much trouble." That might seem passive-aggressive to some, but to be a woman, a Filipina woman, to be forthright with what you desire, is much too intrusive. Instead, she must perform her needs and wants in a way that seems palatable and not too bothersome. The performance continues when society acts against her, and expects her to take hardships with grace. At the back of her tongue she swallows the sourness of remarks about her gnarly smile. She swallows the saltiness of men and their wandering hands. She swallows the bitterness of her choice to become an OFW. She swallows the sweetness that comes with that sacrifice and the celebration of her body as an exported good.

There are things Ma does not know.

In mapping out her body, I know there are things her body holds that are beyond her comprehension. Her pelvic floor, for example. There, in the centre of her centre of her centre, she holds the collective memory of the women before her. They are there, in the fascia, the muscles and ligaments, guiding her. Ma thinks this is her intuition. But really, it's them. And there are many. All of them in their most beautiful state. Some as old as black-and-white photos. Sometimes, Ma hears songs in her head, like Lola Daning's favourite tune by Sam Cooke. When she hears the flourish of strings in the intro, Ma thinks it's just the memory of Lola turning up the radio and singing along as she restocked the shelves of the sari sari store. But no. It's the spirit of Lola Daning, saying, "I am long gone but still here."

Well, that was a lot. What else should I mention? Sorry. My focus is fading. I think I'm hungry. Shall we return to this conversation later? Please say yes. Not sure if you noticed, but I'm squirming. And look. See this? This is me, rooting. Can't you see me desperately turning my mouth to the side, looking for my mother's chest? Please. Call her to me. Go on! Call her. I need her. I promise to continue this conversation, but seriously. Where is she?! Oh great. I have to resort to crying. Here goes. This is me cryyyyyyiiiiiing! Can't you hear me? Can't you tell a hungry cry from a wet diaper cry? For the love of god, feeeeeed meeeee!

# 2

The last thing I remember is falling asleep at Ma's breast, but where am I now? Oh, I see, it's you. We're on the porch, you and I. You holding me close. A blanket draped over us both.

I love this spot. I know you do too. If you position me outwards, I'll be able to see the bright autumn leaves brittle like paper up in the trees. Well, at least the general shape of them. I can't quite make it out just yet. I am a newborn baby after all. I can hear them though. Please. Hello? Please position me outwards, for the love of god. Don't you see me squirming? Please position me outwards. I can't see. I'm so bored looking at your chin and the buttons on your dress. Squirming. Crying. Yes. Thank you. That's much better. Finally. There it is. And who is that? Oh hello, Ma. I think I can see her raking the front lawn. Is she waving?

"Dina! Dina! Are you being a good girl? Who's my big girl?" I hear her say in the same tone she sings that godawful song, "Patty Cake." I'm confused. Does she want me to be good or big? Whatever. I give her a smile.

"Did you see that? Was that a smile?" Yes, yes it was. I see her removing her gardening gloves to run inside. Where is she going? Oh, there she is again.

"Say cheese!" She struggles to figure out her new digital camera. She bites her lips while pressing random buttons.

"Were my eyes closed?" I hear you ask. Your voice is raspy enough that I startle, but not enough for Ma to notice. "Did you hear me, dear? I think my eyes were closed." You cough a wet cough.

Ma manages to check the digital camera's small playback screen. "You're right. I'll take it again." Damn it. Here we go. "Dina! Dina! Can you smile for Mommy? Can you smile?" She says "smile" in this upward lilt. It starts down low in her chest and ends in this high pitch that practically makes my eyes water. I can feel the edge of my left cheek pinch upwards until she says, "There it is! Got it."

She has no idea how hard it is to coordinate your own facial muscles to make this happen, but she certainly knows how to manipulate me to do this smiling thing. Sigh. Although, it could be gas, as I feel things happening down there. Before I have to have a diaper change (which is soon, I have to admit), shall we continue?

We've already mapped my mother's body. Now we will map her journey to you. Are you still with me? Are you listening? Okay. Here goes.

The journey started with a long lineup.

Ma stood in a long queue of women that she had to get through before making it into the actual waiting room where there were actual chairs to sit on. Somewhere she could park her aching legs. She could hear the hum of an air conditioner, although she certainly couldn't feel it. Ma looked at the clock on the wall of the waiting room up ahead. It read ten in the morning, but then she realized the second hand wasn't moving. What time was it, exactly? It didn't matter.

Or . . . maybe it wasn't a long lineup. Maybe it just felt long. Let me explain.

That day in the lineup, my mother was menstruating. Heavily. She is a big bleeder. Deep inside of her were others, like me. About a few hundred thousand to be exact. Can you imagine it? All of us Maybe Babies, sitting there inside of her hoping for the chance to become real. Each time her menstruation came, we knew it would be time for one of us to go, and for their dream to be over. Each time it happened, part of me was sad to see one of my Maybe Baby friends go. And part of me felt happy that I was one step closer to entering the real world. It was complicated. Anyway . . . we were all sitting in there feeling the temperature rising. The clammy feel of Ma's skin. Her irritability. Her heightened emotions. The cramps stabbing at her from within.

Looking around, Ma could not locate the nearest comfort room in case she needed to pee or change her soaked maxi-pad. That didn't matter either. None of the women looked kind enough to let her re-enter the line anyway. She understood. If someone else were to ask for this favour, Ma would certainly not have been kind either. Everyone in that room was as eager as she was to find employment abroad. All over the world, people with more wealth than she could ever imagine were in need of help, to tend to their children and to clean their houses. And on that day, Ma was one of countless Filipinas ready to ship out for the promise of financial stability.

A young man began travelling down the line, passing everyone a piece of paper and a pen.

"Fill this out please. Do you need a pen? Fill this out please. Printing only. Print clearly." He approached Ma and began to struggle with separating the form's delicate pages from the rest of the pile. She thought to herself, *Please don't use your spit. Please don't use your spit.* Sure enough, he licked his middle finger and flicked on the bottom corner of the form before handing Ma her copy. Her stomach churned at the sight of the wet spot on the paper. Bile rose in her mouth. She hated spit.

Like the rest of the women in the line, she turned to the wall to begin filling out the form on its surface. Only, the wall closest to her had a poster taped to it featuring an image of a person removing their shirt to reveal a super-hero costume underneath. The words "OFWs are heroes!" splashed across the bottom in comic book font. Not wanting to mark it, Ma, groaning in frustration, used the cover of her address book instead. The pen provided by the agency was spotty and needed a few good shakes before the ink began to flow. Under the flickering fluorescent troffers, she wrote the following:

**Name:** Mary Grace Concepcion
**Age:** 22
**Married?** Yes.
**Children?** No.
**How many?** N/A
**Nanny? or PSW?**

Ma's pen hovered over the blank squares, uncertain which box to check. She turned to the woman behind her in the line.

"Excuse me, ma'am? What is this?" Ma pointed at the letters "PSW."

The fat woman with short hair looked at the form, then over-enunciated, "Pee, ehs, double yoo," as if Ma was silly for not knowing the term. When Ma still looked confused, the woman sighed. "Personal support worker."

"Oooooooh." Ma paused, looked down at the sandal tan on her bony feet. A V shape of lighter brown skin where her toes met. Maybe she should have worn dress shoes like everyone else. "Um . . . ma'am? What does a personal support worker do?"

The woman laughed. "Is this your first time, mare?" Ma nodded. "These people . . . they need Filipinas to take care of their kids. That's a nanny. Sometimes people need Filipinas to take care of their parents because they can't afford the old folks' home. That's a PSW."

"What do *you* do, ma'am?"

"Both. You should too. Babies grow up and go to school. Old people are old people for years. Sometimes decades."

"I don't think I can afford to go to school to be a PSW."

"You don't have to, necessarily. These people don't want someone for their education. They want someone who's desperate," the lady scoffed. "When you get in there, just look into the camera, show you're a nice person who has lots of skills, but most of all, show you are the kind of person who will do what she is told."

Ma watched dozens of women do exactly what this lady

had said. In a small office beside the waiting room, each woman took her turn.

"Sit here," the young man would say, pointing to an office chair. It was the same person who handed out the application forms. Ma stared at the chair from afar, longing for its soft surface to support her tender buttocks. The cramps were getting worse by the second.

A clunky video camera rigged onto a tripod stood beside a utility light that beamed into the face of each subject. And sitting among this elaborate setup was a middle-aged man in a suit.

"Adjust the light!" he would bark at the young man as if he was a big Hollywood director. "One more time, but slowly. Clearly. They want to hear your command of the English language," he said to one woman who was too meek for his liking.

While standing in line, Ma listened in on each woman's taping, hoping to nail down exactly what she would say.

"Good afternoon. My name is Gloria Bautista. I am thirty-two years old. I have worked in Saudi Arabia for six years taking care of three children, ages one, four and seven . . ."

"Hello. My name is Floribeth Cruz. I am forty-one years old. I have worked in Australia, Israel and the UAE. I am an excellent cook and am skilled at running both kosher and halal kitchens and . . ."

"My name is Luz del Rosario. I am thirty-seven years old. I am a graduate of the University of Santo Tomas. I am a formidable caregiver and tutor in mathematics, so . . ."

Ma's brain was scrambling. Kosher? Halal? Mathematics? Most of these women were older than her. What experience did she have? What schooling? And when would this be over so that she could visit the CR?! Her pad grew heavy and warm between her legs.

She reached into her purse to reapply her tinted lip balm. It smelled musty and moist but would leave a soft pink shade on her lips.

"That's not a good idea." The lady behind her leaned on the wall with one arm and fanned herself using the application form.

"Why, ate?" Ma referred to the woman as a big sister, even though she was old enough to be her tita.

"You're young still. Pretty."

"Me?" Ma pressed her lips together to feel the knobs and edges of her teeth.

"Sometimes these mothers feel threatened. Pretty Filipina in their house. They just gave birth and are feeling sad. Then they think their husbands may be attracted to you instead."

"But . . . I'm married." Ma was confused but took the tissue from the woman anyway and wiped the slight rose sheen off her lips.

"Trust me. I've been through this a few times." The woman peeked at Ma's overly simple application form and raised her eyebrows. "Why don't you have more work experience?"

"I was taking care of my mother."

"Perfect." Ma's eyes widened at this. It certainly didn't feel perfect to watch Lola suffer all those years. "Put down that you have experience in taking care of the sick and elderly." Ma turned to an open space on the wall and began writing the woman's suggestions onto the page. "A sari sari store? Yes. Include it. But say you have experience running a small business, dealing with inventory and managing staff."

The woman continued to coach her and, with Ma's pen, wrote on Ma's forearm the main points she was to cover in her one-minute video for prospective employers.

"Next!" the young man finally called from within the office. He gestured for Ma to sit down. Instead of feeling relief, she worried her pad would leak as soon as her bum touched the upholstery. Ma grimaced, hoping her crossed legs would keep her from staining the chair.

"Don't be scared," said the middle-aged man by the tripod, a tinge of contrived wisdom in his prolonged, breathy vowels. He reached out his hand towards Ma. She thought he wanted to hold her hand and comfort her. But when he frustratedly pointed at her application form, she handed it to him. "Just talk to the camera like . . . it's one of your friends. Like . . . you're having a fun conversation over lunch." Ma tried to conjure the image of one of her friends but was too distracted by the man's paisley ascot and his pointy, leather mesh loafers, no socks.

"Rowan!" he called out to the young man. His feminine hand gestures and gaudy bracelets made Ma's cheeks burn in embarrassment. He must be one of *those*. Rowan quickly approached, his Jennifer Lopez T-shirt, shorts and flip-flops contrasting with the older man's fancy clothing. "Please adjust the light. It doesn't need to be this bright for her. She's younger and has nicer skin, right?" He winked at Ma and pursed his lips as if they shared a secret. Ma averted her eyes. Did he have tinted lip balm on his lips? "And . . . ACK-SHON!"

Ma realized this was her cue. She looked down at her forearm at the scribbled notes.

"Hello. My name is Mary Grace. I am twenty-two years old. While I am young, I have already had ten years' experience in caring for the sick and elderly. I also have run a small business, helped with accounting and managed staff. I am skilled in cooking halal and kosher foods. I am an expert in running a household, keeping all areas clean and children entertained. Thank you."

"And cut! Perfect. Good job. Next!"

Ma ran to the CR as soon as she could. She sat down and inspected her dress pants. Dampness from her groin to mid-thigh. Thank goodness they were black polyester slacks. She re-dressed and stood up, relishing the feeling of dry cotton at her crotch. At last. A long sigh of relief. In that moment, she finally considered what she had just done. *One day the agency will call me for a job somewhere far away*, she thought to herself.


A year later, Ma was en route to her apartment after a long day of shopping. Two flicks on the roof of the jeepney signalled to the driver that Ma wanted to get off. It was a struggle to crouch down low and hobble past the other passengers while hugging her shopping bags. Once she exited the rear of the jeepney, she hooked her hand around the outside handle and felt the hand of another passenger, a teenage boy hanging off the fender of the vehicle. His sandalled feet were propped on the jeepney's sign reading "Jesus Saves." She recoiled and grabbed hold of another handle before stepping down.

Her foot touched the surface of the asphalt just before the jeepney jolted forward without her, quickly occupying a rectangle of coveted space in the bumper-to-bumper traffic. Ma pulled out a kerchief that was tucked into her T-shirt sleeve and covered her mouth to guard from the diesel fumes before bobbing through oncoming traffic to get to the side of the road.

"Chiclets, ma'am? Chiclets?" a hawker called out to her. Squinting her eyes from the fumes, Ma shook her head and watched him pivot towards another potential customer, his wares swinging from his shoulders. Beneath the cascading clips of snacks, chewing gum and cigarettes, his two small children sleepily followed his every move with their tiny fingers hooked around his belt loops.

The alleyway to get to their apartment was a narrow void between the San Carmen Family Bakery and Magnolia Ice Cream Shop. The other way would have been easier, especially with her shopping bags, but then she would have to pass Ate Dominga's place, where her restaurant clients' endless loads of laundry hung heavy from criss-crossing lines of rope. There, table linens rained cold water on passersby. So she made herself as flat as she could, walking like a crab through the alleyway, hoping no one would enter from the opposite end. Once she cleared the alley, there was a small square of open space, which was the outside kitchen of the Villanueva family.

Ma made eye contact with one of the maids, who sat on her haunches, peeling a large green upo. The Villanuevas would be home soon after closing up their jewellery store, which was why this woman was hard at work to make dinner. Ma never managed to peel things the way this maid did, in one long strip from end to end. A neat pile of melon-green ribbons accumulating between her feet. The set of knives Ma had received as a wedding gift had since dulled, giving each vegetable they came into contact with a good scratch rather than a proper peeling. Ma made a mental note to get them sharpened next time that old man peddler came around with his stone. Then she remembered that by the time the old man made his rounds to their barrio in Quezon City, Ma would be gone. Tonight was her last night at home.

She let out a small sigh and allowed her shoulders to sink for a brief moment. Long enough to let the feeling of apprehension spread from her sweaty palms to the heat in her armpits. Concise enough to not allow the emotion to rip her open into a weeping mess. Ma shook her head and smartened up before entering the apartment, the threat of tears firmly squashed. She didn't want her sister-in-law Ate Marcy to see her upset.

The apartment my father had found for them wasn't much of a formal residence. It was more of an unclaimed space behind the Macapagal auto repair shop. And it wasn't so much an auto repair shop as it was a place where taxicab drivers would get one of the Macapagal brothers to do a short-term repair, just so that they could hit the road and earn cash. Just enough of a repair that those rich families needing a drive to their lavish homes in Forbes Park wouldn't be miffed by the black diesel smoke seeping through the vents.

Out front, men waited for Freon to be transferred from old refrigerators to their cabs' busted air conditioning systems, passing time smoking cigarettes and playing pusoy dos with their fellow drivers. Out back, Ma and Ale made the best

of the storage area, which had been converted into an apartment by the magic of a two-burner hot plate and a flower-
printed dish rack by the sink. A pumpkin into a palace. The
apartment was divided by a half wall. On the far side of it was
where Ate Marcy slept with her two small children, Ging and
Ellie. The only separation between the home and the repair
shop was a door with no lock. It was common for strange
men to open it, in the middle of unbuckling, believing it was
the door to the toilet.

"Sorry, ma'am!" the men would gasp before shutting the
door, although the half inch of space below it hardly kept the
sound of banging and clanging from disturbing them all.

On that last day, Ma went through the back entrance
and walked right into Ate Marcy. Ate Marcy would have
dropped the pot of pinakbet if she hadn't stepped back into
the beaded curtain, which separated the kitchen from their
eating area.

"Ay! Shit. Sorry." Ma backed up into the wall to allow Ate
Marcy to pass. "Are you heading to work?"

"Soon." Ate Marcy placed the pinakbet on the table next
to the small pot of steaming rice, which she drew a cross on
using a wooden ladle. *In the name of our Father, Son and the
Holy Spirit. Thank you, Jesus Christ our Saviour, for this meal.*
"I should be back in time for you and Kuya Ale to have your
dinner out," she added with a sad, tight smile, as if pressing
the weight of the occasion between her chapped lips. Ate
Marcy reached out to gently touch Ma's forearm for a brief
moment and said, "Thank you, ha?"

"You don't have to thank me," Ma replied, even though it
felt good to have her sacrifice acknowledged.

"If I could leave, I would, but I'm all alone—" Ate Marcy's weary eyes guiltily scanned the floor for an alternative solution the way single mothers scan the cupboards before payday.

Ma embraced her sister-in-law. This conversation had happened several times since the agency called Ma with a potential employer in Hong Kong. The only thing that could assuage Ate Marcy's remorse was to hold her tightly. "I'll be back," Ma said, considering the truth of that statement. The only thing that helped her put one foot in front of the other was imagining the satisfaction of sending enough remittance home to move them out of this makeshift apartment. Ate Marcy and the kids could be in a real home without the constant noise of the adjacent garage. And she and Ale could finally have a separate place and have children of their own.

The sound of bickering erupted from the washroom. Ate Marcy left the embrace and called out, "Hoy! Ging? Ellie? Dinner time."

Ellie emerged from the small washroom with the front of her dress damp from the knees to the waist.

"What happened?"

"It was Ging. I was trying to wash his feet because he stepped into the gutter again. He was leaning on the edge of the pail to balance and the pail fell on me. But look at Ging. Still dry!" Ging's mischievous toddler face peered from the doorframe tilted sideways. Ma and Ate Marcy burst out into laughter, wiping tears from their eyes. Ellie crossed her arms.

"Ging? What did Mommy tell you, ha?" Ate Marcy restrained herself and beckoned him using a downward scooping motion with her hand. "What do you say to your Ate Ellie?"

"Sorry, Ate Ellie." Ma was going to miss his sweet raspy voice. The siblings were forced to embrace each other. Ellie a wee bit taller than Ging. Both of them with enormous heads and small bodies. *How did those slender necks support them?* Ma wondered with a grin. The children patted each other on the back, mimicking the action adults do when they forgive. Then all was forgotten.

"Okay. Mommy is going to tutor over at Doña Ramos's house, and I will be back tonight."

"Before bed?" Ellie said while excitedly jumping up and down.

"No, anak." Ellie's shoulders slumped in full disappointment. "But Tita MG will put you all to bed and I will kiss you while you are sleeping."

"Give me awake-kisses, Ma!" Ellie said while wrapping her arms around her mother. Ging copied the action, with one finger in his mouth, soothing himself through this transition. Ate Marcy gently nibbled at their sweet cheeks while the kids cackled in notes almost too high for humans to hear before she ran out the door.

After dinner, Ma gave the two children a bath. They stood in the shower, Ging with a gangly-looking outie belly button. Ellie with a vast, mysterious innie. Ma dunked the tabo into a pail full of ice-cold water that had been dripping from the leaky tap since morning. Ma tipped the cup over them. The two screamed from the sensation, their black hair plastered to their foreheads. A layer of dust travelled in rivulets onto the seafoam-green tile, then down the drain.

"No jumping!" Ma said sternly, although she was watching their every move, taking pictures in her mind, trying her best to remember every fleeting moment. Ma squeezed the last of the shampoo into their palms and demonstrated how to lather their hair. "Keep your eyes closed or else your eyes will sting."

"But Tita MG, how can I do this and close my eyes?"

"You know where your head is. You can find it with your eyes closed, right?"

Ellie shut her eyes, then made her soapy hands do a dramatic journey to her wet scalp. "Oh. Okay. I understand now." Ma rinsed them one more time, making sure there was enough in the bucket for her to shower tonight.

"Do you think I can carry you both?" Ma said devilishly before wrapping them both in a towel and picking them up in one gigantic embrace. Ellie and Ging squealed.

"You're so strong, Tita MG!"

After the kids were dressed in their pyjamas, Ma had them play beauty parlour. Ging at the front. Ma in the middle. Ellie in the back. While Ma brushed Ging's hair into a slick side part, she remembered the image of her father standing at the doorway of the sari sari store. A stranger.

"Tita MG?" Ellie said, pulling Ma's hair into several tangled ponytails.

"Yes, anak."

"When will you be back?"

"Soon."

"Jocey Soledad's mother never came back."

"I'm not Jocey Soledad's mother. I'm your Tita MG." Ma turned around, trying to speak through the swell in her throat and the pain in her chest. "All right. Now it's bedtime."

Ma pretended to leave their side of the apartment. But when the noise at the repair shop stopped after it was closed and she could hear the children snoring, she peeked in at their diminutive sleeping bodies, already thrashed out of their cots and moving towards their mother's floor mattress.

She looked at the digital clock by Marcy's pillow. One more hour until Ale would be back from his shift at the call centre and Marcy would be back from tutoring to stay with the kids. She finally had a moment to take out the funny ponytails Ellie had made in her hair and look at her purchases from the Shoe Mart mall. On her and Ale's bed on the other side of the apartment, she placed a small stack of calling cards in case she had trouble buying them in Hong Kong. Then she tore the tags off her new money belt, large enough to fit her passport as well. A pair of sneakers. Underwear. Bra. Slacks. Ma packed her things carefully into her maroon suitcase before getting ready for their dinner out.

"Sometimes I think they just want an apology," my father said to Ma, sitting opposite her, waiting for the outdoor canteen to finish cooking their meal. The table they had chosen was the least rickety of them all. When my father tried to lean on its edge, it tipped to one side, and when he leaned back, it teetered to its original position. He awkwardly positioned himself closer to Ma, close enough to lovingly pinch at the fold of her elbow. If it was pinching, it didn't count as a public display of affection. He continued. "Especially the old ladies. You can imagine it. The time difference. It's afternoon for them when I'm starting my day. No one else to talk to. They call, they complain, they don't want a solution if it means they need to do something. They just want an apology."

"Do you give it to them?" Ma said, removing a stray eyelash from his cheek and blowing it into the wind. Ale did not answer. Instead he closed his eyes for a brief moment at her touch. He coughed into his hands but Ma could see his face fighting itself. The edges of his lips quivered and he blinked heavily as if beating the muscles into submission, to make the fibres of his face continue this ruse of normalcy around this occasion.

The sound of a bell cued Ale to get up and pick up their orders at the counter. Ale looked at the canteen's bright fluorescent light and its sprays of festive streamers linking the canteen to the nearest electrical pole. He smiled sheepishly at Ma, embarrassed at his sudden show of emotion. "I'll be right back."

The two ate in silence, each spoonful of rice pushing down everything unsaid between them.

That night, they entered the apartment, sneaking past Marcy and the kids sleeping in their cots.

"Let me brush my teeth first," Ale said before heading to the washroom. Ma sat on the bed and removed her jacket, knowing what was to happen next. It's not that she didn't want to make love. It's that she didn't want to make love right then and there, under these circumstances. She didn't want to feel the finality of it all. She didn't want to say goodbye this way. She didn't want to say goodbye at all. But wasn't it her duty? To give of her body, to reassure her husband before her departure? It could be years before she returned to Manila. And didn't she wash herself during her shower for this exact purpose? This last memory of a clean wife and shaven legs? The smell of Safeguard soap on her torso and the smell of Palmolive in her hair?

Ale re-entered the bedroom, eyes red from crying. In the section of the apartment that was theirs, they undressed silently. If my mother could put a microphone to her soul, it would have said:

*Ale, don't let me go. Please don't let me leave. Tell me there is another way for us to survive and I will do it.*

Instead, my mother lay back. My father positioned himself above her and stroked his penis, hoping for an erection. He closed his eyes. The erection finally came. He entered my mother.

Inside of her, the rest of the Maybe Babies and I held our breath. Was this our chance? Some of us bickered at each other. *My turn! No, it's my turn! Leave her be. She doesn't want us right now. Look at her face.* They were right. My mother was not ready. She was too sad to be ready. Too sad to look my father in the eye as he climaxed without a sound.

Ma held Ale's face tenderly, kissing his temples wet with tears. "Ale. I love you, Ale. I'm so sorry."

# 3

The Tsang family's home was a palace in the sky located in Hong Kong's affluent Mid-Levels district. The sprawling penthouse featured seamless picture windows facing Kowloon Bay to the north and Aberdeen Country Park to the south. Connecting the two storeys was a grand staircase with brushed-brass handrails and terrazzo treads, which descended gracefully to a koi fish pond by the private elevator entrance.

Back when Ma first arrived, Mrs. Tsang had apologized for the gaudiness of the staircase, claiming that the previous owners were new-money investment bankers wanting to flaunt their wealth. Rolling her eyes at the monstrosity, she assured Ma that an overhaul of the staircase's aesthetic was a major part of the upcoming renovations.

That was the extent of Ma's direct contact with Mrs. Tsang. The rest of the time, Mrs. Tsang instructed her by pointing to things that needed her attention while endlessly squabbling with people over the phone. Ma wasn't sure what exactly Mrs. Tsang did for a living. She just knew that it required her to use a fancy headset wired to a receiver at her waist. Throughout the day, Mrs. Tsang's voice would change depending on who she was speaking to. Seething, deliberate delivery when she was angry at one person. Jovial and musical conversation with someone she was trying to woo. Some days, it seemed she was going through a checklist of deliverables with her staff with a precise cadence, divided by short moments of silence and "uh-hm."

Ma could not understand any of it as she did not speak Cantonese. But that didn't matter. She was given strict instructions to speak only English to Jia, Mrs. Tsang's two-year-old son, whom she was to call John. And pointing was a universally understood language. While on the phone, Mrs. Tsang would point to a ball that strayed as Ma and John rolled it back and forth to each other. Point at the spilled water on the tiles during John's bath. Point at John's jacket zipper as Ma prepped him for an outing to the Botanical Gardens.

John would practise his English with Ma in a rehearsed conversation. "How was your day, MG?" John would say to Ma on the way to toddler music class.

"I had a really great day!" Ma would reply. "And how was your day?"

"I . . . woke up . . ." John would list the events, counting them on his pudgy fingers. "I . . . uh . . . had my breakfast . . . I put on my jacket all by myself."

"Wow! What a big boy you are." Then they'd high-five. There was a lot of high-fiving.

The music class was more like a chaotic circle time. The only thing neat and orderly was the line of children's rubber boots standing like soldiers by the entrance to the studio and their brightly coloured jackets hooked on knobs set low so that the kids could hang them themselves. It was all downhill from there.

Maggie, an expat musician from Cornwall, England, was a hot mess who liked to wear a selection of ill-fitting cheongsams with her blond dreadlocks. Despite her guitar being sadly out of tune, she sang her heart out to weeping children covering their ears.

"And this song is one I wrote myself," Maggie would say before torturing everyone with yet another ditty about flowers following the path of the sun. Ma would work her abdominals trying not to laugh at this comedy of errors. She wasn't sure if it was a good idea to make eye contact with the rest of the Filipina helpers sitting cross-legged in the circle. If one of them cracked a smile it would be over. Instead they all tried to shake their tot-sized rattles and bang their tambourines to drown out the sound of Maggie's banshee wails.

One day, another helper rushed in fifteen minutes late with her charge. The little girl trampled her muddy shoes into the studio, holding a half-eaten dumpling in one hand. The helper was losing her breath and losing her cool trying to get the toddler to take off her jacket without the child unleashing into a tantrum. Finally, the woman sat down with the girl in her lap, clapping along to Maggie's ear-piercing racket about the sound of a choo-choo train.

The woman met eyes with Ma. They looked at each other. Recognition. It was Rhea. She had the same round cheeks, the same dark-brown skin that was two shades darker than Ma's. Eyes that were continuously squinting from a never-ending grin. She was the same Rhea but in a woman's body. She wasn't much taller than when Ma had last seen her. It looked like the only gift time had given her were her large breasts. They waved excitedly to each other from across the circle.

After class, Rhea and Ma walked their charges towards the Central District Promenade. "You don't use a stroller either?" Ma asked Rhea, keeping one eye on John, who was hopping from one foot to the other just ahead of her.

"No. This way, Anna is tired by the time we get home. She has too much energy." Rhea straightened Anna's pull-up diaper and pants before Anna ran off to hold hands with John.

Ma looked at Rhea and asked carefully, "Did you ever see your father again?"

"I did go back to San Marcelino. It was nice to see so many familiar faces, but no sign of Daddy. I wasn't surprised though."

"Oh yeah? Why?"

"If he didn't die from the eruption, I'm pretty sure he died from drinking." Rhea said this like a joke she had told many times. Ma gave a weak laugh, uncertain of how Rhea wanted her to react. Rhea redirected Anna in the direction of the playground up ahead instead of the litter piled at the base of a tree planter. "Do you like it?"

"Like what?"

"*You're* the maid now."

Ma corrected Rhea with a roll of the eyes. "I'm not the maid. I'm the yaya. I am only in charge of John." Ma told Rhea the story of how Mrs. Tsang's housekeeper, Luz, slapped her wrist when Ma tried to polish the grand staircase to remove John's purple handprints. It was a craft activity that had gone wild. "I understand. Cleaning is her domain."

"So no polishing the floors with a coconut husk for you?" Rhea elbowed Ma playfully. Ma was about to answer when she saw John vomit his morning snack onto his shirt.

Nap times were the most difficult for Ma to get through. John was a champion napper thanks to Ma's persistence with keeping him active. She would stuff her backpack full of his snacks and toys before they headed out on long walks towards areas outside the Mid-Levels.

"Can you balance on one leg, John?" Ma would say, encouraging John to copy the stance of the flamingos at Kowloon Park. The only times John was ever picked up was when they were grabbing snacks in the hustle and bustle of Soho, with John sitting on Ma's lap as he made a mess of a moon cake she had bought.

Once he was down for his nap, Ma would wrestle with thoughts of people back home. She would sit in her helper room across the hall from the nursery, steady her gaze on the cityscape outside her window and daydream. It was like picking at scabs. She'd tortured herself imagining Ale returning home from his shift at the call centre to an empty bed. When the image wasn't satisfactorily painful enough, she'd imagine Ale returning home from his shift at the call centre with another woman lying on their floor mattress. Sideways. The lilt of a ravishing body under a silken negligee. A sly smile. Ale and this mistress making love with the grace and ease of movie stars—a way of moving Ma had never mastered. Sometimes this image of Ale with other women both aroused and confused her and she found herself stroking the dampness at her panties. Either way, it ended with Ma in tears, thrashing about her bed, screaming into her pillow. What she wished she could do during those nap times was call Ale directly just to hear his voice, but the landline was almost always occupied by Mrs. Tsang. Not that she'd let her use it. It hardly mattered though. Ale was at work anyway. Once John's stirring could be heard from the baby monitor, Ma was back at it. It was a relief, really. Watching this sweet little boy stretch himself out of his slumber. Wiping the crusted drool from the sides of his mouth. Leading him slowly to his potty and teaching him to aim his penis into the bowl. Chatting with him about his dreams while he ate his snack, still half-asleep. All of the day's tasks helped Ma pass this test of strength, one paycheque at a time.

This daily ritual ended when the penthouse renovations commenced and Ma was forced to share John's room. The designer Mrs. Tsang had hired envisioned "stealing space" from Ma's bedroom for the butler's pantry. There was no butler, but Mrs. Tsang felt the addition would add value to the property. This way, Luz would do her cooking behind closed doors, away from the eyes of their guests, and the stainless-steel appliances could be kept spotless and unused.

It felt comical combining Ma's adult clothes with John's toddler-sized underwear. Tiny bedtime onesies at one end of the closet. Shift dresses at the other end.

Mrs. Tsang removed her phone headset long enough to tell Ma, "It's easier, isn't it?" Ma nodded even though she was confused as to what exactly would be easier. Mrs. Tsang pointed at the small space between Ma's mattress on the floor and John's bed. "When he calls out to you, you'll be right there."

Two years later, Ma laughed while lifting John over a decorative divider to the penthouse's pool. "If you're just a kid, why are your armpits so sweaty?" She didn't want to chance John's flip-flops getting caught in the meandering footpath again. Like many design choices in this home, the teak boardwalk was stunning to look at but horrendous to use. More like an abstract sculpture than a trail. Plus, the decorative divider was the faster route from the guest bathroom where she had changed him into his swim trunks. After swimming with John almost every day, Ma wanted to let him enter the shallow pool without a life jacket. But Mrs. Tsang was adamant about putting safety first.

As always, Ma entered the pool first, bracing at the cold water lapping over her chest. She wasn't much of a swimmer, but the pool was shallow enough that she only needed to walk. No floating necessary.

"Ready?" Ma stretched her arms out. John nodded his head and bent his knees on his slight legs before launching into the pool. "See? I didn't even need to catch you. You did it yourself!" High-fives.

"Watch this! Watch this!" John said while he paddled from the ladder. His favourite trick was to "flip" himself around. In John's mind, he was like the swimmers in the Atlanta Olympics he saw on TV, doing tumble turns at the end of their lanes. But in reality, he just closed his eyes, dipped his head under water, turned laterally, then opened his eyes. "Did you see that?" he said with a wide, self-satisfied smile.

"That was amazing!" Ma said encouragingly. John's raspy giggles reminded her of Ging, but she had become an expert at sidestepping painful memories. The process wasn't any easier. It was just faster. As soon as she thought of who and what she was missing back home—the birthdays, the Christmases, the funny conversations—she would scratch at a lesion on the back of her neck. She'd had eczema when she was young, and since she'd starting working overseas it had emerged again, angry and raw, just below the nape, the size of the bottom of a can of cola. She knew this because she often used the bottom of a can of cola to cool the inflammation and it was a perfect fit. The sharp pain radiated to the backs of her ears, making her lobes swollen and hot to the touch. It was a nuisance, especially while swimming in chlorinated water, but it was less painful than the sensation of longing.

"MG, I need to go pee." John had already made his way to the ladder and fought the pull of gravity to step out of the pool.

"Hold it, John. Let me get out and we'll run to the shower room," Ma said, making her way to him.

John was dancing, holding his crotch, his black hair plastered to his forehead. "No! I need to pee now!"

"Ummm . . ." Ma squinted, trying to see through the house windows if Mrs. Tsang or Luz were watching them. She lowered her voice. "Okay, fine. Go. Quickly." John knew what she meant by this. It had happened twice before. Only twice. And now this was the third time. Just three. John rushed to the side and peed a furious stream into a cluster of sculpted boxwoods. He sighed with his whole body. Relief.

After swimming, the two always tiptoed their wet feet back through the foyer into the guest bathroom, where Ma would rinse him off with soap and water and change him back into his clothes. It always felt unsettling to do anything in that bathroom. All four walls were set with mirrors featuring veins of gold from floor to ceiling. When she had first arrived at the Tsang house and used this washroom, she watched her reflection in horror as the mirrors gave her a direct view of her bum on the toilet. Now, she watched herself change John out of his wet trunks while assessing the weight she had gained since leaving Manila. She wondered what Ale would think of her now, if he would still be attracted to her by the time she visited next year. She scratched at her raw neck. Sharp pain. Back to reality.

Ma cleared her throat and spoke in a quieter voice. She knew no one could hear her talk outside since they were so close to the bubbling koi fish pond, but she couldn't take her chances. "Don't do that again, ha? That's why I ask you to pee *before* we swim." As John had gotten older he had a difficult time obeying the rules of the home. When he was a toddler, Ma found it easy to have him follow instructions. These days, he enjoyed pushing her buttons and challenging her boundaries. She added, "Your mommy would be very upset if she found out you peed on her bushes." At this, John merely shrugged and stepped into the shower. It wasn't him who would get in trouble.

Each week, she would head to Hollywood Road to see Rhea and other helpers who gathered by the hundreds to celebrate their Sunday off. Blocks of pavement were transformed into Little Manila. In one area, papered with flattened cardboard boxes, Ate Fely gave fellow helpers pedicures, clipping and exfoliating her clients' tired feet on her newspaper-covered lap. In another, a group of helpers played pop music on a boom box while they line danced. At Rhea's spot, which was situated at the base of an outdoor escalator, she served Filipino food on the sly.

Before joining in on all the exciting, children-free fun, Ma's habit was to call Ale on a payphone a block away. It was by design. She wanted to know as many details as possible about what was happening back home without sounding needy. At an MTR station, she found a payphone and dialed the number on the back of her calling card, then her home phone number. Ehhhh-ehhhh. Ehhhh-ehhhh. No matter how many times she did this, her heart pounded in her chest. *Please answer. Please don't leave me.* Ehhhh-ehhhh. Click.

"Hello?" Ale's voice always sounded like he was far away. A slight buzz hummed throughout their calls.

Ma swallowed hard, scratched the back of her neck. "Ale! It's me. How are you?" She hated this question. How would he be? And how much different would he be from last week?

"I'm okay. Ate Marcy is out working. I'm with the kids." The conversation trudged along like it always did. How was church? The customer did what? What did your manager do about it? I miss you. I miss you too. If Ma could put a microphone to her soul, she would say:

*Sometimes my heart hurts so much I feel dizzy.*

*I fantasized about kissing you yesterday and I wonder if you felt it too.*

*I don't remember how you smell and that makes me sad.*

Instead, she heard Ging and Ellie begging for the receiver.

"Okay, okay. Here. Talk to her then." Ma could hear the phone changing hands. The receiver hitting the floor, then picked up by Ging. Ma could hear his heavy breathing.

"Tita MG? I love you." Another change of hands and Ma could hear Ellie saying through a laugh, "I love you, Tita MG!" Then another click. Ma wondered if Ale had walked away from the phone or if he had wanted to chat further. Who ended the call? The kids or him? She wanted to call again, she wanted to find out if they received her last remittance to them, if they received the package of Hong Kong T-shirts she sent them; she wanted to hear Ale say he loved her, but she was running low on calling card minutes.

"Hoy! Ate MG! Over here." Rhea waved down Ma as if they hadn't met at the exact same spot for the last two years. Rhea liked to bend the cardboard box patches in her area so that there was a low makeshift wall. It also helped to keep her undocumented restaurant operations under the table— even though there was no table.

"What's on the menu today, mare?" Ma pressed her lips, touched cheeks with Rhea, then sat down on the cardboard with her. Rhea exhaled sharply out of her mouth, then looked around conspiratorially.

"Keep your voice down. I don't want those hawker control officers arresting me for selling food." Rhea, like many of the helpers in Hong Kong, had to hustle to make extra money on the side. Rhea passed Ma a menu written in marker on a small piece of paper. It was a traditional Filipino breakfast spread, perfect for a Sunday. Longanisa, sinagang, tortang talong. Ma pointed to the full-meal option.

"So. Today the mister arrives?" Rhea asked while she furtively opened three backpacks full of food. Steam escaped as she unzipped them.

"No. He arrived late last night. Today is some big cocktail party to celebrate his birthday," Ma replied, watching Rhea snap on a rubber glove. "I'm glad I'm not there today."

"What about Luz, though? Is she there cooking for them?" Rhea used her gloved hand to scoop the rice, sausage and omelette onto a paper plate.

"No. Mrs. Tsang is going full out with caterers. Mr. Tsang isn't home often and she wanted it to be a big deal." Rhea handed Ma her plate, Ma stealthily handed Rhea cash, which she stuffed into her fake Gucci fanny pack.

Another group of helpers entered Rhea's cardboard establishment, stepping one high-heeled sandal over the low barrier at a time, then sitting cross-legged on the ground. Ma recognized one of them as Ate Lettie, who offered counsel to her fellow OFWs while gently rubbing their backs. Ma would have loved to partake, but Ate Lettie's spot was located smack-dab in the middle of a busy thoroughfare between the ladies who sang karaoke and the ladies who beaded wallets together. She didn't want to open up her heart to Ate Lettie while someone sang a Carpenters ballad on one side and a circle of Filipinas leaned slightly sideways on the other, eavesdropping on their conversation. She had lots to share though. And how many times had she witnessed a woman in Ate Lettie's fierce embrace, wailing away the pain Ma recognized within herself? Even in the least emotional sessions, Ma watched women succumb to Ate Lettie's loving touch, hugging their knees, weeping openly, while their back was massaged, no words exchanged.

"What did you order?" Ate Lettie called out to Ma in Filipino so that the hawker control officers wouldn't understand. Ma told her, and Ate Lettie said, "I'll have that," before passing the paper menu back to Rhea. Like sheep, Ate Lettie's friends ordered the same. Ma's face blushed when Ate Lettie winked at her, then continued her conversation with her friends. Something about someone's employer making them sleep in the kitchen.

On her haunches, Rhea doled out the food. Without making eye contact, she asked, "What will you do once John is too old to be cared for?"

Ma had never thought of this before. Although John had transformed from a toddler with chubby wrists into a sassy young boy, she had imagined he would remain small forever, and forever need her help. With her tongue, Ma fiddled with a kernel of burned garlic wedged between two molars. "I guess . . . I would find another family here."

"In Hong Kong?" Rhea passed the plates to the group of women. The cash passed under the plates into her fake Gucci fanny pack.

"Yes, why?"

"Do you remember my Tito Remy?" Rhea took off her rubber gloves, tossed them into a designated garbage bag and reached for a small bottle of lotion in her fanny pack. Ma had never met Rhea's uncle but remembered the name. After Ma's Lola Edith had already trained Rhea to be a domestic worker, her Tito Remy had come forward, offering to care for the child his brother had long abandoned. By then, however, Rhea was no longer a child. That was what Lola Edith had argued was the reason Rhea could remain at her home. Although in truth, Ma believed, Lola Edith simply loved Rhea and wanted to keep her in the only stable home Rhea had ever known. "He wrote me a letter," Rhea continued, now slathering the lotion over her chafed hands. "His wife is in Canada now, working as a nanny. They have a system where you work in their house, take care of their children, then you can apply to be a permanent resident."

Ma looked down at her half-finished plate of silog breakfast, the elements of the breakfast suddenly looking unfamiliar, the fat waxing at the edges of the sausage. Hong Kong seemed like the natural-choice location for working abroad. It was a short flight to Manila in case there was an emergency. Not that she could afford to return anytime soon. The soonest she could return was the following year around Christmas, given her modest monthly wage of five hundred Hong Kong dollars. Ma scraped together a subo, collecting a small portion of rice, longanisa and omelette onto her spoon to make it the perfect mouthful, and considered this strange possibility for the first time.

"Will you apply?" Ma asked before spooning the subo into her mouth.

"I was talking with Manny and we agreed that the best thing to do is get married when I visit back home next month, then apply. That way, once I get my PR in Canada, I can sponsor him too."

Ma had to swallow hard, the food tasting either too sweet

or too salty, too soft or too hard, it was difficult to ascertain which. "Sponsor? You can sponsor your family?'"

"Yes, mare!" Rhea zipped up her fanny pack at the sight of a hawker control officer pacing along the line of cardboard patches, a look of suspicion turning the ends of his lips downward. "You just have to work for two years. That's all! Just two years."

Two years. Ma's gaze softened over the crowd of Filipinas picnicking along the sidewalk, their collective sing-song chatter dampened by thoughts of an alternate future. Part of her ached at the thought of losing Rhea. She was her best friend, the only one she knew from her old town of San Marcelino. Rhea was like family. But so was Ale, and the possibility of reuniting with him, under the same roof, working towards more stable prospects, made her insides churn with excitement.

"Thank you, mare. It was delicious." Ate Lettie piled her and her crew's paper plates and handed them to Rhea, who threw them into the garbage bag. "Will I see you at my spot today?" Ate Lettie said, looking directly at Ma. The two barely knew each other, and in truth, Ma liked it that way. Ate Lettie's energy gave Ma the willies. Her porcelain skin and the benevolent look she gave to all around her reminded Ma of the religious icons her Tito Crisanto sculpted. But instead of the blue shroud of Mother Mary, Ate Lettie liked to wear simple cotton T-shirts over three-quarter-length slacks.

"Um . . . maybe another day. Thank you." Ma averted her eyes and tried to finish her meal, now too cold to enjoy.

When Rhea ran out of food to sell, the two lay down on the cardboard with their feet up along the side of the escalator.

It felt good not to have to think about whether or not John needed to pee. Whether his face needed wiping. If he was hungry or tired. Rhea's and Ma's feet were propped up beside each other, Rhea's a pair of flip-flops, Ma's a pair of slip-on Keds. The two updated each other about tsismis back home. Who was dating. Who was married. Who was cheating.

"You think he's cheating on Maan? Really?"

Rhea scoffed at Ma's innocence. "Of course Freddy is cheating on Maan. They all cheat. The Philippines is full of men who cheat on their wives."

"Even Manny?" Rhea didn't answer. She just slipped off her flip-flops, let them fall to the ground, and wiggled her chipped pink toenails.

With nowhere to go and no money to spend, the rest of the Sunday unfolded the way it always did: Rhea and Ma lying side by side on the cardboard, napping. They surrendered to sleep in each other's presence with the ease of childhood friends. Not so long ago, they were young girls lying down on Lola Edith's couch for the siesta, whispering into each other's ears about the potential of the future. Now they were women dreaming of a future uncertain.

Ma returned to the Tsang house well before the sun set over the cityscape. She shared the private elevator with two of the catering staff and made herself small against the farthest corner to allow space for their stainless-steel cart. The doors opened to the penthouse floor and the sound of the babbling koi pond. It looked like the caterers were almost finished packing up and heading out. One of them stood atop a tall ladder to remove the balloon sculpture of the number forty. They would be disposed of outside to avoid disturbing the Tsang family with the loud popping noises. But how they were going to fit the balloon banner into the private elevator was a mystery.

Ma tried to creep her way up the grand staircase (now made of Plexiglas, which gave her goosebumps each time she climbed it) to avoid Mrs. Tsang so that she wouldn't offer Ma tasks on her day off. Her eyes met those of Luz, who frowned at her before she entered the butler's pantry to prep for tomorrow's meals. What was that about?

"MG." Ma tried to locate the sound of Mrs. Tsang's voice, now stern and sullen. A warm knot of worry formed behind Ma's belly button. All of us Maybe Babies were inside of her, feeling her body temperature rise, and we all braced ourselves.

Mrs. Tsang sat on a velvet settee in the centre of her walk-in closet. It felt like an intrusion into this place Ma had never seen before. Any place John was not permitted was also forbidden for her. But Mrs. Tsang demanded Ma enter but did not invite her to sit down on the settee opposite her, so Ma stood by the door with her hands interlaced by her waist. The ceilings were taller here in the master suite area, which accommodated the closet's expansive storage. Gowns that Ma had never seen Mrs. Tsang wear hung heavily from their wooden hangers on her right. Shoes that Ma had never seen Mrs. Tsang walk around in were displayed on lit shelves to the left. And at its centre, Mrs. Tsang sat in an emerald-green sequined cocktail dress. Her stilettos lay collapsed on the floor just beyond her feet. Ma wanted to remark about how beautiful she looked and how nice it was to see her not having to wear her headset but thought better of it. Mrs.

Tsang may have worn her dress with her zipper half undone, but the look on her face was a full-fledged sulk.

"Luz told me she saw you come in. I've been waiting to talk to you." We Maybe Babies could feel Mrs. Tsang's power course through Ma's body, the searing sensation of her gaze. We all trembled. "Did you tell John he could pee in the boxwoods?"

"Excuse me, ma'am?" Ma stuttered, trying to buy herself time.

"You heard what I said, MG. Did you let him pee in the bushes? The bushes that cost me hundreds of dollars to buy and hundreds of dollars to install."

Ma's interlaced fingers transformed into wringing hands. "Um . . . yes. I did. I . . . I always make him pee before we go swimming, but he had to go once we were in the pool and I—"

"You just let him pee in the bushes then? Like a savage?"

"I told him he had to go to the washroom but he said—"

"He told me you let him pee in the bushes. Are you lying to me?"

"No. No. But he said that he needed to go now. I didn't want him to slip while running to the washroom, so I—"

"So you let him go into the boxwoods."

There was a long pause before Ma responded, head down. "Yes."

"On this day, during our big party to celebrate Mr. Tsang's fortieth birthday, our guests watched in horror as our son John—the child who *you* are in charge of—peed into the box-woods!" Ma felt the beginning of a laugh escape her throat and she quickly covered it up by coughing hysterically. "Cover your mouth, you monkey!"

Ma's vision blurred a bit until she could hear the muffled sound of Mr. Tsang finishing his shower, the silence between them amplified.

"Have we not treated you like family?" Ma felt herself nodding. "Do you know how lucky you are, living in this lavish penthouse? Hong Kong is a city of tiny apartments, people living on top of one another, and you get your very own bed in John's room. We always pay you on time. You eat what John eats. We don't treat you like a slave like others in Hong Kong may treat you. In this city, there are restaurants where women like you aren't even served. And yet, and *yet*! Here you are, instructing our son to pee in bushes like he is some wild animal."

More noises from the washroom.

"I've always treated my help like family, and I see now that that was a mistake. Now go before Mr. Tsang sees you." Ma rushed out of the closet, the taste of bile at her throat. "Oh! And be sure to give John his bath and put him to bed. I am too exhausted to deal with him."

On her way out, she could hear Mr. Tsang's low voice, with his wife responding in kind, loving tones. Ma shut the master bedroom door and walked (floated?) to John's room, where she had slept for the last two years.

"MG!" John abandoned his train set and ran towards her, still wearing a kid-sized tuxedo. His lapel was smeared with blue icing and the corners of his mouth were crusted with cake. He embraced Ma's legs as he always did, only now, his face burrowed into her abdomen and not her knees like before. He had grown so much. Ma took a look at him and could see the sugar intake making his eyes swirly.

"What did you eat?!" she said, even though it was written all over his face. "Did you have fun?" The contrived joy in Ma's voice managed to hide the shame burning the width of her chest.

John pulled away from her and looked down at his feet. "There was a singer. She sang a song to Daddy. I got in trouble for touching the piano during her song." Ma embraced him and rocked him side to side. Who was comforting who?

"How about we do bath time and we can read as many books as you want before bed? How does that sound?" Ma felt him nod in the folds of her abdomen. "Okay. Get undressed and I will draw you a bath."

That night, yet another plane flew into Hong Kong, its wingspan magically descending into the airstrip without touching the city's skyline that hugged it on all sides. Ma watched the angle of lights streak across John's bedroom ceiling as she tossed and turned on her floor mattress beside him. She rubbed away a line of sweat that gathered in her neck crease. What was happening back home? At this time of the night, there would be one more hour until the rooster at the Duvals' house, whose left foot had been eaten by a hungry rat, would crow at the first sign of sunrise. Kuya Rollie at the San Carmen Family Bakery would be punching down the siopao dough in time for breakfast delivery. The night shift at the call centres would be over and a wave of tired workers would be heading home, while the day-shift workers would be heading out. Ale. She needed to call Ale. And she had to do it quickly before Mrs. Tsang caught her. She didn't like Ma using the line even when Mrs. Tsang wasn't working, which was rare. The few times she did use the phone, Mrs. Tsang liked to stand close by with her arms crossed and her lips pursed.

Ma put her calling card in her sweatpants pocket, then slowly turned the knob of the bedroom door to keep the latch bolt from making a sudden sound. She tiptoed down the grand staircase, feeling like she was floating on air with its Plexiglas treads. Another plane took off from the middle of the skyline as Ma scuttered past the grand piano in the living room, past the floor-to-ceiling wine fridge, past the immaculate kitchen's waterfall marble island, to the butler's pantry where there was a phone and some privacy. The pantry was accessed by opening a false cupboard beside the coffee bar in the kitchen, decked out with fake jars of colour-coordinated dried pasta that were adhered to its shelves. Ma opened the false cabinet door, entered the pantry, and shut the door behind her, as quiet as a mouse. After turning on the under-cabinet lighting, Ma spotted the telephone. *So this is where Luz called Mrs. Tsang to alert her of my arrival,* Ma thought to herself. She took the phone off the hook and held it in between her shoulder and her ear. The sound of the dial tone made her heart pound. She fumbled with her calling card, dialing the main number on the back.

The calling card's robot lady announced, "You have . . . two minutes remaining for this call." Ma dialed her home number. Ehhhh-ehhhh. Ehhhh-ehhhh. Click.

"Hello?" Ale sounded rushed. Why was he rushing?

"Ale?" Ma whispered.

"Helloooo?" Ale sang back. "I can't hear you."

Ma whispered harder. "Ale! It's me. MG."

"Are you okay? Why are you whispering?"

"I can't . . . sorry, are you busy or something?"

"I'm on my way to work. You know that."

"Oh. I'm sorry, it's just . . ." Ma kneaded the skin on her forehead with the fingers of her free hand. "I'm sorry. I had a bad dream." She pounded her fist into her forehead. *Why did I say that?*

Ale laughed. "MG. My love. You're calling about a bad dream?"

"You have . . . thirty seconds remaining for this call," said the robot lady. Ma wanted to pull the hair from her eyebrows. She wanted to scream. If Ma could put a microphone to her soul, she would say:

*I am scared. I don't want to be here any longer.*

*I've just been disciplined like the family dog.*

*I am so lonely. I am so desperately lonely. I need to end this.*

Instead, Ma sighed and laughed along. "I'm silly. I'm sorry to bother you, Ale. Have a good day at—" click. The calling card was empty. Ma placed the receiver into the cradle. When she turned around, there was Luz in her duster dress, her hands on her hips. Ma covered her mouth in a silent scream. Luz's usual chignon was undone and a silver braid cascaded down the yellow paisley of her dress fabric.

"John was having trouble sleeping. I thought I'd get him some—"

"Stop!" Luz stage-whispered. "All of you young helpers don't know how to work. All you know is how to break the rules and complain. Why are you here? What are you working for?"

There was a moment of silence, then Ma said, "I send money home, just like you."

"We're nothing alike. I know what I'm sending money home for. I have three daughters. All of them are in school. All of them know how to fend for themselves because I've been away since my youngest was eight. I don't work for Mrs. Tsang. I work for them. And that means I do what Mrs. Tsang wants, I obey her rules and I send money home. That's all. I have no time for complaining. I have no time for being lazy. I have no time for calling my daughters in the middle of the night."

"I just needed to call my hus—"

"Enough already." Luz slowly turned back towards the door. She noticed a few crumbs on the counter and used one hand to scrape them into the cupped palm of the other. She tossed the crumbs into the rubbish bin by the microwave. Without making eye contact she added, "Either endure the work or go." She left the pantry.

A year later, Ma helped host Rhea's despedida de soltera. It was the last time Rhea attended the Sunday gatherings. At her usual spot, Ma and the rest of Rhea's friends celebrated her upcoming nuptials. No making cash on the side. No hustling. No cooking. In fact, the crew cooked for her, although Ma could tell by Rhea's modest spoonfuls that she didn't think the quality of the bibingka, pancit and adobo was to her standard. Ma made a point of mentioning that the spread was cooked by Isidra and Nora on several occasions to wipe her hands clean of any mediocrity.

The gals took a roll of tissue paper and crafted a clumsy veil and wedding dress.

"Ready?" Ma said, looping arms with Rhea, pretending to be a proud father. The pair strolled down the centre of the cardboard patches while onlooking helpers sang an off-tune wedding march. *Ba-dum-dah-duuuum. Ba-dum-dah-duuuum. Ba-dum-dah-dum-dah-dah-dum-dah-duh-duuuum.* Applause. Ma looked at Rhea, once an abandoned child, soon to be a wife. "Who will walk you down the aisle, mare?"

Rhea's eyes filled with happy tears. "I will walk with the Lord."

One helper pressed play on her boom box. A ballad by Destiny's Child. The helper turned the volume to max and the crowd swayed to the music. Ma and Rhea slow danced together. One by one, the other helpers pinned bills to Rhea's toilet-paper veil, as they would at a traditional wedding. They were small denominations, but every bit counted.

"What time are you flying home?"

"Tomorrow morning. Early. Wedding on Saturday. Then Canada on Wednesday." It was all so quick. Rhea's Tito Remy had managed to find her a family to sponsor her caregiver application.

Ma embraced her childhood friend. "I'm going to miss you so much, Rhea."

"Why don't you come to Canada with me? All of our families can be together." Ma playfully spun her around to side-step a response. The crowd cheered.

After Rhea unpinned the money and placed it in her fake Gucci fanny pack, after the toilet paper was removed, after the food was consumed, Rhea hugged Ma one last time and went to her employer's home to prepare for her journey. Ma sat on the empty cardboard patch and looked out at the sea of domestic workers, now going about their business as usual. In one corner a group giggled while turning the pages of a magazine. On another patch, a group held hands in prayer. Ma took off her Keds and lay down on the ground. She put her feet up on the wall of the escalator, wishing for Rhea's feet to couple with hers. *Canada,* she thought to herself.

On the side of my mother's right palm lives the memory of hiding from my father. It was with this small section of her hand that she leaned on a pillar at the arrivals exit at Ninoy Aquino Airport another year later, her life in Hong Kong now a painful chapter closed.

"They told me they would wait for us here with the car," said a woman in sunglasses who pushed past Ma. Behind her was her husband trying to keep pace. The couple made their way to the large crowd of people waiting for their loved ones to return home. The husband's suitcase wheel ran over Ma's sandalled toes. "Sorry, ma'am!" Ma nodded to assure him it didn't hurt even though the pain made her eyes water.

Ma peeked at the crowd through the cloud of diesel smoke. One man paced impatiently, looking at a chit of paper and at the sea of people exiting the airport. One group of women waved frantically at another woman and her son, welcoming them in a tight embrace, their arms intertwined through the gate. A hawker, covered in dust, sold plastic flowers to another couple in the crowd. They exchanged pesos while the hawker's cigarette dangled between the gap in his two front teeth. As an added touch, the hawker added a small balloon that read "Welcome home!" Another large family rushed by Ma with three carts of balikbayan boxes full of presents to give to their relatives. Ma curled her toes at the sight of the carts' wheels as they passed her.

"Taxi, ma'am?" one of the airport personnel asked Ma. She shook her head and went back to peering out at the mass of people outside, greeting their loved ones. She finally spotted Ale. His hair was longer now, like those grunge rockers Ma had seen on television. It was wavy and split in the middle. He leaned on the gate with a soft gaze over the crowd, zoning out but not searching for her. Ma watched him long enough to see him shift from one leg to another impatiently. A murky sensation brewed in her chest. It felt too vulnerable to walk out into the open, hoping he would at least see her and wave her down, eager to hold her again after three years of being apart. The murky sensation spread to her armpits and she could feel the moisture pooling there, the Manila humidity thick enough to cut with a knife. She strategized.

Ma walked along the gate, keeping her body neutral and not needy. This was difficult since Ma's suitcase, unlike everyone else's, did not have wheels. But she managed to keep a pace that gave her an air of nonchalance. She remembered how casual her parents were each time they were reunited after Lolo's long gigs in the Middle East. They never leapt into each other's arms. They never fawned over each other at the dinner table. They acted like being apart for years at a time was perfectly normal. Ma took a breath and tried normal on for size. It did not work. Ale did not call out to her.

Out of the side of her eye, she saw him in the crowd, still day-dreaming, not paying attention.

She tried again, circling back to the exit of the arrivals gate and walking past Ale. This time, she ran her fingers through her hair.

"MG!" she heard him cry out at last. Ma wanted to embrace him through the gate, but he gestured to the side. Ma's stomach sank. Did he not want to hug her immediately? Had he not dreamed of this moment every day like she did? The two met at the end of the gate and hugged. He smelled different. "I didn't recognize you with your short hair." Ma touched the tresses of her chin-length bob, the sensation of relief coursing through her veins. *Yes. It was my short hair. He didn't recognize me and that's why he didn't wave me down.*

Without telling her he liked the new haircut, the new haircut she got to impress him, he took her suitcase and the two sought out a jeepney outside the compounds of the airport. In the crowded cabin, they sat beside each other, their arms touching on one side and touching strangers' arms on the other. Across from them, an elderly man read his Bible. He frowned at the sight of Ma's suitcase taking up space on the floor. She would have placed it on top of the jeepney had it not been taken up by three other passengers sitting on the roof, hanging on for dear life. With every bounce over every pothole, the various trinkets on the driver's dashboard swayed and clinked.

Ma stole a look at her husband. His once clean-shaven face had the beginnings of a beard struggling through his pores in sparse patches. She desperately wanted to touch his face but feared he would flinch at this public display of affection. He looked older now, no longer the little boy from her hometown. No cigarette sitting at the top of his ear. His elbow felt sharp against hers as he flicked the roof of the jeepney twice for them to be let off.

With the remittance Ma was sending to Ale, he and Ate Marcy had been able to find a larger place to live. Originally Doña Ramos's maids' quarters, the cinder-block building sat behind the old woman's mid-century home. She was the widow of a renowned war hero, and her lush garden reflected her comfortable life. It was here that Ate Marcy had worked as a tutor to Doña Ramos's grandchildren. With all of Doña Ramos's children and grandchildren moving to the United States, Ate Marcy became Doña Ramos's caregiver, cooking her meals, cleaning the empty house and reading her the newspaper. The old woman had no need for any other help and offered Ate Marcy the maids' quarters—for a fee, of course. The rent was more than the room behind the repair shop. But outside in the fenced-in courtyard, there was a proper stovetop where Marcy could cook and a clothesline for them to hang their laundry.

Ale hugged Ma's suitcase and walked the meandering stone path through Doña Ramos's garden. Brain coral poked out between unfurling ferns. Orchid roots twisted around rotten logs while their blossoms caught the splinters of sunlight through the waving palms.

"Ah!" Ma exclaimed as her foot missed one of the stone steps. She reached her hand out, hoping Ale would steady her.

He did not. Ale gulped at the sight of her hand and hugged the suitcase tighter. "Watch your step."

They made their way to the back of the home to the maids' quarters. Ma could hear the traffic from the back alley. Ale opened the door.

"Go ahead," he said. No eye contact. Ma entered and inhaled. The smell of stale food was familiar even if the place was different. With the small window on one side of the building, there was little circulation. The air was stagnant and quiet. Ale gave a short tour. Their bed lined the wall on one side of the main room, with storage cabinets underneath. A Formica kitchen-table set and armchair stood opposite. In the one bedroom was Ate Marcy's queen bed, which she shared with her children. Taped up on the walls was artwork from Ging and Ellie, with the occasional A+ test (teacher notes reading "Great Job, Ellie!").

"Where's Ate Marcy and the kids?" Ma asked.

Ale looked shyly at his feet. "She flew to Aklan to accompany Doña Ramos to a funeral. The old lady offered to let her bring her family too." Ma tried to smile as if it was a relief that they had the house to themselves. She was certain Ate Marcy had agreed to the arrangement to give Ale and her privacy, but she had hoped that the kids and their funny antics would thaw the ice between them.

Their grumbling tummies and the high sun signalled that lunch was approaching. Ale suggested they walk to the nearest restaurant to eat. My parents made their way to Juan's BBQ without holding hands.

"Look," Ma said, breaking the silence. In a corrugated metal lean-to, an old man slowly turned the lechon over the fiery spit using a metal crank. "I haven't seen this in so long. I can't wait to eat it." The old man stood for a moment to pour a spoonful of coconut oil over the roasted pig's shiny, crispy torso, then sat back down on his haunches. Through the smoke that wafted from the shack Ma could see the man's eyes, blank yet focused on his hours-long task. When she looked to the side at her husband, she saw that he too had the same vacant face, only his eyes were downcast at his sandalled feet making their way to the front of the shack.

My parents took their places on the restaurant's purple plastic seats and waited for their order. A motorcycle sped past, leaving a cloud of diesel fumes looming over them. Ma reached for her handkerchief in her purse and covered her mouth until the dust settled onto the surface of the road beside them, until it settled over the hawker roasting chestnuts to the right of them, until it settled over the faces of the two small girls begging for alms to the left of them.

"No," Ma shook her head at the children, and they knew to move on to another couple in the open-air restaurant. Their diminutive brown hands were permanently cupped as they walked down the street, one refusal after another.

Just as Ma mustered enough bravery to ask Ale how work was going, the restaurant's waitress, who was also cashier and probably the owner, approached their table with their orders on Styrofoam plates. Ma forced the shape of her mouth to quickly transform from the beginning of a sentence to a delighted smile to not look foolish. My mother and father ate through their meal quietly, making perfect subo spoonfuls of rice, lechon and Sarsa sauce. It felt conflicting, savouring each morsel of crispy skin while her chest burned with uncertainty. Ale still had a few bites left on his plate when Ma stood up and gently rested her hands on the back of her chair.

"What are you doing?"

"Nothing. Nothing." Ma forced a smile. Casual.

"No, really. What are you doing?"

"Um . . ." Ma adjusted her slacks over her hips to minimize her silhouette before she explained. "The other helpers in Hong Kong did this after eating. We all did it. Ate Felipa said it helps the food go down so that we can digest it and we won't get fat."

Ale scoffed. "Sit down. That's nonsense."

"But Ate Felipa was very skinny."

"That may be true, but standing like that after a meal won't help you." Ma blushed. He *did* think she was fat. "Please. Sit down. I can't talk to you while you're standing like that." Ma obeyed, even though he didn't really talk to her during the meal anyway.

They made their way back to the house.

"I wish we could go to the Magnolia Ice Cream Shop in our old barrio," Ma said, a contrived laugh escaping her lips. She had hoped this would signal Ale to think of a place to get something sweet, but he did not respond to her unspoken cues. She walked with her arm swinging freely, hoping he would reach out and hold her hand. He did not. "But this barrio is much nicer."

They approached the Chinese graveyard, which was one block away from Doña Ramos's house. Its tall white gates guarded clusters of palatial mausoleums, capped in encaustic tile roofs, curving upwards at each corner. Ma ran her hand along the cast iron fence but soon removed it, feeling she was intruding on a private resort for the dead.

She yawned, suddenly overtaken by fatigue.

"You're tired."

"No, no. I'm good."

Ale looked at her, his brow furrowed. "Weren't you up early this morning for your flight?"

Ma forced her face into a look of renewed energy. "Yes . . . but I'm—"

Ale opened the back gate to their home and gestured for her to enter. "Then why don't you rest." Ma obeyed. Once they made their way inside their home, she sat on the mattress, looking up at my father, wondering if he wanted to hold her, kiss her, make love. But he grabbed a packet of cigarettes.

"I'll leave you be." He went outside and smoked in the courtyard. Once he closed the door, Ma snuck to the small window and watched him for a moment, wanting a clue, any clue, about what he was thinking. Helpless, she lay back down on the bed. She burrowed her face into the pillows, smelling the scent of Ale's hair.

She awoke to the sound of rain on the corrugated metal roof. "Ale?" she called out. Ma looked outside. The heavy droplets of rain fell on an empty courtyard. Ale's ashtray was filled with muddy water. *He left me,* Ma thought to herself as she turned around and saw him asleep in an armchair. It must have been a piece of Doña Ramos's hand-me-down furniture, judging by the beat-up leather and weathered armrests Ale slumped over. "Ale?" Ma said again, although he could not hear her over the sound of the downpour. A bolt of lightning struck, followed by the boom of thunder.

Ale finally came to. "Are you okay?"

"Yes. Sorry to wake you," Ma said, even though the thunder wasn't her fault.

In the premature darkness, Ale tried to flick on the lights. "Another blackout." He searched the drawers in the bathroom for candles and matches. Nothing. "I'll get some in Doña Ramos's house. Give me a second." Ma followed him into the rain like a puppy. "MG. Go back inside. You'll get wet." Ma pretended not to hear him, and both of them walked through the courtyard, necks bent against the torrent. They entered Doña Ramos's back French doors just as another bolt of lightning flashed through the sky.

Ale headed to the kitchen, while Ma looked around the old woman's stately home. The wall-to-wall mahogany dampened the sound of the rainstorm outside just enough that she could hear the delicate tick-tock of a grandfather clock. Built-in cabinets displayed Doña Ramos's sepia family photos. In one old group portrait, two rows of women sat in three-quarter turn to allow for the width of their butterfly sleeves. In another photo, Doña Ramos sat in a high-backed chair while her late husband stood proudly beside her. Her 1940s cocktail dress with a sweetheart neckline was hand-coloured an emerald green. Her husband's army uniform was hand-coloured a khaki brown. Turning from the photos, MG surveyed the rooms. Just beyond the long dining room set was a plantation rocking chair with an unravelled wicker backing. Its extra-long armrests were meant to accommodate a plantation owner's tired legs as well, as he surveyed his land. The way it sat there, empty in the darkened room, made the hair on Ma's forearms stand on end. A cockroach scurried across the floor, opened its wings and flew past Ma's head. Ma screamed.

"Are you all right?!" Ale ran to her, blackout supplies in his arms. Ma dismissed her fear with the wave of one hand and held her thumping heart with the other.

"Here. Let me help you." Ma took a few of the jar candles from Ale's grasp and put the lighter under her shirt to keep it dry.

"Ready?" Ale held the doorknob of the back door. Ma nodded. "Let's go!" The two ran across the courtyard to the maids' quarters as fast as they could, the rain now coming down in unrelenting sheets. They were both soaked, with Ale's jeans heavy at his waist and Ma's bra showing through her shirt.

"Shit!" Ale used a bath towel to cover the bottom of the front door, now leaking water. He approached the small kitchen table, now piled with candles and flashlights. Ma passed him the lighter from under her shirt. Standing over a Mother Mary candle, Ale grappled with the spark wheel of the lighter. "Damn it!"

"Let me try." Ma reached out, but Ale pushed her hands away. He tried again. And again. And again. He finally threw the lighter across the room.

"I told you! I told you to stay here and keep dry!" He pinched the skin between his eyes.

"Ale. I'm sorry, mahal. I should have listened." Ma reached for his shoulder and he ducked from her touch.

"You should have stayed!" He howled in anguish, his voice cracking. His face contorted, squeezing sorrow through his

73

downward pout. Then, finally, he released a sob so deep Ma thought it was another person's voice, in another room, from another time. He collapsed into the armchair, hiccupping from his weeping. Ma approached carefully until she was standing in front of him. He leaned forward and cried into the softness of her belly. "If only my job . . . if only I could . . ." Ale's hiccups were deep enough to shake them both. Ma rocked him side to side until he was quiet again.

Ale looked up at her with his swollen eyes and red nose. His hair was starting to curl as it dried. Ma's hair was still painted to her forehead from the rain. He eyed the shape of Ma's bra through her tee, the cup slightly misshapen in the damp. Ma's cheeks flushed as she arched her back. Ale's hand reached up to undo the clasp. Ma helped him out by looping her arms out of her bra straps and pulling it through her sleeve. Ale let his thumbs encircle Ma's brown nipples through the wet cotton shirt until they were hard enough for him to bite. Ma gasped.

They both removed their bottoms in a flash and Ale sat back down in the armchair, welcoming Ma to sit on top of him. She had never done that before and it felt clumsy mounting him on this old piece of furniture, but she managed. Breathing heavily, she held his erection in her hand and guided it into her, his warmth a confirmation. *He still loves me.* Their kisses were messy and hungry. There were times Ma could not tell if Ale was sweating or crying. But when they were done, something finally shifted.

My mother and father stood by the small window, both of them naked from the waist down, and watched the rainstorm turn into a light drizzle and then stop. During that time, Ma leaned her head on Ale's shoulder and told him about her final days in Hong Kong.

She explained that John had grown to an age where he needed less care. Mrs. Tsang sourced a helper who cooked, cleaned and supervised his schoolwork. Although Ma and Luz were both capable, she sent them both packing in the interest of giving their home "new energy and a new beginning." There was little ceremony around their departures. On the day Ma was scheduled to leave, she thought at least that John would be emotional about it. She was like a second mother to him after all. Had she not toilet trained him? Taught him how to read in English? Spell his name? Was she not the person who soothed him through his recurring nightmares? Ma packed her suitcase, then made her way to the private elevator. John was already running about the colossal penthouse, driving a truck into an army of toy soldiers standing under the grand piano. Mrs. Tsang was busy talking on the phone. Ma had already watched a heartbroken Luz gather her meagre belongings and head out without waving goodbye.

Although she was unsure whether John truly understood that Ma would not be coming back, deep down inside there was a part of her that wanted him to be surprised—no— shocked. She wanted him to ask his mother where she was and watch his mother's pained attempts at explaining her choices. She wanted him to cry, to mourn the loss of her. So with what little dignity she had left, she quietly entered the private elevator and pressed the down button.

"John sounds like he was a brat. His mother sounds like an asshole. Their loss." Ale scooped my mother up and brought her to their bed. There, Ale ran his fingers along the ridges of Ma's naked chest. Ma looked up at the ceiling, the images of Hong Kong intermingling with the sensation of Ale's touch around the globes of her breasts.

"Ale . . . I tried my best to find another employer."

"I know you did." Ale bit into her shoulders.

"But one house, I was sleeping behind their television stand. Another kept delaying my payment." Ma luxuriated in Ale's messy kisses but had to pull away to add, "And that's why I think it's best I try to work in Canada." Ma finally sat up and looked my father in the eye, gauging his reaction.

"Rhea says she can refer me to someone who can sponsor me. Then I can apply for you to join me. We can finally be together."

"But what about my sister? Ging and Ellie?"

"She would have to do the program herself."

Ma watched the possibilities cross my father's face. He looked up at my mother, then sighed at the complications of this conversation. He burrowed his face into Ma's lap. For a moment, Ma thought he had fallen asleep until he slowly moved his lips up her thigh.

For the next several months, my parents went about their daily lives pretending this conversation hadn't happened. In the morning, Ale would commute to the call centre in the Makati Central Business District. To give Ate Marcy a couple more hours of sleep before Doña Ramos was to be tended to, Ma would serve the kids their breakfast and walk them to school before commuting to Happy Hamburger outside Rizal Park. There, she would spend her day dealing with tourists wanting to try the renowned Filipino fast-food chain.

The sunburned tourists would enter the establishment and sigh at the sensation of air conditioning. They'd sort through the unfamiliar pesos and purchase the world-famous spaghetti and hot dogs.

"Weird that you guys are called Happy Hamburger but your bestseller is the spaghetti," the tourist would say, grinning as if it were the first time anyone in the history of humankind had made the observation. Ma would give a noncommittal smile and nod before packing up their order. Two orders of spaghetti and hot dogs. One order of SPAM biscuit sliders. Three orders of mango turnovers. Sarsi cola. Inevitably, the tourist would return to the counter with everything devoured except for the spaghetti and hot dogs.

"It's a bit sweet. The sauce is like ketchup," the tourist would say in a disappointed tone, hoping for a refund. Ma would give a noncommittal shrug before passing them a coupon for a free mango turnover.

At the end of the day, Ma would commute back to the house. The transit fare ate up most of what little Ma earned throughout the day. By the time she entered their house, Ate Marcy would have dinner ready. Ma would help with the kids while Ate Marcy headed to her night job, working as a waitress at a Manila Baywalk bar where she served drinks to tourists who liked to touch her bum more than watch the dramatic sunset over the water.

The day Ma had a miscarriage was the day before Rhea called.

In the courtyard, the kids played with firecrackers, adding to the noise of New Year's Eve festivities throughout the barrio.

"Ready, Ate Ellie?" Ging said with a wide smile of newly missing front teeth. Ellie counted down, then dragged the tiny firecracker under her sandal along the rough texture of the asphalt until a line of sparks crackled on the pavement. The two covered their ears and danced in circles.

"Don't forget to wash your hands!" Ma said to the kids as she took down the laundry from the line and folded it into a hamper at her feet. She didn't want the kids to eat dinner with the firecracker chemicals on their hands. Too many kids got poisoned that way.

The firecracker smoke made her nauseous. With the pregnancy three months along, everything made her nauseous these days, including the smell of the laundry detergent on the newly washed sheets she folded. That was why she chewed gum throughout the day. She usually kept her pack of gum in the back pocket of her pants, but it had recently migrated to the chest pocket of her button-up shirt so that she could reach for a stick and scratch her nipple—without it looking like she was scratching her nipple. Two days before, her nipples had become inflamed and itchy as her breasts swelled into an unrecognizable pair of heavy water balloons. Ma started brushing her teeth topless, letting the Vaseline absorb into her areola, hoping the pain would subside. It did not. Things got worse once her lower abdomen joined in on the fun and became prickly as the skin split to allow for her burgeoning belly. Not that she would complain. Her body was a bit of a sci-fi film these days, but having a baby felt like she had finally arrived as a woman. She was Ale's wife and would be the mother of his child. It was also a relief. Being pregnant meant that any notion of Canada would have to wait. If she were to pursue the program, she wouldn't be able to leave until the baby was old enough to be left in the care of Ale and Ate Marcy. It bought them time as a family, pretending they could afford living under the same roof, the inevitable departure looming over their heads.

Where was I in all this? I was sitting, waiting, along with the other Maybe Babies. I have to admit I was jealous. The Lucky One exited our waiting area that time my mother and father made love in the shower. It was one of those miraculous nights where they had enough energy after work, after the kids were asleep. I pretended to wish the Lucky One well, even though I was envious at the thought that they would get to have a name, have a face and a body, and that they would be loved. But I listened to their new heartbeat play out with the sound of Ma's and I felt broken. Really and truly. I felt broken. Hopeless, really. To make things worse, we Maybe Babies had to listen to Ale speak to the Lucky One, by kneeling at Ma's feet and saying to her abdomen, "I'm your daddy. I love you! I can't wait to meet you!" I wanted to scream.

On that New Year's Eve day, I heard the phone ring through the membrane of my mother's body.

"Ellie? Can you answer that?" The kids continued to giggle somewhere in the house. The phone continued to ring. "Ellie?" Another ring. Ma dropped the pillowcase into the hamper and rushed inside to the phone. "Hello?" It was too late. She didn't catch the call in time. *Oh well. If it's important, they'll call back.*

Children's laughter drew her back to the courtyard. Three young boys were throwing rocks into Doña Ramos's mango tree again, hoping the fruit overhanging the back alley would fall their way. Ma stood on a stool and threw back one of the rocks over the gate. She managed to hit the shoulder of the oldest boy before they ran off empty-handed. "Ha! Serves you right. Don't come back here!"

Ma stepped off the stool and saw that one mango lay on the concrete of the courtyard. Its flesh was soft enough to have splashed into a bright orange mess. She picked it up, sad that the fruit had reached its peak only to be wasted. But when she handled it, she noticed dozens of fat red caterpillars, like moving beaded necklaces, squirming in its fibres. Ma dropped the mango and stepped back. Was it the caterpillars that were making her stomach turn in on itself? She clasped a sticky hand to her abdomen.

By the time Ale came home from work, the fireworks were in full swing, Filipino style. More for the sound than for the spectacle. In barrios throughout the city, young boys hit drums made of plastic bins with sticks made of wooden spoons. Fathers closed their eyes and pointed exploding Roman candles towards the sky as their children squealed with every pop. Ground spinners gyrated on the pavement. People drew their names in the air with sparklers.

"MG?" Ale called out before appearing at the bathroom door. Ging and Ellie stood on either side of Ma, who sat on the toilet. "What's wrong?" Little Ellie had her arm draped over Ma. Ging looked up at Ale, unsure of what was going on. Ma stared at the bloody panties around her ankles. She saw Ale's bag and hit the floor, but she did not want to look up into her husband's eyes. She knew he would be devastated. She just couldn't hold his feelings at this moment. Her feelings were much too large for her to hold anyone else's. Ma swallowed and wiped her numb face with her forearm.

"Come. Ging. Ellie." Ale pointed with his chin for them to leave their auntie alone. The kids obeyed. Ale approached Ma and softly kissed her on the forehead. He whispered into her ear, "It wasn't meant to be." It wasn't until he left the bathroom that Ma felt that her ear was wet with Ale's tears.

That night Ma sat in the old armchair with the door open to the courtyard. Ale placed three coins in each of the children's cupped hands and instructed them to shake them for a prosperous year. Every now and then, a burst of light would flash over Ale's head. Ale turned to Ma and gave her a look, saturated with a blend of love and sadness. The left side of his lips turned up slightly trying to manage a smile. Ma looked away into the dark chemical-ridden smoke that hung low over the city.

Did I want this to happen? Of course not. Okay, maybe. I'm ashamed to admit it. Yes. And I hope in this strange place, this in-between place where we two are meeting, you can try not to judge me. You must understand the pain of longing. To wait with the other Maybe Babies felt like torture, seeing, hearing, feeling things but through the body of my mother. I wanted so badly to take my first breath, to be photographed, fawned over. To have my cheeks pinched. To be punished for doing things I wasn't supposed to do, touching things I wasn't supposed to touch. To be measured against a wall, year after year. To grow taller. To be cheered on every time I learned something new. I wanted that. Could you blame me? I didn't think, in my wildest dreams, that my desire to be human meant the loss of another. It was devastating. Now the Lucky One didn't even get to dream like the rest of us. The dream for them was over.

If the Lucky One had lived, he would have:

- had at least three nicknames

- been born bald but grown a full head of thick, coarse hair

- been an excellent sleeper, but horrible at teething

- been a lover of bananas and rice, hater of beans and fish

- grown to be a taker of chances, leaving school early to start his own business

- had many secrets, including a long list of lovers

- left the church in pursuit of modern spirituality

- called our mother every week to update her on his travel adventures

- sent our mother postcards from exotic locations that read "I love you, Ma!"

As young as I am, I cannot dwell on my regrets. I'm only a baby, and there isn't much time.

It was New Year's Day and Ma was still sitting in the armchair looking out at the courtyard. Ate Marcy was busy cooking in the kitchen, while the children ran about the house holding Ellie's new Barbie dolls by the legs like machine guns and shooting at each other.

The phone rang. Through the soft cloud of Ma's grief she heard Ate Marcy pick it up and chat with someone on the other end. Ma was relieved that her sister-in-law was willing to pick up the slack and answer any season's greetings they were to receive today. Ma wasn't in the mood.

"MG? It's for you."

Ma reluctantly stood and put the receiver to her ear. A strange buzz. A voice from far away. "MG? It's me." Her voice sounded older.

"Rhea?" Ma's eyes filled with stinging hot tears. If Ma could put a microphone to her soul, she would say:

*Rhea, my unborn child just died and took me with them.*

*Rhea, I feel like screaming, what did I do wrong?*

*Rhea, I would do anything to be nauseous again.*

Instead she said, "Hoy, mare. Happy new year."

Rhea had good news. She had accompanied her employers to a week-long getaway to a ski chalet so that she could care for their two children while the adults hit the slopes with their friends. The host had found out she was pregnant and was looking for a caregiver.

"She can sponsor you, MG!" Rhea said.

The receiver felt hot against Ma's cheek. She looked out at her husband in the courtyard, smoking cigarettes. *I will tell him later*, she thought to herself. *Now that he has lost a child, I cannot tell him that he will soon lose his wife too.*

# 4

Everyone applauded when the plane's wheels touched down in Toronto. They had good reason to do so. It had been twenty-nine hours of flying, not including the twelve-hour layover in Seoul. It was supposed to be a short stop, but Ma's connecting flight had had refuelling issues. The mostly Filipino passengers had been herded like cattle into a waiting area where a large television broadcast Korean slapstick comedy. All night, people tried to sleep on the seats with angular armrests or attempted to change the channel to something more subdued. But the television's buttons were protected by a thick panel of glass. When their flight finally took off, they had a bad case of turbulence while flying over Vancouver. More slapstick comedy played over the shared monitors in the cabin. This time, the passengers helplessly watched Mr. Bean stuff a supersized turkey as they were jostled about in their seats. Ma tried to sleep as best she could, but there was little escape from discomfort. When she closed her eyes, she saw the image of Ale's forlorn face as she walked through the gates and waved goodbye. When she opened her eyes and looked out the window, all she saw was the endless ocean, threatening to swallow her and the plane whole. When she looked to her right, she saw the businessman sitting beside her, his legs manspreading into her space. She should have taken Rhea's advice and swallowed a sedative. Instead, she stared at the overhead fan and blinking seatbelt sign, imagining what life would be like in Canada. If she played her cards right, after two years she could apply for permanent residency and sponsor Ale to join her. They could be together. They could try for another baby. Maybe two. Maybe three. They'd have enough money to live comfortably and to send home remittance to Ate Marcy. All of this was worth it. Even the long plane ride.

Ma had two large suitcases for this job, full of clothes that she believed would help her weather the Canadian winter. When they landed at Pearson Airport, however, there was no sign of snow. In fact, many of the people she passed in the terminal wore shorts or sundresses. She pulled her luggage onto the escalators. She had splurged on cases with wheels, but they were so heavy, it didn't make them any easier to move around. She descended to the ground floor, where people patiently waited for arrivals. Among them was a brown woman who held a sign with Ma's name on it.

"Are you MG?" she asked. Ma was confused. Who was this woman? "Ang pangalan . . . ang ko . . . no. Wait." The attempt at Tagalog coming out of her mouth was like mangled metal. The woman stretched her mouth out and tried again. "Ang pangalan ko ay Helen." She smiled the smile of a child that had just recited their alphabet. Ma hugged her awkwardly, more to make her stop than to greet her warmly.

The woman continued, this time, for all of their sakes, in uptight Canadian English. "I'm Helen Levesque. We spoke on the phone?" Ma finally pieced together that the white woman she thought had interviewed her over the phone was actually this Canadian-born Filipina standing before her. She must have taken the last name of her husband. "How was your flight?"

Ma wanted to share the discomfort and sadness of her trip, how nervous she was, but she thought better of it.

"It was okay."

"Here. Let me help." Helen reached for Ma's other suitcase, but Ma waved Helen's hand away. Helen's pregnant belly hung so low that it looked like she was about to rip open. Delicate caramel highlights graced her perfectly blownout hair.

"No, no. Please. I can manage."

"Let's pay for parking and drive out before rush hour starts."

The journey to their home was eerily quiet in Helen's swank SUV. No constant buzzing from motorcycles cutting in front of them. No series of potholes to drive over. The road was surprisingly smooth—even smoother than the affluent Mid-Levels district in Hong Kong—and Helen's easygoing driving matched the calm. Accustomed to drivers zigzagging around each other in bumper-to-bumper traffic, Ma realized her white-knuckle grip around the grab handle was not needed here.

The Levesque family lived in Toronto's exclusive Forest Hill area. As Helen drove into their neighbourhood, Ma marvelled at the wide spaces between the gated homes. The manicured lawns were green enough that Ma wondered if they were made of AstroTurf, but the rhythmic spray of lawn sprinklers confirmed they were real grass.

"Some of these places are so extra!" Helen said, pointing out the car window at the series of mansions and shaking her head. "We hope by the time Pascal is done with our renovations, our place will feel homier and inviting. Not like these monstrosities."

The SUV pulled into a cobblestone roundabout driveway. One half of the palatial building was covered in scaffolding, while the other half's cedar fascia and trim revealed Pascal's vision for "West Coast Lodge."

While Ma learned her tasks for the house, she learned about her employers. Pascal was a renowned French-Canadian architect, and he juggled his time between designing for condo developments in the downtown core and "putting his stamp" on their home, which Pascal deemed "cookie cutter." This meant that one room could look like it had jumped out of the pages of a magazine, while another looked like a bomb had dropped on it. Ma went about her work, stepping over tarps, brushing dust off her clothes and breathing in paint fumes.

Helen (she insisted on never being called Mrs. Levesque) was the former co-owner of the luxury baby store Mama & Co. By the time Ma entered their lives, Helen had just sold her share of the company, determined to be a stay-at-home mother. "I don't want my kid to be raised by some stressed-out lady, with one eye on her laptop all the time!" she explained with a laugh. "I really want to be . . . oh, god. What is it called? Present."

With Helen's pregnancy brain in full swing, most of Ma's conversations with Helen involved filling in the blanks.

"Oh . . . could you pass the . . . that thing."

"Your water bottle."

"Yes! My water bottle. Thank you," Helen would say as if she had won a contest.

The two women tackled the nursery together, a few weeks before Helen's due date. Ma took to painting everything above and below, while Helen painted what she could standing up.

"Pascal wanted to do this room. Could you imagine if I let him? The feature wall would be some custom-made wallpaper with a Pablo Neruda poem on it and a sculptural light fixture." Ma chuckled even though she only half understood. Helen waddled across the tarp to the paint tray and dipped her roller into the robin-egg-blue liquid. "But I needed this. I needed to decorate our baby's room so that I knew it was real."

Helen explained that three years prior, they had lost a baby to placenta previa. There was blood everywhere. So much blood they almost lost Helen too. "It was tough getting Pascal to try for another baby after what happened. I mean . . . we used to live in this sweet townhome in Bloor West, and it was like he wanted to move as far away as possible from any memory of the home birth. The midwives assured him it would have happened in hospital either way. But I think he blames himself." Helen rolled the paint onto the walls, heavy in thought. Ma was perched on a ladder, unable to continue edging the crown moulding, her brush loaded with paint but inert. The image of a splattered mango on concrete flashed through her mind.

"Anyway . . . I got my way and had the same midwives as last time, and Pascal got his way and we're going to deliver at . . . where's that place called? Sunnybrook Hospital. I just wish he could be as happy as I am about it all."

Ma shook her head out of its fogginess and continued her detailed brushwork along the top of the ceiling. After the frigidity of Mrs. Tsang, Helen's relentless monologues about the state of her marriage, the grief around their unborn child and everything in between felt unnerving. She wasn't sure if Helen wanted her perspective or advice. So she attempted to change the subject matter to something more familiar.

"Are you excited about your party?"

"Sort of. Organizing this baby shower is giving me a headache. With my baby brain, I can hardly keep all the details in my head. I just wish Pascal was more present in all of—"

"I can make lumpia for you," Ma quickly offered, hoping to stop Helen from monologuing yet again.

"Really? Are you sure? You don't have to."

"It's no problem. I love making lumpia for parties."

On the morning of Helen's baby shower, Ma set up shop in their custom kitchen to make the lumpia. A deep frying pan filled with vegetable oil came to temperature on the range. Beside it, Ma placed a paper-towel-lined colander on a plate. On the adjacent breakfast nook, Ma arranged an opened package of lumpia wrappers, a large bowl of seasoned minced pork with a spoon and a small bowl of beaten egg. Ma began separating the lumpia wrappers by carefully walking her fingers along the sheets to pull them apart without poking a hole. Out of the side of her eye, she could see Helen, absentmindedly icing a cake.

"I wouldn't have said yes to your lumpia if I had known it was going to be this much trouble. This looks like a lot of steps!" Helen left her lopsided cake and toddled over to Ma.

"It's not too much trouble! I love doing this. It passes the time." Ma put her sheets of wrapper to the side and reconfigured the layout of supplies to bring the bowl of raw minced pork closer to her. Helen stepped closer.

"Do you need help?" Ma looked at Helen's hopeful face.

"Okay. Sure," Ma said with uncertainty. She rarely liked people "helping" her in the kitchen.

Helen excitedly spun around and grabbed another spoon. "I need one of these, right?"

"Yes . . . and um . . . another plate."

Helen went to the cupboards and got a plate, but it was more of a saucer. Ma corrected her. "No . . . one that's larger and flatter so that you can roll."

Helen sat beside Ma at the breakfast nook, far enough from the table to accommodate her large belly, too close to Ma with her elbows brushing against hers.

"I've never seen this done before. My mom always bought it from the nearby Filipino restaurant. She said it would make the house stink to fry them up herself." Helen copied Ma, who placed a sheet of wrapper on the plate in diamond formation. She used the spoon to scoop out the pork, placed it in the middle of the diamond, then used the bottom corner of the sheet to tuck it tightly into a roll.

"You need to make this tighter," Ma instructed, slightly annoyed that this would make her task more complicated and slow her down, but she could not say no to Helen's child-like wonder at the process. "That's the most important part.

If it's loose, then the pork will escape the casing." Helen managed to tuck in the pork, then folded the right and left corners before rolling it to the top corner. Ma showed her how to use the beaten egg to seal the parcel. She placed the first two lumpia side by side on a baking tray to eventually bring to the frying pan.

"There. See? Our lumpia are almost the same size. That's what you want. You want them all to be the same size, not too much meat, not too much wrapper. And you want to ensure that there is no leftover pork to waste. Good job!" Ma said with finality, hoping Helen would go back to icing her cake or putting flowers in water or whatever women do to prepare for their baby shower.

Helen remained at the table, her elbows infringing on Ma's space as she tried her hand at another lumpia. She held up the spring roll to her face and smiled. "I did it again!" Ma had to admit, Helen was pretty good at it, but she insisted that she alone would be the one to fry everything. She didn't want Helen to get splatter on her gorgeous knee-length silk robe. As Ma placed each spring roll into the oil, she wondered what kind of Filipino family would not have taught their daughter how to make lumpia. What kind of Filipino family would choose a nice-smelling home over good-tasting food? And would this happen to her family once she was reunited with Ale and they lived their life in Canada?

Ma answered the door as each guest arrived.

"MG, you don't need to do that! The door is open. They can let themselves in," Helen insisted. But Ma wanted to keep herself busy, taking everyone's coats instead of immersing herself in the incessant squeals from Helen's friends.

"Look at your beautiful body!" one woman with hip-length extensions screamed while rubbing Helen's belly like a crystal ball. "You are a goddess!"

Another woman in a linen suit hollered into Helen's belly button as if it were a portal to another dimension. "I am your Auntie Meredith! I'll be the fun auntie. You just wait. I'm gonna spoil you!"

During the festivities, Helen's mother, Perla, approached Ma while she was replenishing the punch bowl in the kitchen. She was a stout woman with permed hair that was dyed a burgundy that reminded Ma of tassels on drapery tiebacks in fancy homes. The same shade of burgundy was caked into her thick lipstick, which she marked around the rims of the several glasses she left half-empty around the house. Sparkling lemon water to begin. Mimosas. Lots of mimosas. A couple of glasses of chardonnay. Sparkling lemon water once her speech began to slur. "Mary Grace! The lumpia was delicious. I heard you coached Helen on how to make them. How ffffun!" she said in her repressed Filipino accent, doing her best to pronounce the "f" in "fun." Ma smiled.

"Whoa. Mom. Lay off the mimosas," Helen's sister, Chelsea, said, halfway through eating another lumpia. She had the same face as Helen, only she held it differently, in a perpetual frown. Her button-up patterned shirt seemed too tight around her thick neck.

A blond white woman entered the kitchen and handed Chelsea the car keys. "Babes. I looked in the car. Nothing. We'll have to drive back and get her the gift another time."

"Another time? Look at my sister, Lisa. She's about to pop any moment. Maybe we should drive home now and—"

Chelsea stopped and regarded Ma, who placed sliced pine-apples into the punch bowl. "Sorry. That's rude. MG, this is my wife, Lisa. Lisa, this is MG. My sister's new nanny."

"Oh, hi! Nice to finally meet you. Helen has nothing but great things to say about you."

"Sorry," Chelsea added, leaning in. "Is that the right term? Nanny? Or caregiver?" Ma found herself smiling wide, looking back and forth between Chelsea and Lisa. Did Chelsea say "wife"?

Pascal arrived three-quarters into the party, holding two bags of ice. By then, Helen was opening gifts while her friends and family sat in a neat circle, oohing and aahing at the adorable sleeper sets and booties.

"Sorry it took me so long, hun," Pascal said as he walked to Helen and kissed her forehead, nudging the paper crown she wore slightly off-centre. He righted his designer black-rimmed spectacles on the bridge of his nose and nervously rubbed his shaved head. "I've placed the ice in the freezer. Hey, everyone." The women all smiled and waved. "Okay. I'll leave you to all this girly stuff and I'll see you later." Before he went up the stairs, two treads at a time, he nodded in Ma's direction.

Ma had already placed the lunch plates in the dishwasher and was able to peek into the living room to watch the rest of the gifts get opened. One of Helen's workers from the baby store explained the nondescript envelope's contents.

"It's a gift certificate for a plaster belly-casting session with Fernando Cosas. Have you heard of him?"

"Are you kidding me? Yes."

"I was able to book him next week before your due date, so . . ."

"That's incredible. Thank you!"

"I mean . . . it was tough getting a present for a former owner of a luxury baby store, am I right?" The crowd of women all groaned in agreement.

Helen placed the certificate to the side, the last gift in the pile. "Thank you all for coming today. I really, really, really appreciate you all. And I know many of you were there for me when . . ." She looked at her guests, choking back tears. "This has been a long road. And sometimes, I wondered if we would ever get here. But now . . . with you all here, celebrating me. It finally feels real. I'm going to be a mom. I'm so damn excited!" The women gave her a gentle group hug. Ma exhaled and returned to the kitchen.

Helen did not make it to her belly-casting appointment with Fernando Cosas.

A few days before her due date, Pascal announced he needed to make a quick trip to the west coast to oversee the design of a new Whistler condo development. In the nursery, Ma did her best to pretend she was stacking diapers in the change table when she was actually eavesdropping.

"Don't look at me like that."

"Like what?"

"If I'm needed at work, I need to go."

"I'm due on Wednesday, Pascal."

"I have a job, okay? I'm not like you. I didn't get to sell my shares of a successful business. I have to show up when they need me to show up."

"Isn't that convenient? Just when I'm about to give birth."

"What? What the fuck are you talking about? What are you? Some kind of therapist?"

"No. But you need one."

Ma began earnestly hanging onesies in the closet as Pascal rushed past the nursery doorway, suitcase in hand. Helen followed him as fast as her swollen legs would allow.

"Pascal. This isn't going to be like the last time. I promise you."

Ma could hear Pascal's voice quivering. "You can't promise me that."

"Pascal? Pascal!"

Steps to the foyer. Door closing. Ma shuffled to the nursery window and saw a cab reversing down the driveway. Ma found Helen sitting at the top of the staircase, her head in her hands. She approached her carefully, sat beside her and placed a cautious hand on her shoulder. Helen immediately melted into Ma's neck, sobbing in uncontrollable wails.

The next day, Ma agreed to accompany Helen to get her belly cast. After hearing what it entailed, Ma was hesitant.

"Are you sure? Maybe this is a private thing. And I have to do the laundry."

"Fuck the laundry!" Helen said from behind large sunglasses. She drove them both to the nearest McDonald's and lowered the window to place her order. "Two number ones with Coke, three apple pies and a hot fudge sundae, please." Then she turned to Ma. "And what do *you* want to order?" They sat in the parking lot to devour their food. In between bites, Ma would pass Helen tissues as she cried, then ate, then ate and cried. Helen used her finger to remove a splatter of barbecue sauce that stained her shirt. Instead of using the napkin Ma handed her, she licked it off her fingers. "Holy shit, that tastes good." And that's when it happened.

"Oh jeez."

"What?"

"Fuck. My water broke. Fuck." Helen used the crank under her seat to pull herself away from the steering wheel. "Oh god. Oh fuck." She turned slightly, pointing to her purse. "MG, can you please use my cellphone to call for an ambulance? I don't want to give birth in a goddamn McDonald's parking lot."

Helen's contractions were intense enough that by the time they reached Sunnybrook Hospital, Ma had to fill out all the paperwork. "MG, don't leave me. Please."

"Don't you want me to call your mother? Maybe she should be here."

"Hell no!" Helen said, another contraction cresting through her body. "I FUCKING HATE MY MOTHER! SHE IS SUCH A HOITY-TOITY BITCH! DON'T CALL HER OR I WILL KILL YOUUUUU!"

"I'll keep trying Pascal, then," Ma said, scrambling to find an exit strategy.

"FUCK PASCAL! His flight won't land until later."

"I don't think there's time for any phone calls. I need you to hold Helen's leg up during her next contraction," said Esme, Helen's midwife. "This is going faster than we want it to. And with precipitous births, our goal is to ensure Helen doesn't push too hard or it may cause a nasty tear," Esme said as she and her assistant quickly tied up their smocks and snapped on rubber gloves.

"I'm in the room!" Helen said with her eyes closed. "I can hear what you're saying about me."

"You're right, I should have included you." Esme apologized

and adjusted the lamp towards Helen's crotch, now splayed open for all to see.

Ma couldn't help but look at the small bit of scalp that poked through Helen's vaginal lips every time she pushed. Esme circled her fingers along the inside, trying to clear the path for the child.

"Three, two, one. Good! Exhale. Great job, Helen. I can see the baby crowning. Did you want to touch the head of your baby?" Esme guided Helen's hand towards her own crotch. Helen's eyes widened, then shut closed, another contraction taking over. "Take a deep breath in, now push. Ten, nine, eight . . ."

Ma watched as Helen's pelvis widened for the briefest of moments. A flower blossoming. The baby slipped out of her in a wave of blood and silky water, their tiny face squinting at the light. Esme placed the baby on Helen's chest, now crying a raspy cry, its hands grasping at the air. Ma let go of Helen's legs and stepped back, the scene of joy too much to bear.

That night, after Helen and baby Andre came home, Ma cried herself to sleep in her room. In her dreams, I came to her. It was the least I could do. It was at three in the morning, the easiest time to cross into the physical world. What I truly wanted to do was lie next to her, the way she once did with my Lola. But I hadn't a body yet. Instead, I snuck away from the rest of the Maybe Babies and crossed into Ma's dreams. In it, she was trying her best to get on top of a bar stool at the Magnolia Ice Cream Shop. But because she was just a little girl, she couldn't reach. I came to her as another set of hands helping her patent leather shoes step up onto the seat.

"Thanks!" she said to me. I took the shape of another little girl. We were both wearing white lace dresses, as if we had just returned from church. I made two large halo-halo desserts appear before us. We took our long spoons and poked the layers of jackfruit and tapioca pearls until they became a homogeneous mix of ice and evaporated milk.

"Are you my cousin?" Ma said, her voice delightfully small. I hadn't heard that voice in years. I had almost forgotten it.

"No. I'm your baby."

"You're not a baby!" Ma said, trying to get the macapuno fibres onto her spoon.

"I'm not one now. But I will be one day. Maybe. If I'm lucky, you'll be my mother."

"What do I have to do to be a mom?"

"You just have to wait and be patient. That's all." Ma turned to her halo-halo glass and saw that it was empty. She woke up, her hands still curved along the frosty glass of her dreams.

I went back to the other Maybe Babies and waited. And hoped.


Ma's time with the Levesque family was short-lived. Just as Ma had developed a system around documenting Baby Andre's feeding schedule, cooking Helen's meals, doing the family laundry and shopping for groceries, Pascal was transferred for his job. The west coast development's new investors meant the project quadrupled in size and Pascal needed to take the helm in Vancouver. There, Pascal's stepmother had offered to help with the baby full-time.

Helen hugged Ma until the breast milk soaked through her pyjama shirt. "Goddamn it! I'm sorry," Helen said, looking down at the two wet circles on her chest. "I'm gonna miss you so much, MG," was as much of a goodbye as Helen could manage before the baby monitor in her bathrobe pocket began to broadcast the sounds of Andre waking up from his short nap. Helen sent Ma away with a glowing letter of recommendation and a couple of referrals of families that needed caregivers.

# 5

"MG!" Rhea waved from the playground sandwiched between two subdivisions. She pushed a small baby on a swing, the infant stuffed tightly into the black harness. A toddler dug holes in the sandbox with the blunt end of a branch. Ma slowly made her way to Rhea, dragging her two large suitcases through the muck of autumn leaves and mud. Before moving to her next contract, Ma had packed up her things and taken the commuter train west to Oakville for a brief visit with Rhea. Although Ma had been in Canada for almost half a year, this was the first time they'd been able to meet, as their days off didn't match. They embraced.

"You smell funny," Ma said, pulling away from Rhea with a look of concern.

"Toby ate too much cereal this morning. Right, Toby?" Rhea turned to the toddler and nonchalantly dug her finger into his mouth and retrieved a piece of broken beer bottle. Rhea threw it into a garbage bin and pointed an authoritative finger at Toby. "No, thank you. We do not eat glass."

Ma's eyes widened. "My god. Maybe his mouth is cut?!"

Rhea waved off Ma's concern, rolling her eyes. In Tagalog she replied, "This kid. I'm not sure if his mouth is made of leather or he's just evil, but finding pieces of glass on the ground and sucking on them is his favourite activity."

Toby gave Ma a naughty smile and a look from his creepy eyes that made her hair stand on end before he ran off to dig more holes. The baby kicked her heels and whined, her face grumpy under a knitted hat. "Okay, okay, Rose. I haven't forgotten you." Rhea pushed the baby and looked at Ma. "You're fat now."

Ma looked at herself through the thick of her jacket, suddenly unaccustomed to the razor's edge of Filipino observation. "Yes. That Canadian-born Filipina you found me really loved pork adobo!" They laughed. Rhea looked like she had actually lost weight. When Ma witnessed the circus of wrangling the two kids to sit down at a picnic table for snack time, she understood why. First there was a washroom emergency, with Toby thinking he needed to go poo, then changing his mind, then changing his mind again with Rhea rushing him to the nearby porta-potty with seconds to spare. Then there was Rose and her habit of throwing her head back during her tantrums, often hitting Rhea square on her left eye. It did not help that the baby was dressed in the most slippery outerwear that made her feel more like a floundering fish than a child.

The four finally sat down to a snack. Toby stuffed cubes of cheese and blueberries into his mouth in breathless bites on one side of the picnic table. Ma and Rhea sat on the other side with Rose slip-sliding up and down Rhea's lap. Rose drank the milk in her sippy cup by tipping it up and throwing her head back in violent thrusts.

With one arm, Rhea opened a side pocket on her backpack and took out two boxes of calamansi juice and two snack bags. "So where are you headed now?" Rhea poked the straws into the juice boxes and opened the bag of corn nuts. The intense smell of garlic lifted into the air.

Ma took out a transit map from her pocket and unfolded it. She pointed to an area east of Toronto's downtown core. "Helen referred me to a family here. Somewhere called Riverdale."

"Wow. You can take the streetcar to the CN Tower!" Rhea passed Rose to Ma so that she could fish another piece of broken glass out of Toby's mouth, then sat back down. Rhea said something, but Ma couldn't hear her over the crunchy sound in her mouth.

"What did you say?"

"I said you should make friends with the other nannies in your area." Rhea took Rose from Ma and placed her on her lap in a way that signalled Rose to begin her nap. The baby's eyes became heavy as they continued their conversation. "It's not like in Hong Kong where we can gather together and take up space. But you can make friends with those who have the same day off as you. Or even share a house."

"But we're living in our employers' homes, so why would we need to share a house?"

"Some families kick their nannies out on the weekend and they have to find a place to stay. So the nannies pool their money to rent a place together. Do you know if your new family will allow you to stay in your room for the weekend?" Ma shrugged her shoulders, suddenly worried. Rhea placed a sleeping Rose into the stroller. Toby was now lying down on the playground's gravel. "I should get going. Toby's nap time is soon. It's my favourite part of the day."

The Meaford family lived in a detached red-brick home separated from their neighbours by pencil-thin alleyways on either side. The house had a lot of stairs. Even getting into the home involved Ma climbing the wide stone steps through a cascading manicured garden, into a mudroom that ended in another set of stairs that led to a living room with a staircase in the middle. It was like the home was a lighthouse, with Mr. and Mrs. Meaford shouting demands at one another from the bedroom at the eaves all the way down to the creepy basement.

Mrs. Meaford was a plain woman who liked to describe her equally plain children as "charming." Ma wasn't so sure. Judith, the almost-four-year-old, possessed her mother's mousy-brown cropped haircut. Ma was instructed to give Judith as much attention as possible and to not interact as fully with the six-month-old Lucas.

"Since the baby was born, Judith has been acting out. And who can blame her? Having a younger sibling is traumatic," Mrs. Meaford explained during the phone interview. "Our family therapist has instructed us to show her, through our actions, that she still is the centre of our life. For her to know we are all on the same page, you would need to do the same." This meant, according to Mrs. Meaford's long list of demands, meeting Lucas's needs while making more eye contact and conversation with Judith.

When Ma was introduced to the children, she knelt down to meet the eyes of Judith.

"Hi, Judith! My name is Mary Grace, but you can call me MG."

Mrs. Meaford looked down at Judith, who hid behind her. "Judith? Would you like to say hello to your Ah-tay MG?" She shifted to look at Ma with a tight smile. "That's how you say it, right? The word for 'big sister' in TAG-ah-log?" Ma didn't have the heart to correct her pronunciation, so she just nodded to appease the woman. Judith peered from behind her mother's legs, her chubby finger digging into the depths of her nostril.

"It's very nice to meet you, Judith." The smell of poo suddenly filled the air like a leaden brick hitting all of their faces.

"As you can smell, Judith is rebelling against her brother's arrival by regressing. She was toilet trained by two, but now, she refuses to use the potty. And this week, she started nose-picking too. Right, Judith?" Judith did not look up at her mother's matter-of-fact delivery since she was in the middle of pushing, her cheeks flush with effort.

Ma's stomach churned. She almost looked at the baby to distract herself from this awkward moment, but the way Mrs. Meaford closed her eyes for a brief moment with the slightest shake of the head made her stop. It was as if the two adults in the room were held hostage by this knee-high human, digging into one orifice and pushing out of another. "I've been assured by the ladies in my parenting group that as long as we centre Judith's needs, she will eventually even out her behaviour. Several of them have experienced the same thing, and now their kids are perfectly normal."

A man's voice from the master bedroom two floors above called down to them. "Ava, hun? Is that the new nanny?"

"Yes, Arthur. Can you come down and say hello? We're just in the middle of—"

"Welcome, MG!" Mr. Meaford sang down the staircase. "Avaaaa, are you going over the schedule with her? Do you need me there?"

"Yes. Caaaaan you please come doooown? I'm going over the schedule noooow."

"Okay. Cool. Call me if you need me."

"Arthur? I'm goiiiiiing. Over iiiiit. Nooooow."

"Awesooooome. Thanks, Ava. See you later, MG."

Mr. and Mrs. Meaford were chartered accountants who worked from home. Under the pressure of auditing dozens of organizations at a time, they observed a highly structured schedule in the hopes of achieving what they called a "better work–life balance." Ma had a schedule of her own.

**5:45 a.m.**

Awake from a too-short sleep, which was disturbed by Lucas's nighttime feedings. Silently tiptoe out of room and walk one floor down to prepare everyone's breakfast. Baby monitor in pocket, volume low. Judith: steel-cut oatmeal and mixed berries, sippy cup of almond milk. Lucas: rice cereal and bananas. Bottle of pumped breast milk to defrost on the counter. Mrs. Meaford: half a grapefruit sprinkled with a packet of sweetener. One half bagel to defrost on the counter. Mr. Meaford: smoothie cup cleaned and dried on counter. Smoothie machine plugged in and ready.

**6:00 a.m.**

Walk up one floor. Wake Judith, change her diaper, dress her for the day.

**6:30 a.m.**

Walk down one floor. Sit Judith down in the kitchen with her breakfast. Walk up one floor and wake Lucas up. Change his diaper, dress him for the day at lightning speed.

**6:45 a.m.**

Bring Lucas down to the kitchen and seat him in his high chair far away from Judith so as not to upset her. Spoon-feed Lucas his cereal while chatting with Judith so that she doesn't feel abandoned. When Lucas is ready to drink his milk (now to room temperature), let him hold his own bottle as Judith is rushed to the powder room adjacent to kitchen to brush her teeth.

**7:00 a.m.**

Let Judith choose between playdough or painting as a quiet morning activity. While she chooses, administer Lucas's medication for his gastroesophageal reflux disease (GERD) by squeezing his plump cheeks and injecting a syringe of orange fluid past his tongue. Sit him upright in his high chair for another thirty minutes to make sure he doesn't vomit. Give him his favourite giraffe toy to chew on to encourage him to swallow.

**7:15 a.m.**

Toast bagel. Play with Judith *quietly* so that when Mrs. Meaford comes down for her breakfast, the cacophony of loud toys such as dump trucks or musical instruments doesn't aggravate her chronic migraines. Listen to Mrs. Meaford complain about her poor night's sleep while playing with Judith—quietly. "Look, MG. I made a face with the play-dough. Look, MG. I made a dog. Look, MG. I made a tree. Can I mix the colours?"

**7:30 a.m.**

Manage Judith's tantrum as Mrs. Meaford heads to her office upstairs. Allow Mrs. Meaford the joy of her child missing her enough to roll on the floor and scream, "Mommy! Don't go! Mommy don't leave me!" Give them space as Mrs. Meaford makes promises about treats after her workday, whispering into Judith's ear as she cries. Do not inform Mrs. Meaford that the tears end as soon as she's gone.

**7:45 a.m.**

Let Judith play with the dump trucks and musical instruments so that when Mr. Meaford comes down for his breakfast, he can say proudly, "Sounds like my girl is having lots of fun!" Take Lucas out of his high chair and place him in the playpen with his infant toys. Do not pay too much attention to him so as not to upset Judith. The only interaction is saying, "YAY!" each time Mr. Meaford uses the smoothie blender machine so that the baby doesn't get scared by the loud noise.

**8:00 a.m.**
In the sweet spot when the parents are both in their respective offices working and children are happily playing, go into kitchen and prepare the snack bag. Fish crackers. Sliced cucumbers. Cheese strings. Full sippy cup of milk. Another bottle of breast milk, defrosting in the bag.

**8:15 a.m.**
Say to the kids, "Are we ready to go?" in the most cheerful voice. Be the only one to respond with "Yay!" because this means Judith has to help clean up. Sing that godforsaken clean-up song while Judith pretends to help, even though she's really just kicking building blocks to the corner and calling it a day.

**8:30 a.m.**
Walk the children up one floor, holding one child at each hip. Change Judith's diaper. Change Lucas's diaper while Judith cries that no one loves her anymore. Reassure Judith that she is loved. Clean up any spit-up on Lucas because his GERD makes him vomit each time he lies down.

**8:45 a.m.**
Walk the children down one floor, holding one child at each hip. Ask Judith to put on her rainboots

because it's raining outside, she doesn't want to catch a cold, does she? Dress Lucas in autumn outerwear of insulated onesie, quilted hat and leather shoes. Ask Judith again to put on her rainboots because it's raining outside, she doesn't want to get wet feet, does she?

**9:00 a.m.**
Chase Lucas, who has crawled into the kitchen, and attempt to get his leather shoes on again, but where did the left shoe go? Listen to Judith scream that no one loves her, they only love Lucas, look I found the leather shoe, but I'm not going to give it to you because you love my brother more than you love me.

**9:15 a.m.**
Put alternate pair of shoes on Lucas to spite Judith. Put Lucas into car seat and snap him into the stroller. Get dressed in outerwear and stand by the mudroom door, giving empty threats about leaving without Judith. Smell poo in the air.

**9:30 a.m.**
Leave Lucas in the stroller in the foyer to walk up one floor with Judith on one hip, poo in her diaper. Try and change her diaper even though she is actually quite tall and is kicking your face during the process. Listen to Lucas cry, cross your fingers Mrs. Meaford isn't disturbed by the noise. Walk back down to the mudroom where Lucas is crying, wondering where

the hell everyone went. Let Judith wear the sandals if she wants to. Once outside, finally, wrestle with the stroller down the stone steps to the street. Listen to Judith complain that her feet are wet because it's raining.

**10:00 a.m.**
Enter play centre two blocks down the road and nod hello to all the other caregivers with their charges. Undress Judith, who is crying that her feet are wet. Encourage her to go play with her friends. Let her have a tantrum on the floor while you undress Lucas and let him play in the baby area with other babies.

**10:30 a.m.**
That godforsaken clean-up song is sung by the centre's facilitator, and all the grown-ups are expected to sing along. Ask Judith to clean up. Ask her again. And again. Listen to a short storytime and sing along during circle time. Place Lucas in a high chair during circle time because Judith wants to sit in your lap.

**10:45 a.m.**
Snack time. Sit the kids at the table far away from one another so as not to upset Judith. Give Judith her portions of fish crackers, sliced cucumbers and cheese strings. Give Lucas his bottle. If well-timed, Lucas's diaper will need changing while Judith is busy eating. If not, listen to Judith cry about not being loved while changing Lucas's diaper.

**11:00 a.m.**

More playtime. Drink coffee from the carafe that has been sitting on the centre's counter since 8 a.m. Put two sugars in. Heat it in the microwave. You need it. Complain with the other caregivers. Laugh. Speak your language.

**11:45 a.m.**

Say to the kids, "Are we ready to go?" in the most cheerful voice. Be the only one to respond with "Yay!" because this means Judith has to get dressed. Ask her if she wants to wear her rainboots this time so that her feet don't get wet. Feel satisfaction when she reluctantly says yes because she learned her lesson.

**12:00 p.m.**

Get back to the house. Undress the kids from their outerwear. Place Lucas in playpen away from Judith so as not to upset her. Get Judith to choose three books she can read (i.e., flip through the pages) quietly while you heat up lunch. Mashed sweet potatoes (running low). Beef mechado and rice leftovers. Blueberries and yogurt for dessert.

**12:30 p.m.**

Another round of diaper changes. Carry both children up one floor, a child at each hip, to prepare them for their naps. Judith must have her Benny Bunny and blanket. Curtains closed. Sound machine. Have a good nap. But I don't want to sleep. You don't need to sleep. Just close your eyes. Lucas is given one more bottle before nap time, which he can barely stay awake for. Place him in his crib where you sleep too, in a single bed in the opposite corner. Vague sounds of Mr. and Mrs. Meaford lunching downstairs in the kitchen.

**2:15 p.m.**
Awaken to the sound of Judith screaming your name. Rush over to her bedroom and see that she has a diaper full of poo. Diaper changes for both children.

**2:30 p.m.**
Snack time. Quiet crunching of granola bar and halved grapes. Another bottle for Lucas.

**3:00 p.m.**
Slow walk to nearby playground. Listen to Judith cry that Lucas is in the stroller and not her, she doesn't want to walk. Stand and watch Judith have a tantrum on the sidewalk. Reassure concerned passersby that the child is all right. Arrive at playground and push Lucas in the swing. Intervene when Judith hits other children. Teach Judith how to go up a slide and come down on her own. Intervene when Judith takes another child's toy.

**4:00 p.m.**
Say to the kids, "Are we ready to go?" in the most cheerful voice. Be the only one to respond with

"Yay!" because this means Judith has to walk. Stand and watch Judith have a tantrum on the sidewalk. Reassure concerned passersby that the child is all right.

**4:30 p.m.**

Arrive at the house and undress the kids from their outerwear. Place Lucas in playpen so as not to upset Judith. Set Judith up at the easel with four paint colours, a brush and a smock. Make dinner (Filipino beef steak, extra onions) and more baby food for Lucas (more sweet potatoes, peas, carrots). Every now and then say, "Wow, Judith! That's a beautiful bird/house/car."

**5:00 p.m.**

Hear Mr. and Mrs. Meaford come down the stairs from their offices. Listen to Mr. Meaford make an excuse not to join for dinner and head out for the night. Something about some buddy from college being in town. Watch Mrs. Meaford's jaw tighten as she sits down at the table and falls silent, looking at the wall as her husband exits. Watch Judith pick her nose, hoping her mother will stop her. Cut Judith's food into bite sizes. Watch Judith throw food onto the floor, reminding her mother of the treat she had promised. Listen to Mrs. Meaford sidestep this with "No treats for table manners like this!" Spoon-feed Lucas.

**5:30 p.m.**

Clean the kitchen while Mrs. Meaford announces that she will watch some TV with the kids. Wonder why Mrs. Meaford is not watching TV with her kids in the living room and is, instead, standing by the dishwasher overseeing how it is being loaded. Not this way. This way. Yes. That's much more efficient. Not this way. It'll block the jets and nothing will get cleaned. Have you never used a dishwasher before?

**6:30 p.m.**

Play with Judith now that her one hour of television is over. Watch Mrs. Meaford climb the stairs up to the master bedroom to read a book in peace and quiet. Maybe there's a storm coming. My head is pounding, she says.

**7:00 p.m.**

Bath time. Put both children into warm water, naked as the day they were born, which was not that long ago. Tell Judith there is a difference between splashing her brother playfully and splashing with intent to drown. Play with the bubbles. Make Santa's beard. Make funny hats. Please don't hit your brother.

**7:30 p.m.**

Bedtime. Only two stories and that's it. No more. But just one more. Okay, then. Judith must have her Benny Bunny and blanket. Curtains closed. Sound machine. Have a good sleep. But I don't want to sleep. You don't need to sleep. Just close your eyes. Lucas likes an empty crib. Good night, Lucas.

**8:30 p.m.**
Sneak downstairs and see if the living room is available to watch some TV after such a long day. Arrive at the bottom of the stairs and see Mr. Meaford eating a bag of chips, the bag of chips Mrs. Meaford told him to throw away because they're supposed to do the South Beach diet together. Watch him hide the bag, then continue to eat, realizing it's not his wife but his kids' nanny. Head back upstairs to your bed, which is in the corner opposite Lucas's crib. Sit in the darkness unsure of what to do next. Fall asleep trying to figure that out.

**5:45 a.m.**
Repeat.

The monotony of each day was broken up by the occasional Girls' Night Out when Mrs. Meaford would meet with her friends from college and would return home late at night, pretending to be sober. This did not happen as often as Ma thought it would. Ma wondered about this. Mrs. Tsang and Helen had no issue with leaving their children with her for hours at a time. With Mrs. Tsang, she would take "mommy vacations," which would mean Ma staying home with John, even on her days off. With Mrs. Meaford it was different. She loved to be present in the home; not to be with her children, but to oversee Ma's tasks.

Mrs. Meaford had exact standards when it came to laundry. She expected underwear and the armpits of button-up shirts to be sprayed with stain remover. Soiled clothes were to be divided into piles based on colour and care. Darks. Whites. Brights. Blacks. Greys. Delicate machine wash. Delicate hand wash. Towels. Bed linen. Each pile was assigned a specific setting on the machines, which were located in the home's low-ceilinged basement. Mrs. Meaford would stand a few feet from Ma as she handwashed appropriate items in the laundry sink. Scrubbing not soaking for Lucas's onesies. Dabbing not wiping stains on Mr. Meaford's dress pants. Squeezing not wringing Judith's cardigans.

Ma noticed that the micromanagement would get worse each time Mr. Meaford headed out for his "business meetings" with clientele.

"If you want the mortgage to be paid, I wouldn't complain," he'd say, slipping on his corduroy jacket (spot treat and dry clean) over his crew-neck tee (machine wash, inside out to spare the screen print). It was the way he gave himself one last look in the mirror before leaving that made Mrs. Meaford suspicious. He would check the symmetry of his beard and assess his ensemble while his wife glowered on the living room couch.

From the kitchen, Ma would pretend to clean while watching Mrs. Meaford tighten the belt around her plush housecoat (machine wash alone to keep a balanced load). "I'm not complaining. I'm wishing you a wonderful night out with these supposed clients who want to meet late at night at a sports bar."

Once he was out the door, Mrs. Meaford would march on

over to Ma and lord over whatever she was doing, as if to control something, someone, anything, in her inability to control her husband.

"Just a reminder that the texture has to be velvety smooth to keep him from choking," she'd say while Ma made Lucas's baby food.

"I think a good scour with the bristle brush before sanitizing makes more sense than simply washing it with a sponge, don't you?" she'd say while Ma cleaned the kids' toys.

"I feel like you're focusing too much on the cooking and not enough on Judith's playtime," she'd say while Ma swept up the brown rice Judith threw on the floor during lunch.

Needless to say, these times Mrs. Meaford spent out of the home were a welcome reprieve for Ma.

"Okay, MG. I put my cellphone number on the fridge in case you need me," she said one night, distractedly looking at her new flip phone and seeing that her husband had not called her while out. She slipped on her Blundstone boots and turned to Ma with a smile that said she wanted a favour. "Can you do me a favour?"

Ma was in the middle of washing Lucas's high-chair food tray, but she nodded yes.

"Can you please call me when Mr. Meaford comes home?" Ma was confused as to why she would want her to do this, but nodded yes. "Awesome. And hey. We should get you a cellphone too. Whatcha think?" she added, her smile wider.

"Me?"

"Oh, everyone should have one. It's good for emergencies. I don't know what I did without it. And those payphones will be obsolete one day, so you might as well, right?"

Ma shook her head. "I don't have the money."

"Are you kidding me? We'd pay for it."

"No, no. I don't want to be a bother."

"It's not a bother at all. You deserve one." Mrs. Meaford put her hand on Ma's shoulder and tilted her head to the side as if to blur an unspoken boundary between employer and friend. "That way, I can call you to get updates about the kids."

Once Mrs. Meaford was finally out—as in out-out, not out-then-in-I-forgot-my-lip-balm-okay-bye kind of out— Ma turned to Judith. Judith sat at the kitchen table, enjoying a bowl of arroz caldo.

"Is that yummy?" Ma asked. Judith nodded enthusiastically. Ma looked around, as if, at any minute, the parents would walk in on her, descend the stairs or round a corner. "I was wondering. Could you help me?"

Judith used her top lip to shovel stray grains of rice into her mouth. "Okay."

"Awesome. I've been having trouble feeding Lucas." Ma stood and looked at Lucas across the table, who smiled back at them. "Could you do it for me?"

Judith thought for a moment with her brows knitting under her short bangs. "Oh, I know how to do *that!*"

Ma applauded. "Thank you." With her foot, Ma undid the brakes on the high chair's wheels and rolled it close to Judith. "There we go." Ma handed the spoon to Judith. "Sometimes he still gets food on his cheeks when I feed him. Maybe you can do a better job than me."

Still sporting a bib herself, Judith got up and stood on her own chair. She dug a spoonful of the rice cereal and jabbed it into Lucas's mouth. "Careful, Judith." Ma thought Judith was being too aggressive, but the baby laughed and clapped his hands.

"Good job, Lucas!" Judith said, loading the spoon again. She jabbed it back into his mouth, then expertly used the spoon's edge to clean her brother's cheeks and then spoon the surplus back into his mouth. The siblings laughed at this new game. They laughed at the sound of each other's laughter. Lucas's fingers twiddled in the air, delighted by the interaction. Ma watched them in wonder. It was the first time she had seen the siblings looking at each other, eye to eye.

Later that night, while enjoying Judith's allotted one hour of television, Ma cuddled with her. "Judith, thank you so much for helping with Lucas. I could not have done it without you. You're such a big girl now." Judith nestled into the space between Ma's armpit and her breast, one finger hooked into her mouth. "Lucas has to have his diaper changed because he's a baby. But you're not a baby, are you?" Judith shook her head. "From now on, I hope you can help me change his diaper. Does that sound good?" Judith nodded. "And you can use your potty." Ma hugged Judith extra tight while saying this. "Lucas and I can help you. How's that?" Judith stood on the couch and wrapped her arms around Ma.

"Mommy, I need to go pee."

Ma did not correct her. "Okay! Lucas, let's go watch your sister go pee!" She unbuckled Lucas out of his bouncy chair and they rushed to the powder room.

"See, Lucas? This is how you go pee," Judith later said, slouching on the toilet, her legs dangling. Ma held Lucas on her hip at the powder room's doorframe. He grinned at his sister, fist in his mouth.

A week later, Ma approached Mrs. Meaford in her office during nap time. The small space had been a storage closet originally, but Mrs. Meaford had made the best of it by placing files in numerous banker boxes along the shelves that lined the top of the walls on all sides.

"Is something wrong?" she said, still looking at her spreadsheet on the desktop computer.

"Nothing is wrong. I have some good news," Ma said, quietly. Mrs. Meaford spun her office chair around slowly. She looked odd with her reading glasses on. Like she had borrowed them from an old man. With eyes looking abnormally large under the magnification, she scanned Ma over.

"Okay. What's up?"

"We need to buy Judith big-girl underwear." Ma smiled.

"Why?"

"Because . . . she's now able to go to the washroom instead of using her diaper."

"You potty trained Judith?"

"Yes, ma'am."

"Without asking me."

"I didn't think you needed me to—"

"MG. I had told you already she was not to be rushed."

"But I didn't rush her."

"I told you she would even out on her own accord. Am I imagining things? We had this conversation, right?"

"Yes."

"So who brought this up, then? Did it come about in conversation? Did she ask to use the toilet?"

"I told her she's a big girl now, so—"

"You led her towards using the potty, then."

The office suddenly felt half the size. Ma stepped back. "I just said that—"

"Are you hearing yourself? You went against my wishes and pressured my daughter to be potty trained." Mrs. Meaford took a deep breath and made a T with her hands. "Let's pause for a moment. I'm sorry I'm shouting at you." The pause was long enough that Ma's emotions caught up to her and her eyes began to burn with tears. She swallowed hard to keep the water from flowing. This didn't feel like an apology. It sounded like the beginning of an explanation. "It's just . . ." Now Mrs. Meaford was fighting back tears. She removed her large glasses to wipe her face dry. "You have no idea how difficult it is with people questioning your every decision as a mother. First, they questioned the fertility treatments, then the extended breastfeeding, then using a nanny. In the eyes of my mother-in-law and the entire world, it seems, I am a huge failure. Our family therapist had strict instructions and then you . . . anyway. It's done now, I guess."

Ma wasn't sure what to do next. Comfort her? Was that also part of her job?

"Mrs. Meaford? Judith . . . she's very proud of herself."

Mrs. Meaford looked to the side with disappointment transforming into a look of guilt. "I'm glad she's proud of herself. That's awesome you were able to bring that out in her. I wish I could do the same."

Her last remark didn't have the desired effect, so Ma added, "Even at night she—"

"Oh great. Does this mean we have to deal with nighttime visits to the toilet?"

"No. She sleeps *through* the night. No accidents. That's why we need to get her underwear."

Mrs. Meaford sighed heavily and slowly spun her office chair around back to her computer. Without looking back she said coolly, "So you're asking for money to buy them?"

Ma wilted. "Yes, ma'am."

"Fine. There's cash in my purse downstairs." Ma moved to exit. "And MG. I need a receipt of what you buy."


The only computers in the Meaford household were in the offices and held "very sensitive information." That's why the next Sunday, as with all Sundays, Ma bundled up and spent the first part of her day off travelling to the nearest internet café to check her email. It wasn't the most ideal situation. While it was only a few blocks away on Danforth Avenue, the café was filled with all sorts of shady characters. Usually, there would be a man on one side surfing porn and on the other would be some person who struggled with technology and assumed Ma could help them.

"Do you by any chance know how to send this to the printer?" "Do you know how much they charge per sheet for printing?" "If I print something in colour, does it cost more?" "I sent this to the printer, but nothing is happening. Is something wrong? Is it the connection? Should I send it again?"

This Sunday was no different. At first, Ma felt lucky finding a desktop in the corner against one wall, which cut the chances of porn man/needy person in half. But when a man with a braided beard sat next to her, plugged in his head-phones and tilted the screen slightly away from her sight, she knew her luck had run out.

She logged into her Hotmail account and waited patiently for the page to load. From behind the service desk Ma could hear the sound of a fax coming in, which thankfully drowned out the faint moans coming from Braided Beard Man's headphones. It had been a few months of having this email account and she had fantasies of this type of communication being faster, easier, more visual. It was always a heartbreak-ing thing, just listening to Ale's voice on the phone but not seeing his face. There were three emails sitting in her inbox. One email promised to help her lose twenty pounds without dieting or exercise. One email was from a prince in Nigeria imploring her to help him gain back his kingdom. She knew well enough to erase those messages. The final message was from Ale. Ma's heart raced. In increments of pixels and lines, the email's text finally materialized.

> My love. The internet café here is full so I will keep this short. Did you get the card Ging and Ellie made you? How are you? Is it snowing there? Please take a picture so that we can see. Please see attached photos from Ellie's birthday. Doña Ramos let us use her house for a small party. I love you. Take care.

Ma scrolled down and saw that two photos were loading. And loading. And loading. She hovered the cursor over the refresh button, tempted to end the torture of waiting. The first photo finally loaded, but its enormous size forced Ma to move the toggle bar right and left. There was no sign of Ale. Just a group photo in Doña Ramos's mahogany dining room, with Ellie smiling behind a Sans Rival cake, two young women behind her (most likely her schoolmates since Ma did not recognize them), Ate Marcy in the middle of a laugh and Ging making a funny face. Ale must have been behind the camera. Ma bit the inside of her cheek, as if she could chew the disappointment away.

Another photo loaded, and this time it was very small and pixelated. It was of Ellie clasping a locket with its thin chain around her neck. She held it towards the camera as if to show her new necklace. She showed all the signs of womanhood emerging, especially the tilt of her head and poised smile, like a facade she was expected to create for all those around her. And beside her was Ale. The sight of him, no matter how small, took Ma's breath away. Ale. There he was. She wheeled her chair closer to the monitor to peer at the image. Ale looked like he was in mid-sentence, his lips open and slightly to the side. It was a habit of his, speaking out of the side of his mouth, after years of talking and smoking a cigarette at the same time. His sparse beard was still sparse. His hair had grown slightly, and it surprised Ma how unkempt he looked, especially for a birthday party. He wore the imitation Lacoste golf shirt Ma had sent him from Hong Kong, with its buttons undone.

Ma looked up at the dusty ceiling of the internet café, willing the tears in her ducts to be absorbed back into her body. The raw wounds from last week's email exchanges had only just patched over, only to be ripped open with news of things happening so far away. Straightening herself up on the worn office chair, she took a deep breath and pressed reply.

*Good morning, my love. No snow yet, but I am told it should come soon. Did you receive the package I sent you?*

After a day at the library and a meal in Chinatown, Ma returned to the Meaford home to find the door unlocked and the two children playing by themselves in the living room.

"Judith? Where's your mommy?"

Judith was distracted by the cartoons playing on the TV and casually replied, "Mommy's having a bad day." Lucas sat in his exersaucer chewing on his leather shoe. Ma took the leather shoe and replaced it with his giraffe chew toy. He cried. She replaced the chew toy with the shoe. He smiled. Ma's mind raced, conflicted over the situation. It was her day off. But the kids . . . why were they left alone? Should she intervene? Ignore them? Go upstairs and pretend she didn't see?

"Judith. I'm going to look for your mommy, okay? I will be right back." Ma speed-walked up the stairs. Office. Empty. Bathroom. Empty. She walked another flight up and stopped in the middle of the stairs, knowing the master bedroom had no door.

"Ma'am? Ma'am? Are you there?" No answer. Creeping up the stairs, she could hear the sound of running water. "Ma'am?" Ma said louder this time. "It's MG. Are you all right?"

Mrs. Meaford appeared at the top of the stairs, still in her pyjamas, blowing her nose. "MG. Thank god you're here." She gestured for Ma to meet her at the landing. Ma ascended the stairs and saw the room in a complete state of chaos. Clothes were strewn around the room. Shelves were emptied, with the contents dropped on the floor. Behind her, the bathtub in the ensuite washroom filled dangerously close to the brim. "You would not believe what happened. Remember how I got you that cellphone? Well, to save money, the cellphone provider suggested we consolidate all three of our plans, and that's what I did. So I started receiving one bill, with all the charges and all the phone call records on one piece of paper. You understand?" Mrs. Meaford shaped her tissue into a cone and stuck it up one chafed nostril, then the other. It didn't help because she started crying and her nose started running again. "And that's when . . ." She squeezed her eyes shut, her face contorted. "I saw this number coming up again and again on Arthur's call log. And I . . . I called the number. I did it, okay? I called it. I don't care how crazy that sounds. I don't care. I had to. I knew deep within my soul that he was cheating, but I had to confirm it. It was some woman. What I did was I called and didn't say anything. Just to see what she'd do. And when she answered the phone, she said, 'Hey, babes'! Hey. Babes." Mrs. Meaford threw the soggy tissue to the side, where many other tissues lay in a messy pile, before collapsing on the floor in long, soul-crushing wails.

Before tending to Mrs. Meaford, Ma rushed to the bathtub and shut off the water. She returned to Mrs. Meaford's side, kneeling on the floor beside her. "I don't know what I'll do! I'm so humiliated!" Ma thought of touching the woman's shoulder as a way of showing support since there were no words that were coming to mind. But she thought better of it.

Ma began to sort the room out, starting with placing the pile of tissues into the bin, the books back on the shelf, the duvet cover back on the bed. The bathtub looked delicious, especially after Ma had just been out in the crisp grey weather. Ma wished she could soak in there while the woman cried on the floor. Instead, she said, "Ma'am? Would you like to take a bath before the water gets cold?"

"You're right, MG. You're always right." Mrs. Meaford got up slowly and shuffled herself to the bathroom. Before she closed the door, she looked at Ma. "I'm so sorry for being such an asshole lately." Ma fought the urge to reply, "That's okay," because that would imply her agreement that she was in fact an asshole. Ma shook her head in a half-hearted attempt to disagree. "It's just . . . my marriage . . . and I didn't know how to deal with it all. I'm sorry to take it out on you. I knew I could count on you. Thank you." Ma gave her a closed-mouth smile. "I'll be down by the time dinner is ready." It was Ma's day off, but she nodded yes anyway.

During the process of their separation, the home's energy drastically shifted. It wasn't so much Mr. Meaford's things being packed into misshapen wine boxes and left in the mudroom for him to pick up. Nor was it the wine Mrs. Meaford consumed before packing her soon-to-be-ex-husband's things into them. It was a change in Ma's role in it all.

"Come!" Mrs. Meaford would say to Ma while patting the sofa beside her. These days, her tone towards Ma was always a hybrid of BFF and family dog. "Sit! Sit!" Ma looked back at the steel-cut oats simmering on the stove in prep for tomorrow's breakfasts. Another three minutes. She sat down on the edge of the sofa, readying herself for the sound of the pot boiling over. Mrs. Meaford took another sip of her chardonnay, then placed the glass on the coffee table beside the Christmas acorn/candle centrepiece. Excitedly, she repositioned herself on the sofa so that she was cross-legged, facing Ma. Like two girlfriends during a sleepover, chatting about boys. "Now that Arthur is officially moved out, I was thinking we should have a celebration." Her eyes twinkled at Ma. "I mean . . . there's a lot to celebrate. We have New Year's Eve coming up, I'm a proud single woman . . ." Ma nodded. "So I want to invite our neighbours and their families for a big Y2K celebration. All the food, all the music, all the games. What do you say? Could you help with the food? Your cooking is amazing." Ma blushed, happy that she liked Ma's cooking yet unsure of how many guests Mrs. Meaford had in mind. When Helen had her baby shower there were about thirty people, and that was challenging but doable. Ma nodded. "Perfect! I'll get the invitations out ASAP."

Mrs. Meaford showed Ma a detailed list of the invitees. But when they sat side by side to write out the first few cards, Mrs. Meaford was in awe of Ma's penmanship. "Oh my god! Can you imagine if two of our neighbours show each other their invitations? It's like mine was done by a toddler and yours was done by someone from the eighteenth century or something." Ma didn't disagree. Penmanship was an important skill to ace in Filipino schools. "Could you take over the rest? I'd hate for someone to get offended by my chicken scratch." Ma was confused about what exactly was offensive about bad handwriting but agreed to take it on nonetheless.

This gave Mrs. Meaford more time to "find herself" and "heal the hurt" at yoga classes and support groups. Between diaper changes, cooking and housecleaning, Ma wrote out the invitations. Then she addressed the invites and delivered them to their neighbours, with children in tow. Between tantrums, laundry and reading to the children, Ma answered the phone and kept track of the guest list.

"How are we doing so far?" Mrs. Meaford said, patting the sofa beside her. Ma sat down, removed her dish gloves, still wet from scouring the pasta pot from dinner, and reached inside her apron pocket for the paper guest list. Mrs. Meaford perused the check marks and strike-throughs. "Hmmm. I was secretly hoping Radna's family would decline because those kids of hers are terrors, but wow, I'm jazzed Ollie and Carol will make it." She took a sip of her cabernet sauvignon and placed it back on the coffee table, now clear of Christmas decor thanks to Ma's work the day before. She gave Ma a covert look. "Truth is, they're part of the parent/teacher association at Fenners Green, and it would be killer to get an in on that school for Judith next year." Mrs. Meaford closed her eyes and touched a hand to her chest. "Ugh! My heart. I have not felt this happy in . . . in forever, really. When Arthur was here, it felt like every day was this torturous, monotonous cycle of ignoring each other. And now . . . wow. To dream about the future? To celebrate with *real* friends? It's amazing." She leaned over and rubbed Ma's knee. "I couldn't have done this without you, Emmie," she said before wrapping her arms around Ma.

*Where did this weird nickname come from?* Ma wondered to herself while the woman embraced her. Oh yes. She traced it back a few weeks to when Mrs. Meaford asked her to drop off Mr. Meaford's odds and ends at his new condo in Liberty Village on her day off. At first, Mrs. Meaford would sing "Ehhhhhm" each time she summoned Ma to her with another envelope of Mr. Meaford's mail to add to the give-back package. Then, it evolved to the song "Ehmmmeeee" each time Mrs. Meaford was heading out the door for her Buddhist meditation workshops but Judith needed to go potty. Now, Ma was knighted "Emmie" and was expected to answer to it. And make a delivery in an expensive taxi half-way across the city.

"Say, would you like a glass of wine?"

Ma didn't want to wash another glass. "No. That's okay. Thank you."

"Ah, come on! Please. The kids are asleep. It's just us girls. I hate drinking alone." Mrs. Meaford was already up and walking towards the kitchen. Ma got up from the sofa. "No, no. Sit. I can get you a glass if you're game."

"Oh. Um . . . okay." Ma was a lightweight. A "cheap date" as Ale used to say, preferring the taste of cola over beer.

Mrs. Meaford returned with another wineglass in hand. She sat back beside Ma and filled the glass halfway with liquid. One sip in and Ma could already feel her head swirl.

"I got this bottle on our last trip to Niagara-on-the-Lake. I love this vineyard." Mrs. Meaford tipped the glass enough that her nose poked into the bowl of it, then sipped it. With a small amount still swishing around her mouth she said, "I detect notes of . . . what is it? Cherry? Yeah. Cherry." Ma took another sip herself and detected notes of cough syrup and hairspray.

Mrs. Meaford put her glass down and leaned on the sofa sideways. "Okay. Since we're sharing a bottle of wine, you have to dish about your personal life!"

Ma shook her head and sipped again. Notes of nail-polish remover and bathtub cleaner. And cherry? Was the wine getting tastier? Maybe.

"Come on! We live in the same house, Emmie. Like . . . tell me about your family. Why you're here."

Ma's lips were a bit clumsy, but she managed to say, "I have a husband in the Philippines. No kids yet. When I finish the Live-in Caregiver Program, I can apply for him to come here."

"That's so heartbreaking! Do you miss him?"

"Of course. I miss him. Every day." Ma usually didn't divulge such personal things, but the wine was making the words loose in her mouth. "It's worth the sacrifice. I send money home to support him, my sister-in-law and her two children."

"Two of them! Emmie, you're a saint."

Ma laughed a little too loudly. Another sip of wine. All cherry. "A saint? No. No, not me."

"Just think of those kids, though. Because of you they get to live their lives with stability. They have you to thank for that. If you didn't have this job, what would happen to them?"

"Well . . . what would happen to all of us? I would have been home, yes, but then we would be struggling to make ends meet. Any job we would find, if we could find one, would only pay enough to live day to day." Ma set her glass down on the coffee table. "Yes, I am far away, but at least they can live with confidence that rent will be paid, food will be there. For that, I am thankful for this opportunity."

Mrs. Meaford closed her eyes and touched her hand to her chest again. "Wow. Thank you. Thank you for sharing your truth with me."

It was hardly truth. There were a lot of things Ma wanted to say, but the words were slurred, muddy and squishy between her tipsy lips. The way she has replayed, over and over again in her mind, the sensation of turning the key in the door of their future home. No more waiting. No more time apart. Watching Ale leave for work and knowing he would come back home in the evening. Chatting about each other's day over dinner. That was truly the opportunity she was talking about.

Clumsily, Ma managed to say, "I'm just . . . doing my job, Mrs. Meaford."

"Hey." Mrs. Meaford held Ma's hands and looked right into her eyes. "Call me Ava. I insist. I'm not going to be Mrs. Meaford for much longer anyway. After this divorce is finalized I'll be back to being Ava Brown."

On the day of the New Year's Eve party, Ma took all two hundred of the lumpia spring rolls (wrapped the night before once the kids were asleep) out of the freezer to defrost them on the counter. She chopped the vegetables and chicken for the pancit bihon noodles (pancit palabok was Ma's favourite, but she grew tired of Canadians asking, "This is delicious but what is this crunchy stuff on top?" and Ma responding, "It's pork rinds" and them leaving their plates half-eaten). She punched down the dough for the pandesal. Ava offered to "treat" Ma to some alone time to get the cooking done by taking her children to a nearby play centre for the day.

The neighbours arrived at six that evening. Winter boots were tossed about the mudroom and flashy silver Y2K hats were worn. Ava expertly greeted guests at the door. "Holy cow, you look fabulous!" "Spin around. I have to get a good look at this dress!" "Happy holidays. Come on through. Shut the door behind you before the cold gets in." "Judith is playing in her room. Go find her. Have fun!"

Ma kept everyone's wineglasses full. She replenished the cutlery. Washed used serving dishes. "Your food is delicious!" a man in an ugly Christmas sweater said, squeezing her trapezoid while Ma wiped wineglasses of lipstick residue.

Ava called out for Ma, or rather, Emmie. Ma stopped icing her sponge cake and made her way to the solarium. In that cold room that Ava had decorated with her collection of Moroccan lamps sat a circle of six women drinking wine. The women all stopped talking and looked up at Ma, smiling.

"Hi, Emma," one woman said. She was young-looking in the face, but her hair was completely grey and coiffed into a high bun.

"Oh, it's Emmie. It's *my* nickname for her. It's a long story. Sort of an inside joke between us. But her name is actually Mary Grace, or MG," Ava explained as she reached her hand out to Ma. "Come." Ma stepped forward into the room and her toes curled at the sensation of chilly tile. Still holding her hand, Ava continued, "This is Carol. She's the wife of Ollie?" Ma looked back into the living room, where she could see Ollie putting ice into his mixed drink. She looked back at Ava. "Her kids Winnie and Keegan are the ones wearing the reindeer onesies, remember?" Ma nodded. "We thought, since they get along so well with Judith, they'll come here to play too."

"Together?" Ma asked.

Ava nodded excitedly. "Exactly! Every afternoon! They're like three peas in a pod." Ma thought the expression was two peas in a pod, but maybe she was mistaken. "When Judith has other playmates, she's way easier to take care of. And Winnie and Keegan are so fun!"

"I don't know if 'fun' is the word I would use to describe them," Carol said with a roll of her eyes. The other women laughed. "But they are pretty easygoing kids. They just play. I can't wait to see you after the holidays."

And that was that. Ma walked (floated?) back to the kitchen to ice the cake. Since she'd left it, the buttercream had begun to separate. She continued as quickly as she could, her hands shaking. From the solarium she could still hear the women talking, this time in stage whispers.

"No really. She's amazing with the kids. I could not have survived the separation without her."

"But what does she charge?"

"Well . . . What can you manage?"

"How about . . . I dunno . . . how about five hundred dollars a month?"

"Sure."

"Do I issue the cheque directly to her?"

Ava paused momentarily. "Since she's under contract with me, it's best you give me the five hundred dollars and I will add it to her paycheque. I wouldn't want her to get in trouble."

"Perfect."

Ma placed the sliced strawberries on the cake, and a sudden feeling of relief washed over her. She would be paid five hundred dollars more. That would make it worth it. Five hundred dollars more a month to send back home. Maybe a little to keep, to enjoy on her days off. She could go shopping. Buy new shoes. A nice meal. Maybe she could treat Rhea to a meal out in Oakville. Five hundred dollars. Yes. She could do it.

She did do it. Four children. One in diapers. Two out of diapers. One potty training. Through the dirty snow they went, to library storytimes, to play centres. Morning snacks at Carol and Ollie's home (plastic cups and bowls that all smelled like spoiled milk). Lunch and nap times at the Meafords'. Keegan was in a kindergarten prep program, which meant Ma had the tricky task of feeding the kids, dropping him off at the program and rushing back to the house without Lucas falling asleep in the stroller. To keep Lucas from ruining his nap, Ma would get the kids to sing all of his favourite songs extra loud on the brisk walk. She became an expert in lining the children up to go potty (pants down, bum on seat, kid leaning forward between her legs while she wiped their bottom, "Next!") and lining them up to wash their hands ("This is the way we wash our hands, wash our hands, wash our hands . . .").

A month into this chaos, Ma heard Ava's nasal voice calling out for her. The kids had just been put down for their nap and Ma rushed to Ava's office. She knocked on the door softly. "Come in." She opened the door.

Ava tried to turn around in her office chair, but the breast pump was getting in the way. She held the breast shields in place as the machine whirred away.

"Yes, ma'am?"

"Your cheque." Ava pointed her gaze at an envelope on top of her printer.

"Thank you, ma'am." Ma took the cheque and stepped out of the office. She looked at its contents. A heat in her throat and cheeks. She stepped back into the office, careful with the tone of her voice, careful not to cry. "Um . . . Ava?"

"Yes?"

"Is this everything?"

"Everything what?"

"Is this all of my pay?"

"This is what I always pay you. What?"

A ringing in Ma's ears. "Keegan and Winnie. I thought—"

"Hey, MG. I forgot to ask you," Ava quickly interrupted as she detached the breast shields and turned off the machine. "How's your family doing?"

"My family?"

"Yeah. Your family."

The cheque was damp in Ma's hands. "Good. My husband is good. My sister-in-law is—"

"That's amazing. I'm glad. I imagine your husband looks forward to you completing the program."

"Yes."

"What an opportunity for him. I bet he looks forward to being reunited with you after you sponsor him."

"Yes."

Ava opened the breast pump and unscrewed the bottle from its interior. "Here, Emmie." She handed the warm bottle to Ma, after securing its bottle top. "Can you put this in the freezer?"

Ma would deny ever fantasizing about Ava's death. But we Maybe Babies knew the truth. For months, deep down inside of her were these flashes of light, these images, scenes in which Ava would be huddled in the corner of a room, Ma standing above her and swinging a baseball bat to her head. Ava running through a wheat field while Ma steadied her rifle's sights on that bitch who did her wrong. The temperature inside Ma's core was balmy, but her extremities were icy cold. We were all kind of scared, to be honest. We had never seen Ma this angry before. But what was most disturbing was the presence of something new, a stranger to all of us. Not another Maybe Baby. Something else.

Ma played out these revenge scenarios in her head throughout the day, while dealing with Winnie, who picked her nose so hard she got blood all over her face. While dealing with Lucas, who was teething and miserable. While dealing with Keegan, who refused to leave the playground. While dealing with Judith, who liked to climb to the top of slides and announce that she needed to go poo so could Ma come and get her?

One morning, she woke up and crept to the powder room downstairs to have her morning pee. A trickle. Sharp pain. Her colon contracted as if a bowel movement was occurring, but just as the sensation hit its apex, another sharp pain. Nothing. Ma looked down into the toilet bowl, her brow wet with perspiration from the effort.

She tried to continue the day as if nothing was happening. Breakfast. Playtime. Library. Lunch. Another sharp pain happened while Ma was placing Lucas into his high chair. She managed to buckle him in before she rushed to the powder room, thinking she was finally going to have a bowel movement. Nothing. Sharp pain, this time strong enough that she doubled over. The Maybe Babies all braced ourselves inside of her. Ma tried to poo again, pressing down on her swollen abdomen. Nothing. Sharp pain, this time strong enough that Ma couldn't help but let out a low-pitched groan.

"Ate MG? What's wrong?"

Ma wanted to say "I'm okay," but she could only let out another moan. She sat on the toilet for another minute until the pain subsided into a dull ache. If she walked bent over, the pain was not as severe, which is what she did to get the kids dressed, walk Keegan to the prep program and rush back home for naps. Her cellphone rang in her pocket.

Ma flipped her phone open. "Hello?"

"Hi, Emma. It's Carol. Listen. I know you just dropped off Keegan, but they called and said he has a funny rash on his back. I don't want him to miss the program because he gets grumpy about it all. So could you run and get some ointment at the drugstore and put some on his back?"

"Ointment?"

"Yeah. Like one of those cortisone creams. Just buy it and I'll pay you back. Okay, gotta go. I have a meeting. Thanks, Emma."

Ma walked to the nearest drugstore and bought the ointment. Lucas had already fallen asleep. His nap would be ruined. Winnie and Judith were getting tired and petulant, their winter boots dragging on the pavement. Ma and the kids returned to the prep program, she applied the ointment on Keegan's back and said what Carol had instructed her to say. "Carol says it's not chicken pox. He just has eczema."

The program workers suspiciously shepherded Keegan back to the classroom, and Ma made her way back to the Meaford home. By this time, Ma could barely walk. Ma used her phone to call Ava. "Please come and get the children. I need to go to the hospital."

In the ER, Ma lay on a bed sandwiched between two women wailing in pain. The torturous throb kept Ma from even speaking. It was cold in the room, but she could barely move let alone slip under the tightly done white sheets on the bed. It didn't matter though. She could not figure out how to lower the angle of the bed, and the buttons on the bed's side seemed dysfunctional. So she just curled up in a ball and prayed the doctor would see her sooner rather than later.

Ma was given an emergency appendectomy. The first thing she did when she awoke was to vomit onto her lap. The second thing she did was ask a nurse where her cellphone was so that she could call Ava.

"No need to make calls right now, Mrs. Concepcion. Just lie back down until your nausea stops."

When she finally came to, a doctor informed her that it would take a while for the sutures to heal. "That means no heavy lifting, okay?"

"None?"

"None."

"But my job . . ."

"I can write you a note that you can show your employer. Seriously. You can't overextend yourself. We just cut you open. It will take you time to heal."

Ava used her old-man reading glasses to scan the doctor's messy handwriting. "What does this mean, no heavy lifting?"

"I can't lift anything . . . heavy."

"Like a baby?"

"Yes, ma'am."

"Well. That's unfortunate." Ava crossed her legs and removed her glasses. Her eyes were back to their regular size, but her cheeks were starting to flush. "Because that's what I pay you for. That's what Carol pays you for."

"No. Carol doesn't pay me. She pays you." Once the words slipped out, Ma felt her arms go numb with regret.

"Are you upset? Is there something you want to share with me? If you have an issue, I'm listening." But Ava's expression wasn't so much listening to her as it was challenging her. Her eyes tightened, waiting for Ma to respond. Daring Ma to respond.

Ma looked down at the floor, her focus suddenly soft. "No, ma'am. Nothing."


Before entering the internet café that Sunday, Ma used the payphone outside.

"Shit, MG," Ma heard Rhea say through the sticky receiver. Ma made herself smaller to avoid the streak of spit on one wall of the phone booth and the drawing of a penis on the other. "Are you thinking of leaving?"

"I have to. I can't do this anymore. Lucas is crawling now and getting into everything. And that other kid, Keegan, sometimes when he doesn't want to leave the playground I have to pick him up and he's so heavy. I can feel my stitches coming apart even if I'm coughing. How can I do the laundry? Or put Judith on the toilet?"

"Do you think she'll give you a letter of reference? And do you think she'll let you stay in her home while you heal?"

"Probably not."

"Are you sure you can't just endure this? Maybe no carrying as much as you can? It's so hard to find another employer if you don't have a letter of reference. And there's only another year before you can sponsor Ale." Tears stung Ma's eyes and ate their way down her already chafed cheeks. Rhea was right. It was just like what Luz had said back in Hong Kong: "Endure the work or go."

When Ma returned to the Meaford home, she expected Ava to ask her to prepare dinner. But when she arrived, Mrs. Meaford was at the stove making pasta.

"Hello, MG." She turned and called out, "Okay, Judith. Mama has made your favourite." Ma realized the table was set only for two and Lucas's high chair. Ma guessed she would have to make her own meal and eat later when they were all done. As Judith climbed a chair and sat down, Ava pointed to an envelope sitting on one of the bookshelves in the living room. "That's for you."

Ma opened the envelope and saw a letter of reference. Despite the ink cartridge running low, it managed to print out its sparse praise, which progressively faded by the bottom of the page. Satisfactory. Decent. Suitable. Sufficient.

"El Padre phoned," Ava explained while cutting up Judith's noodles. El Padre (which she pronounced "PAH-dray") was the codename she gave to Mr. Meaford when the kids were present.

"No! I wanna swirl it on my fork like Ate MG showed me!" Judith screamed.

Her mother continued to cut the noodles. "And he's offered funds for a housekeeper and another occasional babysitter. Since Judith is going to school this fall, it makes the most sense. We don't need someone here all the time. Otherwise you'd be bored to bits during the day." Lucas dropped his bottle on the ground and leaned over his tray to look down at it. He reached his fat hands towards the bottle. "By Wednesday we'll be all sorted," she said, smiling at Ma. She handed a spoon to Judith, who was pouting at the sight of the massacred noodles.

Lucas was crying, still reaching for the bottle as Ma walked slowly up the stairs to the bedroom she shared with the baby. Was this a blessing? She did get what she wanted: an escape and a letter of reference to boot. But the sudden departure left her feeling empty.

Once the family was done eating, Ma finally felt it was appropriate to head downstairs to make herself something to eat. She crept past Ava on the couch, watching a reality-television show, cradling a bowl of popcorn on her lap. As Ma entered the kitchen she saw the pile of dishes on the counter, stained with tomato sauce. Caked-on noodles at the bottom of a large pan. Wineglass. Scattered Parmesan cheese. The popcorn maker. A jar of kernels left open.

"Thanks for cleaning," Ava said with her mouth full. Ma cleaned the kitchen before she made herself a sandwich.

# 6

Rhea's Tito Remy lived in an area east of Toronto called Scarborough with his wife, Tita Connie. Ma took one streetcar, two trains, one smaller train called the SRT and two buses to get there, with her two suitcases rolling behind her. The warm spring weather made the long commute somewhat pleasant. Their apartment was on the ground floor of a low-rise that faced the dumpster, which meant that throughout the day, one could hear the banging and clanging of recycling being thrown into the bins. Sometimes it landed. Sometimes it missed. When Tita Connie opened the door, Ma could immediately smell the delicious scent of fried bangus.

Tita Connie reached up to embrace Ma, who was a foot taller than her. "My god! You made it! Come in, come in!" Tita Connie helped Ma wheel her suitcases in and guided her to the balcony, where Tito Remy was frying the fish on a two-burner hot plate. Tito Remy stood up from his small stool and zipped up his jacket. He had the same eyes as Rhea. Continuously squinting from a never-ending grin. Only his eyes were framed by deep crow's feet and his hair was salt and pepper. Tita Connie, however, looked like she had just dyed her tresses black, since her roots were a telltale red where the grey had been concealed.

"Have you eaten yet?" Ma shook her head enthusiastically. Like a good Filipina she had arrived hungry.

"You know, this does not surprise me," Tita Connie weighed in over lunch while pinching a subo of rice and fish with her right hand. Ma tried her best to listen even though she was enraptured by the taste of the fatty fish belly melting in her mouth. "When I came to Canada, I thought at first, wow, people here are so nice. Much better than the abuse I endured when I nannied in Dubai. They tell all their friends that they treat you like family. But you know what? Canadians are so good at expecting more, more, more, even on your days off, even when their kids act like monsters." Tita Connie put the subo in her mouth. Ma felt for fish bones in the flesh and placed them in a small pile on her plate. "I have to say, though . . . my last family. I loved those two little girls. Can you believe they're now in college?" Tita Connie pointed with her lips to a photo adhered by a magnet to the refrigerator. Two young women. One wearing a graduation cap. Thumbs-up at the camera. "And their mother taught me how to drive. I really liked my time there. They were very nice."

Tita Connie insisted Ma stay as long as she needed until she could find another employer. A bed was made on their faux-leather taupe couch using linens that were spared the smell of food because of the scented fabric softener sheets tucked between the folds. It was on this same couch that the three of them watched television together each night until

Tito Remy would call it a night. He always had to hit the road the next morning for his trucking job, and Tita Connie had her job making food at the nearby hospital. Ma sat on the couch until her sutures healed, until her wrists stopped throbbing from all the child carrying, until she forgot that Judith's naive last words to her were "No, Ate MG. I won't miss you. You'll come back here."

Their Saturdays were spent in and around Highland Park Mall, located a five-minute drive away from the low-rise. It wasn't so much a mall but a collection of rundown shops connected by sticky brown walls and a rusty escalator. Ma would accompany Tito Remy and Tita Connie for their grocery shopping. It always felt like a carefully coordinated expedition. Tito Remy would drop off the women at the mall's dilapidated front doors so that he could go to the Allmart to get bulk items such as toilet paper and laundry detergent. Meanwhile, Tita Connie would head to Gary's Groceries for things like eggs and milk, and Ma would walk across the parking lot to the Sampaguita Filipino store for things like frozen longanisa, patis and haw flakes. The expedition would inevitably end with them sitting on the plastic scoop stools at the mall's food court eating fish and chips. Ma would always feel uncomfortable not paying for the meal, but Tito Remy would insist it was his treat. It had been a month of trying to find another family to hire her, with no luck.

One summer Saturday, Ma proceeded to the tiny shop with windows covered in advertisements.

"Send money home fast!"

"Balikbayan boxes: 2 for 1 special!"

"Lita's Home Cooking. Available for all your catering needs!"

A dusty brass bell on the door signalled Ma's entrance.

"Hello, good afternoon," said the store owner, JP, as he turned the page of the latest issue of *Pinoy Ekspres* community newspaper. On the counter before him sat a crate of live crabs in various shades of red and blue. Ma peered inside at the creatures with their claws bound in thick rubber bands. JP used his hands to push one of them back into the crate. "It's a special order. The guy is picking this and an order of lechon up for his daughter's christening."

The sight of the crabs and image of them steamed in black bean sauce and garlic made Ma's stomach grumble. She shook her head to focus and continued her way down the narrow aisles with her wire basket looped over her arm. As she reached down for a bottle of spicy vinegar on the bottom shelf, she heard the door's brass bell chime.

"Hello, good afternoon," JP said, switching to English.

"Hey. Do you have a bulletin board? And do people check it? Like nannies and nurses?" said a man's voice.

"Yes, sir. It's over there. By the bags of rice, sir."

"Damn it. I forgot my stapler. Do you have any push pins or something?"

"Here you go."

Ma walked to the spice aisle and perused the soup packets for sinigang and kare-kare mixes. She looked up for a moment and saw the white man pinning a notice on the board. It was crowded, so he had to rearrange some of the other notices to fit his, printed on yellow paper with black lettering.

At the opposite end of the store, Ma watched a tall old woman creeping towards the counter. It was you, Liz. It was you!

"Crabs. Someone is picking them up for a party," JP explained, his brow furrowed in curiosity. Ma could see in his face he was trying to figure something out about you, like you were a riddle he could not solve. Your long white hair. Your stained summer dress. Your large feet. Your towering height. JP's face changed, like he had closed the shutters to his eyes and made his body impenetrable by placing a "Keep out" sign at the edges of his energy. You reached for one of the crabs, and JP immediately took the crate away. "No, sir. Do not touch!"

"Justin, look!" you said with the glee of a young child. Ma stepped side to side trying to peer at you between tins of SkyFlakes and bulk bags of White Rabbit candy. Why did this woman talk like a man? Why did she have this voice?

"Mom. Stop. Let's go," said Justin, as he turned from the bulletin board and rushed over to the counter. He grabbed your biceps firmly and you resisted him. "Come on. We don't touch things that aren't ours, do we?" The tone he took with you was similar to the tone Ma took with Judith. Your body wilted with shame.

"Please don't block the entrance, sir." JP was suddenly curt, his lips pressed together, his chin jutted out. The message was clear. You and Justin shuffled out of the store. Another ring of the brass bell. Ma watched JP march towards the bulletin board and rip down the notice Justin had pinned up. He looked at Ma and shook his head.

"Can you believe that? They're looking for someone to take care of that bakla. But here in the ad it says 'elderly woman.' Some people have no shame." JP crumbled up the paper and threw it into the trash can by the counter before heading to the back of the store to restock the shelves. When JP wasn't looking, Ma took the ad out of the bin and stuffed it into her purse.

After Ma made her purchases, she headed outside the store and looked at the ad, smoothing out its wrinkled texture on the brick wall by the parking lot. Ma absent-mindedly waved at Tita Connie, who was walking towards her with her arms full of groceries. On the ad it read "Personal support worker needed to care for elderly woman. Live-in. Cooking, light cleaning." That sounded easy enough. Well . . . it sounded easier than caring for a bunch of rowdy children. Sure, it was for a bakla, but from Ma's experience, most of them were meek and girly, right? What did she remember Father Paul saying during his sermon way back when she was a child? Oh yes. "Love the person, not the actions," he said in reference to a scandal involving a San Marcelino husband being caught in bed with his male co-worker. "We need not judge homosexuals. We can let God judge them and their choices." As long as this person didn't force her into living this perverse lifestyle, then no harm would be done. And this elder seemed too old to do the things the younger ones do. Not that Ma knew what those things even were.

Ma arrived early for her job interview because she didn't want to risk being late. Even though Tita Connie and Tito Remy's low-rise was just ten kilometres away, getting to your house using Scarborough transit involved two buses from different lines that each came every forty-five minutes. She found the right address and walked down the long, flat driveway and sat on the porch of your home. Even though it was summer, the garden beds were a tangle of old growth and rose bushes that were mostly thorns, no blooms. The white siding on the bungalow was stained a dirty grey, and the roof smiled from soggy tiles and a bad foundation.

"You're early!" Justin said, jogging from his SUV to the porch. He was a goofy-looking man in his forties. His belly, exposed under his too-short shirt, jiggled with every step towards her. He lifted a small white plastic bag he was carrying as an explanation. "Sorry. I wanted to grab some lunch while my mom was napping. I'll just eat this later." Justin put the bag down on the ground for a moment to shake Ma's hand. It was a strange handshake that included not only the grasp but him cradling Ma's elbow with the other hand. The touch was repellent enough that Ma's shoulder instinctually lifted towards her ear, but she tried her best to accept the awkward intimacy with a smile. At last, Justin let go and used his forearm to wipe away the sweat gathering at his receding hairline before opening the front door. The stale smell of unwashed bodies and urine permeated the air as soon as Ma stepped inside. When Justin placed his takeout bag on the entrance table, the mélange of foul odours and fast food made her eyes water. Ma was about to sit down in the foyer to remove her sneakers but noticed Justin kept his sandals on. "Here's the living room. We have cable TV." He stepped onto the carpet. It felt strange to Ma to step onto carpet with her shoes on, but given the numerous mysterious stains, she was fine to keep them on. "The house is sort of like a circle. Down this hallway are the two rooms, one for you, one for Mom. Then this office, where I work sometimes, which circles back to this kitchen." A shade of white paint plastered over the dents and imperfections of the cabinets. The door fronts sat crooked on their hinges like loose teeth, leaving every cabinet slightly ajar. A counter opposite the greasy cooktop was covered in piles of unopened mail, receipts and magazines. "And here is the living room." Justin stepped into a modest room with a couch on one side and a table and chairs on the other. A wide window looked out over a backyard with an overgrown lawn.

Ma's jaw dropped at the sight of a wide river beyond the expansive yard. Cattails and bulrushes. Lily pads. "I know, eh? It's stunning out here," Justin said. He pointed out the window. "That's the Rouge River. The hill on the other side is Pickering. We're at the very edge of Toronto. It used to be a cottage before I winterized it and made it a four-season dwelling so that my mom could live in it. The old house is a pain in the ass with all the repairs it needs, but with this view, I thought my mom would enjoy it."

Ma tried her best to focus on what Justin was saying, but she found it difficult not to gape at the scenery outside. An old swing wavered in the wind under a towering willow, its chain grown into the tree's ancient limbs. An arrow of geese flew past in arrhythmic honks. "My mom has Alzheimer's disease. She's had it for, gosh . . . maybe ten years? I've lost count. Not that you can count. There were signs for a while that she was losing it. But who knows how long her memory was failing her. I don't remember the last time she's made any sense. Since I live downtown, I had to hire someone to care for her. We've had a couple of ladies before. Maybe you know them? They were also Filipina. Yolanda? Mercy?" Ma shook her head. "Yolanda had to head back to the Philippines because her paperwork got screwed up, and Mercy got her permanent residency and moved to another part of the city. Anyway . . . she definitely needs someone to live in. It's not a huge amount of work. Mainly, it's cooking her meals, making sure she's eating, changing her diaper, bathing her. That kind of thing. She's not on a ton of meds. She's mobile most of the time. But there are moments, when she's not so lucid, when there may be heavy lifting."

Justin droned on while Ma looked around the living room. Cobwebs sat in the upper corners of the room. Old frames filled with family photos and tchotchkes sat on built-in bookcases on either side of the fireplace. They weren't on display, really. Rather, they sat haphazardly, as if they were taken out from a moving box recently and meant to be organized one day, long before the dust settled on them. Ma noticed that a square of dirty carpet had a round handle on it.

"Oh. Are you looking at the hatch?" Justin followed Ma's curious gaze and walked towards it. "This is how you get downstairs." He hooked his finger around the handle and lifted it up. The smell of mildew and mould. Ma stood cautiously and examined the tight concrete staircase painted in a faded and chipped red leading to a dark basement. "That's where the washing machines are. You have to do laundry when Mom is asleep. She's slipped down these stairs a few times." Ma's toes curled in her shoes. Justin closed the hatch and gestured for Ma to sit on the couch and took the spot beside her. He leaned his elbows on his knees, his face closer to hers.

"And now . . . let's discuss what you're probably thinking." Ma's cheeks grew hot. "Yes. My mom is my dad. But she told me she was a she when I was about twelve and has insisted I call her Mom ever since. So I just play along and call her whatever. Otherwise she gets upset. You know what I mean?" Ma tried to make a face that pretended this was all normal to her even though it wasn't. She remembered seeing one bakla back home, eating at the food court at Shoe Mart. He sat and ate his fried chicken, all alone, while a crowd gathered to stare at him. People laughed at him crossing his legs as he gracefully used the plastic fork and spoon to make subos of chicken and rice. Ma was amazed at the way he ignored everyone hissing and pointing at him. His thin fingers ending in long bright-pink nails. She wasn't sure if she should stop everyone from ridiculing him or join in. She ate her meal quietly, pretending it wasn't happening. Ma shuddered, thinking how awful it would be for Ging to turn out that way. Alone. Different. Seen with disgust by all those around him.

"You'll notice some mail coming in here under her old name, Louis Cahill, but you'd have to call her by her female name: Liz or Lizzy." Justin suddenly slapped his forehead. "And what about you? Damn it. Here I am jabbering on about the job and I didn't even ask for your qualifications. Do you have experience taking care of elderly people?"

"Yes. I cared for my mother for many years before she died of Parkinson's."

"I'm sorry to hear that."

Ma shrugged her shoulders as if the sentiment wasn't needed, even though she was surprised at the sensation of sorrow swelling at the base of her throat.

"Who's there?" you said from your bedroom. Ma followed Justin towards the sound of your fearful whimpers. Justin opened your door, with glass panels painted over in white paint. You sat up in your bed and held the quilted duvet cover in your two fists, tucked under your chin, like a child who had awoken from a nightmare. A beige vinyl pull-down blind, ending in scallops and fringes, wavered from the breeze outside. Justin tugged at the blind and it shot right up into its roll at the top of the pane. You used your arm to shield your eyes from the bright sunlight. Ma could finally see the state of the room. The night table was crowded with soiled tissues, ointments and used notepads. Dead flowers stood in a dirty vase on top of a dresser drawer opposite the bed.

"Hey, Mom. Did you have a good nap?" Justin handed you a half-full glass of cloudy water that sat on your bedside table. Ma watched you take the glass suspiciously and lower your lips to the liquid, barely taking a sip. After scanning your son up and down, you looked at Ma and handed her the glass. "I'm ready to eat now."

Justin laughed and took the glass instead. "Mom! This isn't Mercy. This is another lady. This is MG."

Ma smiled nervously at you. In response, you side-eyed your own son and whispered to Ma, "This one wears too much cologne. I don't like him."

Justin attempted to land a kiss on your forehead. You pulled away. He laughed again. "Oh, Mom." Justin turned to Ma and said, "She's always the most out of it when she wakes up from her sleep. Let's look at your room." They walked down the short hallway to a slightly larger bedroom. The bed had been stripped of linens. A strange stain on the mattress.

Despite your needy whimpers in the room next door, Justin continued. "I know it's strange, you having the larger room, but she really doesn't like this one. Maybe it's the weird sink. But she hates this room." Justin pointed to the sink in the corner behind a sheer curtain. Ma didn't know what was kookier: a random sink in a room or the need to put a drape in front of it—and a sheer one at that. Nothing in the room made sense. The bay window was too high to sit at to look out at the front garden (not that there was anything to admire other than the size of the anthills outside), and the built-in drawers below it were too shallow for socks. The wood-panelled closet doors were too sticky in their tracks to slide open wide.

Justin suddenly sat on the bed with a bounce, his arms to the side like he'd completed a gymnastic routine. Ta-dah. It was as if he expected Ma to sit down beside him on the lumpy mattress. Something about his smile scraped a sharp sensation inside Ma's chest, and she took a step back. Before she could honestly consider her reaction, Justin said, "So? Can you do the job?" Justin had mistaken Ma's split second of silence as a negotiation tactic and outlined the generous pay (more than her nannying jobs had ever paid her) and the ease of the job (comparing his own mother to a house plant with the occasional attitude). Ma had only just given the smallest of nods before Justin was up on his feet giving her a bear hug. He did wear too much cologne. Ma held shut her mouth so as not to breathe it in as his embrace lasted a few seconds too long. "When can you start?"

*

Ma's last night at Tito Remy and Tita Connie's apartment was spent eating celebratory takeout from Kora's Kwizeen. Ma told them over platefuls of dinuguan and turon that she had gotten a job taking care of a senior but left out the part about your identity. She was too embarrassed. They didn't need to know anyway. She reassured them she would be by to visit on her days off since she was only two buses (albeit extraordinarily slow buses) away. Before they made a bed out of the faux-leather couch, Ma watched Tita Connie pluck Tito Remy's white hair from his head as she did each week. Tito Remy laid his head in his wife's lap and she got to work. Using a rat-tail comb to divide thin sections, she isolated the offending hair and plucked it before placing it in a pile of other twig-like strands beside her. He always fell asleep luxuriating in the sensation of his hair being touched, the light of the evening news twinkling on his tranquil face. Ma loved witnessing this weekly ritual. She had never seen her father and mother touch one another, even after he returned from his years-long contracts abroad. To see Tito Remy and Tita Connie together, loving each other, gave her hope. Thanks to this new job, she could complete the program and be reunited with Ale. One day, they would have their weekly rituals too.

So that's how she found you, Liz. And that's why she stayed. I want to tell you more, but I feel like my eyes are dry. Are they dry? I'm just going to rub them a bit. That's better. Wait. No, it's not. My eyes. They're closing. Can you help me? Yes. Hand me to my mother. Thank goodness. Hello, Ma. Ma, could you maybe . . . I dunno . . . sit me up so I can look at something interesting? No, not that. I've seen that wall before. And that window. Is this all you got? Sit me up, please. Yes. Maybe walk around a bit. I like a little bounce. Crap. My eyes are still closing. The bounce is making it worse. Stop. My eyes. Closing. I like that song Ma is singing. Good tactic. That'll keep me up. She's got a nice voice. Great vibrato. Wow. She's good at this. Wait. My eyes. The softness of Ma's shirt. Maybe if I just nestle in here for a moment I can enjoy her voice, but from her chest. My eyes. They're closing. What a beautiful voice she has.

# 7

Hello! Holy moly was that ever a good nap. I don't want to brag or anything because I understand that sleep gets progressively crappy as we age, but wow. That was restorative. I think I grew a little. What do you think? Does this onesie look tight on me now? Have my cheeks gotten fuller? I feel fuller.

We'd better get started as I'm already feeling foggy about where we left off. This is going to happen, I'm afraid. I was reminded by the Maybe Babies that the more I come into this new body of mine, the less I will remember. And they were right. It happened just the other day, when I learned how to open and shut my hands. Ma was standing over me singing some godawful repetitive song. I found myself copying her movements, manipulating my fingers like hers to mimic twinkling stars. It's a silly song. I don't know why it ever caught on. I copied her, Ma started freaking out like I had invented the wheel. She squealed and took pictures. When the flash went off, there was this shift. Like . . . how can I describe it? There was a flash, and then there was a section of my memory, my Before Memory, that was erased. No.

Not erased. Dulled. Like, I remember the basic shape of Lola Daning's face and the small moles that dotted her neck. But the sound of her voice. What was the sound of her voice?

Okay. Back to what I have to tell you. And this part is important. It's important, but it's also difficult, I'm afraid, as all apologies are. She made mistakes with you, Liz. Lots of mistakes. She treated you like a nuisance. There was something about you being an elder rather than a child that Ma had to adjust to. While engaging with kids was easy for her, she found talking to you difficult at first. It did not come easy. You would call her Jane. She did not know who Jane was, and she did not want to play along and would correct you. And correcting you would inevitably make you nervous and scared, especially when she had to touch your body, like when she bathed you or brushed your hair. The entire day would be ruined with you fighting Ma over the smallest things such as putting on your shoes or swallowing your food. If Ma wasn't Jane, then who was this person puttering about the house? Your confusion frustrated her. Maybe even angered her. Instead of playing this annoying game of correcting the demented old lady, she did her job, thinking that cooking, cleaning and physically caring for you was the job.

Ma would wake up at seven and get your breakfast ready. Two squares of toast, one with margarine and cheese spread, one with peanut butter and strawberry jelly, just the way you like it. Start the coffee machine for her, the kettle for your tea. Not at the same time, to avoid short-circuiting the badly wired kitchen. When she heard you moaning in your room, she would silently enter and begin your morning hygiene routine. A short greeting. Change your diapers. Dress you in one of the four sweatpant ensembles Justin gave to you. Brush your bottom and top dentures, left in a cup on your bedside table. Brush your actual teeth (over the bathroom sink if you were agreeable, in your bed if you were grumpy). Then breakfast (in the dining room if you were agreeable, in your bed if you were grumpy).

It was like clockwork. An efficient engine to meet your most basic needs. As Justin said, you were like a houseplant. Nothing more. Someone she could place in front of the television while she did her weekly walk to the nearby grocery store. The only thing that inspired her diligence was to clean the home to the point where she would feel comfortable walking on the carpet without shoes and not see dust on the shelves each time the sun shone through the windows.

Every other week, Justin would randomly drop in, without warning Ma in advance. He would never stay long enough to give Ma a break—she worked twenty-four hours a day, no weekend respite—but long enough for him to annoy her.

One day, Justin barged through the door singing, "Hello, hello, hellooo!"

Ma had just exited the kitchen with two plates in hand. She was about to serve lunch for you and herself. Two fried eggs. Two pieces of toast. Two pieces of bacon. Justin sat down at the table across from you. "Wow, this looks amazing," he said, eyeing the meal. Ma clenched her teeth and handed him the spoon and fork she was about to use. "Aw, thanks," Justin said and began eating. You crossed your legs tightly and ate silently, serving your son suspicious looks as always.

While Ma headed back to the kitchen to make herself a sandwich, she heard Justin add, with a mouth full of food, the food that was intended for her, "Nice day today, eh?"

Ma stood by the counter eating the cold sandwich filled with last night's SPAM.

"You can eat here if you want," Justin said, gesturing to the other chair.

Although Ma abhorred the sight of people talking with their mouths full, she joined the two of you at the kitchen table, with her eyes down, not wanting to hurt Justin's feelings.

A stretch of silence ensued.

"You ever find it weird?" Justin pointed between you, eating your lunch quietly, and Ma. "You know . . . talking to her and all?" Before Ma could redirect the conversation to include you, he continued. "It's hard when she doesn't recognize me. Sometimes I feel like . . . what's the point?" He coughed to hide the fact that his voice cracked with emotion.

"Well," Ma tried her best to articulate a mistake she made herself. "She's right here and—"

Justin waved his arms as if to sweep this moment under the rug. "Enough of that. I have your paycheque." He reached into his pocket and placed an unsealed envelope on the table. The paycheque always made his bothersome visits somewhat tolerable.

"Thank you." Ma took the envelope and then added delicately, "There's something I hope you can help with. I think there's mould in the ceiling close to your mom's bed."

Justin groaned. "Yeah . . . that's just a bit of moisture. We had a roof leak a year ago, but we patched it up. Nothing to worry about."

"But it's black. On the ceiling. If it's not too much trouble, could—"

"Just spray it with some bleach and you should be fine. I'll leave you some extra cash if you need to buy a bottle of it." Most likely he heard Ma's sigh because he quickly said, "Don't worry. I'll have my buddy Paul come take a look at it."

This buddy Paul never came. Ma did manage to keep the bloom of mould at bay, though, at least at the surface of the drywall, spraying the area with bleach a couple of times a month.


She began measuring time in increments of mopping the floor and disinfecting garbage bins the way a prisoner tallies days on a cell wall. While it was easy to find other caregivers to gossip with in the park while the kids played on the slides, taking care of an elder was isolating. Ma's voice would grow raspy from days of not talking until she began narrating her activities.

"One trick is to use a sharp knife," she said to herself, imagining she was the host of a cooking show. "That way, the onions don't make you cry when you cut them." The blade nicked the side of Ma's thumb, and the pain made her snap out of her fantasy. She looked around and found herself in the empty kitchen, all alone. From your bedroom, she could hear the sound of you snoring softly through your midday nap.

Ma wanted company. She just didn't want *your* company. Not yet. It wasn't like taking care of Lola Daning. At least she had something in common with her own mother. You were a stranger and she liked to keep it that way. The relief of you going down to sleep for the night was short-lived because it meant she had to face the endless night, watching episode after episode of mindless entertainment. The intrigue of these new reality-television shows gave her fleeting sensations of joy, anger, anxiety. It felt good to feel but sad to feel things that weren't real, sitting alone on that lumpy sofa, channel surfing from one drama to the next.

Sometimes at night, when the loneliness was overwhelming, Ma would splurge on using her calling card to phone home, hoping to catch Ale before work.

"How are things over there?" Ale's voice said on the other side of the world.

"Good, good." Ma swallowed hard. Speaking to a lucid adult felt foreign and wonderful.

"Oh! I went to Western Union and the control number for the funds was incorrect. Can you double-check, please?"

Ma frowned, wishing her husband would focus on more romantic things rather than details about remittance. He didn't even go so far as to ask about her job. Or about you. Not that she would tell him who you were. Not that she even knew how to describe your identity.

This will be difficult to hear, but I must tell you. Okay, here goes. She did not believe you. To her, your gender was some kind of make-believe game. She played along like she had played tea party with Judith, pretending to fill their cups with pretend tea, toasting each other and sipping thin air with their pinkies upright and proper. To her, your gender was a lie she was forced to go along with to appease you. Even saying your name felt funny. Unnatural. When you were sleeping, she would sometimes look at you and squint her eyes, wondering what you looked like as a man. She even nosed around the house trying to find pictures of you from before, as if to confirm this ruse. But she only found photos— piles of photos—of you with another person who seemed just as confused as you, wearing a dress. On the outside of one of the envelopes of photos was scribbled "FOR PICKUP: JANE LOUGHLIN."

This monotonous machine ran for over two months before the doorbell rang, out of the blue, one Monday morning.

You were sitting in front of the television, watching an interior designer give tips on installing wallpaper to a talk-show host. Ma was downstairs, switching the laundry. As always, she had to lift the hatch and walk down the tight stairwell into the dark depths of the basement. She hated this chore. The low ceilings infested with spiders had her wearing a hoodie and rainboots to keep the creepy crawlies from scurrying up her pants or down her sweater. She was spraying your shirt with stain remover, trying to get rid of the tomato soup splatter, when she heard the doorbell ring. Or she thought it was a doorbell ring. She paused for a moment and heard nothing but the sound of a zipper on a pair of pants rotating in the dryer. She continued spraying. Another ring. Someone really was at the front door.

As she rushed up the stairs and closed the hatch, the person at the door knocked, assuming the doorbell wasn't working.

"Just a sec," Ma called out, obviously not loud enough because the person knocked again. This time it was insist-ent, slow and deliberate. Ma opened the door.

"Hello!" said the person on the porch. Ma was frozen. Was this person a boy or a girl? They shifted the paper bag they held to one arm in order to shake Ma's hand. "You must be Liz's new PSW. Awesome to meet you." Ma looked them up and down. Their hair was buzzed short on the sides and left curly at the top. A chain linked from their belt loop to their back pocket. When Ma saw their chest bound under their flannel shirt, she thought to herself that this person was a woman pretending to be a man, just like you were a man pretending to be a woman. All of this was so complicated and annoying, having to keep track of everyone's deceptions.

"I meant to arrive earlier, but those buses take forever around here." They gently pressed past my bewildered mother to sit on a bench in the foyer and remove their shoes. They pointed at the paper bag. "I hope you don't mind, but I got some supplies from this amazing organic grocer downtown. I thought I could bake Liz a cake." When Ma gave them an awkward shrug and smile, they chuckled. "I didn't even introduce myself. What was I thinking? You must have been all, like, 'Whoa, who is this person?' I'm Ash. I'm one of Liz's friends. I try to come by every month just to check up on her and hang out. But things have been a bit chaotic lately and I haven't been able to come by until now."

"Hello, Ashley. I'm MG."

"Oh. I'm Ash. Just Ash. And I go by they/them pronouns." Ma was confused. Not only did she have to pretend this person was a man, she wasn't to use the term "him"? And there was only one of them. Not plural. This made no sense to her. Perhaps it was Ma's face that made them add, "I don't identify as a woman or a man. Just a person." This still didn't make any sense to Ma.

Ash changed the subject. They turned to you with a smile, with arms outstretched, hoping for a hug. "Hey, Liz! It's me. Ash." You didn't turn away from the television. Ash didn't take it personally. Instead, they let their arms rest back at their sides and looked around the house in shock. "Wow, MG. You did an amazing job fixing the house! I tried to clean up a bit last time I was here, but Justin had left hiring a new PSW for so long that the place was definitely in a state of disrepair. Wow. Look at these carpets." Ma followed Ash to the kitchen. "And the counters. No more papers. Holy cow! Thank you." Ma's chest puffed out a bit in pride, listening to Ash's praise. She had never heard someone admire her hard work before.

Ash placed the paper bag on the kitchen counter. "Did you have any plans today?" Ma thought about this. What plans would she ever make with the old woman other than to keep her alive? "Because if it's okay with you, I can help you dress her up and we can walk to the mouth of the river. She loves looking at the marsh."

You shuffled your feet towards the kitchen and began opening cupboards at random. "Hey—" Your voice was raspy. You coughed a bit into your fist and tried again without the frog in your throat. "Hey, Ash."

"Hey, Liz."

"What brings you here?" you said casually, without making much eye contact with anyone and opening the refrigerator. Ma gently closed it and redirected you towards Ash.

"I came to visit. Want to make a cake together?"

"I love cake."

"I know you do."

"But only chocolate. Vanilla is for losers."

Ash's guffaw was so loud and sharp it startled Ma. "I can't agree more. But before we bake a cake, did you want to go out to the mouth of the river? Maybe we'll see a heron again."

"Maybe. If we're lucky. Sure. Okay," you mumbled before heading back to your favourite spot on the couch in front of the television. This time the talk-show host interviewed a style expert on how to wear low-rise jeans tastefully.

Ash turned to Ma with a softer tone so that you couldn't hear. "It's nice when she recognizes me. Sometimes she doesn't. I try not to take it personally, but it really feels good when she can remember my name and face."

"Sometimes she calls me Jane. Who is Jane?" Ma asked, also in a low voice, taking the pork chops out of the freezer to defrost them in time for the evening's asado.

"That was her sister. Her chosen sister." Ash leaned on the counter and assessed Ma's face, as if to see if any of this was registering.

"Chosen?"

"Yes. As in not related, but they chose to be each other's sister. Lots of us have chosen family because . . . well . . . lots of our blood families chose to kick us out because of who we are. I always say, 'Blood is thicker than water . . . but so is a milkshake.'" Ash shifted their focus to you in the living room. "We'd better get her dressed."

"She is dressed." Ma scratched the back of her neck. Who was this person disrupting their daily schedule?

"Um . . . that's not dressed. She's in her pyjamas, right?"

"No. Those are the sweatpants that—"

"Let me guess. Justin bought them."

"Yes."

Ash rolled their eyes. "Yeaaaaah. I don't think we should take any fashion advice from *that* dude, do you?"

*Fashion? Why would Liz need fashion?* Ma wondered.

Ash led you to your bedroom. Ma followed but stayed at the frame of the door. A game of dress-up she wasn't invited to. Ash opened your closet. "Where did Justin put your dresses, Liz?"

"Who?" you said, bracing on the bed frame to lower yourself down onto the mattress.

"Justin. Where did he put your beautiful dresses?" Ash walked past Ma to the hallway and opened the linen closet. "Aha! Found them. Of course he puts them behind the hand towels. The fucker." Ash began sifting through a pile of brightly printed dresses still creased from their neat folds. "How about this one?"

You assessed the yellow floral dress with empire waist. "Nah. I want a long one so that it can wave in the wind."

"I agree. Is this one long enough?" Ash showed you a slender blue midi dress with bell sleeves. As soon as you had it on, you gave it a twirl. Ma watched Ash French braid your hair into a neat plait that descended down your back. "How does that look?" Ash handed you a mirror and you nodded with quiet satisfaction.

"Okay. Let's go to the river. You can't wear a dress like this and not show it off."

At the speed of molasses, you three made your way down the street, past all the old converted cottages, past the trees turning colour in the autumn wind and waning tiger lilies towards the entrance of the river park. Ash in the middle, holding your arm. Ma on the other side of Ash wondering how long this walk was going to be. Ma tried to make conversation with Ash. "Was Jane . . . was she like Liz?"

"What do you mean?"

"Was she also a man?"

Ash held their hand up in a gesture that was both kind and firm. "Let's wait until we're down by the river and she's settled so we can chat, okay?" Ma looked down at her shoes, embarrassed. "It's best we don't talk about her like she's not here."

The three of you entered the park by descending a steep paved hill towards the river marsh. Ash took your arm as you walked down, each step of yours careful but determined. A family of swans walked past, with one of them honking your way like a threat.

"Okay, okay. I'm not gonna touch your babies. I get it," you said as they completed their crossing from the parking lot of the park towards the shallow water. You put your hands on your hips and giggled at the sight of them. That was the first time Ma heard your signature laugh. A cross between a song and a wheeze.

"Did you hear the city is going to build a path here, Liz? They're going to build some kind of walking path that will connect Scarborough to Niagara-on-the-Lake. Can you believe it?"

"But then everyone will come here. Ruin things."

"Yup. Isn't that always the way?"

"I guess I better enjoy this peace and quiet while it lasts." And then you went towards the shoreline of the river to skip rocks. They mostly fell into the water with a loud kerplunk, but it kept you busy while Ash turned to Ma with a look of compassion.

"Hey. MG. Can we talk?" Ma nodded, afraid she had done something wrong. "Look . . . you're doing an amazing job. I can see she's being cared for, without a doubt. I've never seen the house—or Liz for that matter—this clean, like ever. You don't even understand what a mess it was before you came around. When Liz couldn't care for herself anymore, Justin plopped her here, away from all her friends, all of her support people, in this dingy home he rented out. He's hired two caregivers so far, and one of them was a disaster who had few skills and even less patience with Liz. If I wasn't in school, I would have stayed here with her. You have no idea how thankful I am for you." Ash positioned themself to face Ma directly, their hands in their pockets. "It's super important to understand that Liz is a woman. She's not lying. She's not pretending. She's a woman. A transgender woman." Ma looked at you from a distance, kicking at the mud, trying to source flat rocks for skipping. Ma pretended to look at you out of concern for your safety, since it was her job, but in truth she had to look away because what Ash was saying made her feel uncomfortable. She crossed her arms. Ash continued, "But she's so much more than that, MG. Liz is one of my heroes. She's inspired a lot of people—like, a lot of people—to be who they are. She and Jane produced films. They founded organizations. They marched. They were arrested. They kept marching. That's why I visit as often as I can. It's important to me that she's treated with respect, especially since her own son doesn't think much of her."

Ma nodded, unable to make eye contact. "Please don't take this personally, okay?" Ma was surprised by the tenderness in their voice. "I don't truly know what life is like for you, but I imagine in your line of work, people don't often see you as a human being with needs and feelings, am I right? But you deserve to be treated with respect. It's the same with Liz. She deserves to be seen as a person. The more you get to know her, the better this arrangement can be." Ma nodded again, this time looking at Ash. It made no sense that there were tears in her eyes. "Can I give you a hug?" Ash asked. Ma had never been asked. When Ma agreed, they embraced. The smell of clove and body odour.

Later that evening, Ma cleared the table while you and Ash made a mess of decorating the cake.

"Liz! You gotta stop eating the icing."

"But it's yummy," you said with white gloop all over your face.

"It'll be yummier on the cake itself, hun." Ash tried to collect the spatula from you, then gave up. They spread what remained in the bowl and announced that dessert was ready. Ma wasn't so sure she wanted any. Not only had you dipped your fingers into the bowl, but Ash had said the cake was gluten-free and the icing was free of dairy. She took a slice anyway and was surprised that it tasted somewhat okay. More like a sweet piece of bread, but the icing was as yummy as you said it was.

"When will we see you again?" you said to Ash, your voice growing agitated.

Ash licked their fork clean. "Well . . . I don't know if you remember, Liz, and it's okay if you don't . . . but it's my last year of midwifery school, which means I am now on call assisting births." From across the table, Ma saw your leg start to shake, your gaze become vacant. "So I'm going to be quite busy for the next few months. However, when I graduate, it means I'll have much more of a flex schedule to see you again. For now, I'll just have to drop by when I can. Sound good, Liz?"

You slammed your plate on the table. Cake crumbs on the carpet.

"You okay, Liz?" You slammed it again. "Hey. Liz. Let's not spread crumbs everywhere. MG works hard to keep this place clean, all right?"

"I'm going to my room. I don't want to see you." You stood up and left.

Ash smiled at Ma. "She always gets upset when there's a transition. She does this each time I leave. I get it. I'm amazing." They laughed, then added, "Shall I help you clean up?"

"No. Don't worry about it. I will clean." Ma didn't like the way Ash had cleaned one of the mixing bowls. There was still a milky film on it, and the insides of her dish gloves were wet because Ash had left them lying in the sink. Best not to set herself up for disappointment.

Before Ash caught the GO train back downtown, they took the paper on the fridge that listed Liz's family doctor and Justin's contact info and scribbled their phone number underneath. "Okay. Off I go. Stay strong, and if you need anything or have any questions about Liz, just call me." They tossed the pen Ma had lent them on the counter and marched out the door.

Changes in Ma's behaviour towards you did happen, albeit slowly. She started with hanging your dresses in the bedroom closet and having you select which one you wanted to wear each day. To keep from overwhelming you, she'd show you only two dresses at a time.

"This one," you'd say, pointing to your choice for the day's ensemble. "The V neck shows off my clavicles."

Even when the weather became crisp and the light started to dim, she would slip the dress over a layer of pants and sweater to keep you warm. Each time you wore a dress, you'd act like it was the first time you had tried it on.

"Behold!" you'd say, turning in a slow circle, waiting for Ma to praise your appearance.

Ma would nod with both thumbs up. "Looking good, Liz."

It was obvious from the get-go how this transformed your mood. Instead of sitting in front of the television most of the day, you had the energy to accompany Ma to the dollar store to purchase things like cheap bathroom cleaner and new dish gloves. You loved loitering in the hair accessories section, constantly asking Ma, "What about this one? Or this one?" while modelling various types of barrettes and clip-on ponytails.

"Okay, Liz," Ma would say cautiously. "Just remember that we have a budget of ten dollars and we still have to get a mop from the other section."

Fellow customers who meandered through the aisles inevitably stared at you and whispered among themselves. They would linger in the crafting section, even though they were assessing you from afar. "Faggot," some of them would whisper before pushing past you.

One time close to Halloween, you were in the cosmetics area, selecting a nail polish.

"I think I'll keep it simple this year. I'll be a witch. But the best witch I can be," you said with resolve while painting your thumb with the sample bottle's brush. Out of the side of her eye, Ma noticed a teenage boy with red curly hair eyeing you down with a look of disgust. He flagged down his friend with a shaggy haircut from another aisle to join him in ogling you. Ma's cheeks went hot and she found herself hunching her shoulders, conflicted about whether she should hide or confront them.

"Maybe we should move on, Liz," Ma said, gently touching your shoulder. You locked eyes on the boys. Long enough that they both took a step backwards. You then painted the nail of your middle finger and flipped them the bird.

"Jason? Andrew? Where are you?" said a voice from another location in the store. The boys rolled their eyes and walked away.

"We'll see those fuckers at Pride ten years from now, won't we, Jane?" you said while wiping your freshly painted nails on your gingham-print dress. You spritzed the air with perfume that smelled like lemons and walked through it, your eyes closed for a moment. "I'm sure they're already giving each other hand-jobs, so . . ."

Another change Ma made after Ash had visited was to stop correcting you. She noticed how your eyes lit up when Ash went along with your ramblings about gossip from long ago that involved people neither Ash nor Ma had ever met. She realized there was nothing to be gained by telling you your memory was failing other than to have you shuffle out of the room frustrated and confused.

She began making this face. It took some practice, mind you, but after a while she figured it out. When you'd tell a story, she noticed that you were searching her eyes for recognition that what you were saying was true. It wasn't so much a smile. No. You could see through Ma's smiles when she was placating you. She actually had to visualize what you were saying, see it, claim it as a memory of her own and react to it. Laugh like it was a shared joke. Shake her head at a shared tragedy. It was difficult to get her face just right, but when she did, it was astounding what a difference it would make. And when it was paired with phrases like "Of course I remember!" or "Really? That's amazing," or "Can you believe it?" it would make your day. Sometimes, you'd lean back and look out the window, suddenly somewhere far away but pleasant.

There were some days that were not so pleasant.

One night, an unseasonal cold snap hit. Ma did her best to seal the thin windows with plastic film in time for the windstorm that was scheduled to move through the Rouge River area that evening. After putting the double-sided tape and plastic over each pane, Ma went through the house with a blow-dryer to shrink-wrap the frame. Even then, the wind was starting to pick up and push through the ineffective insulation. Ma could see you were getting agitated by the noise.

"Just a few more to go, Liz, and I'll be done with the blow-dryer," she said while you covered your ears and paced the living room floor.

That night you refused to brush your teeth or get dressed for bed. You tried to lock Ma out of your room. When she finally opened the door, she made the mistake of trying to touch your shoulder to comfort you. And that's when you bit her. Ma held her wrist in shock.

"Liz. Please don't do that," Ma said, swallowing hard. It wasn't so much that it hurt her skin, but it hurt her feelings. She didn't mean to scare you. She felt like she had failed.

The next morning, she entered your room. It seemed premature to have put the insulating film on the windows because it was strangely sunny outside, and Ma could hear birds chirping in the almost-bare raspberry bush outside. You had already gotten yourself up and made your own bed. Your teeth weren't in yet, making your face sunken and forlorn.

"Jane. I'm so sorry. I didn't mean to make you come with me. I lost track of time, making out with that Suzanne lady, and next thing I know you've up and gone. Did you make it home okay?"

Ma made the face. "Yes. I did."

"You're not mad at me, then?"

"No."

You stood up and held Ma's hands, a naughty smile dancing upon your concave lips. "Good. Because I got fucked so hard and I wanna tell you all about it."

Ma covered her mouth in shock and laughed at your audacity.

In those first several months, she quickly learned that while you had most of your mobility, there would be days when a fog would move in across your eyes. It was like the mischievous woman she knew had stepped onto a boat and drifted off somewhere far away to the remote regions of your mind, for hours, sometimes days.

Perhaps you could hear her, entering your room in the morning. She would see your slack jaw and vacant eyes and know. Unlike when you were lucid, Ma would take over and get you ready for the day, talking through every step. She'd set you up for a bed bath. It was tight but she managed to fit a bowl of warm water, a squeeze bottle, washcloths, towels, soap and shampoo on your nightstand. Turning you onto your side, she'd place towels under your bum and under your head before rolling you on your back.

You always groaned in pleasure when she washed your hair, combing her fingers into your scalp and loosening the dandruff from the thin skin at your temples. "You like that, Liz? Is that temperature okay?" Ma would ask as she rinsed the suds in small drips of water from the squeeze bottle. "When you're back, you can wash your nice long hair in the shower by yourself." You also liked Ma's aggressive scrubbing under your neck and behind your ears.

Your face, however, was another story. You didn't like Ma wiping the sleep from your eyes or the dried saliva at the corners of your mouth. "I know. I'm almost done," Ma would whisper.

She'd remove your diapers, taking extra care to clean at the folds of your groin as you were susceptible to skin irritation. "Oh no, Liz. That must hurt," Ma would say while applying zinc oxide cream to any rashes. "We need to get more cream when we're out. You know what that means. Another trip to the dollar store!"

After the diaper change, Ma would look hard into your eyes, checking if you were any closer to arriving back to the present, back into your bedroom, in this rundown home in

Scarborough. She knew you preferred to shave your own face and do it in private. But foggy days meant Ma doing it for you.

That's when she knew she had finally grown to like your company. When you were away it meant the conversations stopped. Even though those conversations weren't meant for her, Ma loved to chat with you and listen to your stories. Sometimes the stories were disjointed and absurd. Sometimes they were full of adventures. Ma would affirm them either way and even add general details until the conversations felt like they belonged to her too. When you were gone, there was no one to pretend with.

On one of those foggy days, Ma was singing to herself, lathering the tips of her fingers with cream and daubing it onto the growing prickles of your face. She dipped the razor (you hated the sound of electric ones) into a bowl of water, then moved the blade down your crepe-like skin, with one thumb planted at your cheekbone to keep the surface taut so she didn't nick you. When she moved to your chin, you suddenly stood up and began talking mid-sentence.

"You're not listening, Jane! I can't put my finger on it. I just don't trust him!" You looked at Ma, who was frozen in bewilderment. You felt for the shaving cream on your face, snatched the razor from her hand and booted towards the bathroom to complete the job in privacy.

By the time Ma's second Christmas in Canada was approaching, she had settled in with a general understanding of your schedule and your needs. Or so she thought. There were always opportunities to humble her.

You were sitting in front of the television listening to the news anchor and meteorologist's banter about the damage done by the previous night's snowstorm.

"After a metre and a half of accumulation, you'd think Mother Nature would spare us what's coming, Nick," the anchor said while Ma tried to dress herself in the snow pants she'd found in the basement. Was she supposed to tuck the pants into her boots or leave them out?

"Sadly, no, Ronald. As you can see here, the cold front that just hit the state of New York is heading north of the border with a balmy low of minus twenty degrees and wind speeds of up to sixty kilometres."

Ma looked out the front window and saw that the neighbours across the street and beside them were already at work shovelling their driveways. At the sight of the rapid accumulation of snow, Ma decided to try to do the same before it got too high, just in case there was an emergency. She zipped up her ill-fitting coat and put her hands into her mittens. "Okay, Liz. Just stay here. I'm going to shovel the snow. And when I get back, we'll have soup." Ma tried her best to put on her hat and made a mental note to put her gloves on last next time. When Ma opened the front door, the push of the wind swung it open and slammed it against the wall. She shut the door behind her and braved the gusts of air, cold and biting against her cheeks. Each step through the waist-high snow was a Herculean task. *Oh, the snow pants are supposed to go* outside *your boots,* Ma thought to herself, feeling the icy wet at her ankles.

She dug around for the handle of the shovel, now buried under a blanket of white. It was stuck under a frozen pile of leaves, and by the time Ma yanked it out, two inches of plastic was chipped off one of its corners. Ma slowly made her way to the end of the driveway and shovelled the snow in arduous, horizontal strips towards the lawn (wherever the lawn was). The strips became narrower and narrower, the snow too heavy for my mother's slight body to push. At least the clearance now was wide enough for a car to drive in and for someone to walk onto the porch.

Ma entered the house out of breath.

"My eyelashes have icicles. And the inside of my nose is frozen!" Ma said, stripping off her soaked coat and hat. She looked at the empty couch. "Liz? Where are you?" A funny feeling at her belly button. Ma frantically kicked off her boots and ran to your room, still wearing her oversized snow pants. Empty. She ran to the washroom and there you were, sitting on the toilet with your diaper stuck at your knees.

"I tried to get this damn thing off in time but I couldn't," you said through tears. Your own feces streaked across your thighs and smeared onto the toilet paper roll, which you most likely had used to try to clean up. Your head hung low as you wept. "I'm so sorry. I made a mess. I'm so, so, so sorry."

"That's all right, Liz," Ma said cheerfully, although she was breathing through her mouth to avoid the stench. "Let's get you all cleaned up."

After Ma had sanitized you and the area, she drew you a warm bath, and you played with the water as if nothing had happened. This was another face Ma had mastered. It was the face that said there was no trouble, she was happy to help, when inside she was bone-tired.

"Close your eyes and look up," Ma said, pouring a cup of water onto your hair. You did as she said, and it reminded Ma of little Ellie, although she was far from little anymore. How old was she now?

"Jane," you said to Ma, lightly touching her wrist with your fingers, now raisin-like from the water. "I have to tell you something." Ma repositioned herself on the closed toilet seat so that you knew you had her full attention. "I can't go back there. I don't care how long ago it happened. But I can't face him. Not today. Not ever."

Ma made the face and said, "Why not?" Her heart started beating heavily in her chest, worried you might answer. Most of your ramblings seemed delightfully disconnected and nonsensical. But your serious tone and grave look made her nervous to know this truth about you.

"I saw it all. I admit it. Right from the beginning. Do you understand? We were only kids. Little Polly had just had her bath and walked into Mom and Dad's bedroom. Dad was lying on the bed. I don't remember if he was having a nap, but he was lying there. I was sitting at Mom's dresser, filling in the spaces in my colouring book. Mom was in the kitchen making something. Cake? No. Something savoury but baked. Chicken pot pie. Yes. Chicken pot pie. She called to Polly to go get into her pyjamas. Polly didn't listen. Instead of getting dressed she hopped onto the bed and jumped on it, laughing. She said, 'I'm gonna jump on you, Daddy!' Next thing I know, things are quiet. Then . . . out of the corner of my eye I saw it."

You were silent for a moment and Ma heard herself saying, "Saw what, Liz?"

You hugged your knees in the water and looked off in the distance. "I saw my dad put his hand on Polly. Right down there. Right on top of it." Ma's stomach turned as you cupped your hand over your own crotch. "He had this look in his eyes. Like his eyes got all soft and gushy. It was the same way his eyes looked when he would try and come up on Mom from behind and sneak a kiss. But it was on little Polly." You took a handful of water and splashed it on your face before looking at Ma. "Then my mom walked in. She froze. My dad froze. Then she said, 'Polly, didn't I say to put on your pyjamas?' and then went back into the kitchen. Jane. He shouldn't have done that . . . he shouldn't have done those things again and again . . . right?"

Ma tried to make the face but couldn't. She realized her mouth was open and closed her lips shut. She nodded. "Yes. It was wrong." Although . . . was it? How much did Liz actually remember? And what did she actually see? Sometimes fathers are affectionate. Sometimes children misinterpret things.

"Then you won't judge me for not going? I mean . . . none of those people have seen me since I went through the change. I don't want people to focus on me. I want them to celebrate my mom."

"I understand." Ma noticed your lips were turning blue and your chin was shivering, but there was a part of her that just wanted the conversation to end. "We'd better get you out of this water before you catch a chill."

She helped you stand up so that she could wrap a towel over your shoulders. Your voice now quivering in the cold of the air, you said, "If I could go back in time, I would have beaten the shit out of that man. Stopped him, dead in his tracks. I don't care if he was my dad. Polly deserved better. She was never the same."

Justin barged in early on a December morning when Ma was massaging you on your bed. Your sciatica was acting up, and Ma positioned you on your side to rub liniment on your bare buttocks. The scent of eucalyptus reminded Ma of Lola Daning, making her strokes into your pained muscles all the more tender.

She heard the front door open with Justin's usual "Hello, hello, hellooooo!" which annoyed the hell out of her. His boisterous announcements of his own arrivals occurred any time of day, even when you were sleeping. This day was no different, only it was accompanied by a scraping sound and his dramatic dragging of something large through the doorway. "Did someone order a Christmas tree?" he bellowed cheerfully. Ma rolled her eyes. She wanted to yell back that you'd both be out in a moment, but she didn't want to startle you while you were enjoying the massage. It didn't matter. Justin strutted right into the bedroom, with his usual ta-dah arms outstretched, as if he expected Ma to cheer for him.

"Justin. Your mother is . . ." Ma gestured to your naked body, trying to get Justin to respect your privacy.

He cut Ma off, rubbing his hands together in excitement. "Once I get the Christmas tree up, we can decorate it together." He exited as quickly as he'd entered, puttering about the living room while whistling an unidentifiable tune.

Ma looked down and found you gripping the bedsheets in two tight fists. Your eyes looked suspiciously at the door. "I'm telling you, Jane. I don't trust him."

Ma stopped herself from correcting you and assuring you that he was your son. Instead she said, "I'll keep that in mind. Thanks, Liz."

You refused to decorate the tree and stayed by the television. This did not keep you from side-eyeing Justin as he shoved the bottom-heavy pine tree into its stand.

He pointed to a stack of mildew-covered boxes he had retrieved from the basement. "These are all I could find. The others I'll have to toss out because they got ruined last year when the basement flooded. I have to find a better place to store things because it floods every spring. We're just too close to the river." Ma nodded. That explained the mould line downstairs. He passed one of the boxes of ornaments to Ma. The miniature birds in cages looked splendid as Ma looped each decoration onto the tree. "Hey, look at this!" Justin showed Ma his box filled with Santa heads. "You're supposed to fill the inside with a candy, and if you squeeze its cheeks you get a Hershey's chocolate kiss," he said, demonstrating the mechanical jaw. He stepped closer to Ma and bopped the Santa's lips to hers with a "boop!" then giggled. Ma laughed along even though she turned and wiped her mouth. The ornament smelled musty and old, but she didn't want to offend him.

Justin held the ornament in his hand, a look of wistfulness washing over his face. "I can't believe how old these things are. I remember buying these at Kmart when my parents were still together. Before . . . well . . . you know."

Justin moved on to another box filled with tinsel. As he looped the cord around the tree he said, "I've got good news and bad news. Bad news is, the consultation company I worked for had a staff shuffle and I've been given a package. Don't worry. You'll still get paid. Because the good news is, this gives me more time to manage my rental properties."

Ma wasn't sure what this meant, so she continued to arrange plastic poinsettias on the branches of the tree. "And you know what that means." Ma didn't like the way Canadians did this guessing-game structure to their sentences. She had learned to wait it out until the person provided an answer to their own question. "I can help out more around here. I'll come by every day. I've been meaning to set up my office in the third room. I'll get my desktop and the internet set up, and you're welcome to use it if you'd like."

Ma's eyes lit up. No more internet cafés. "Really?"

Justin put his heavy hand on Ma's shoulder, slightly too close to her neck. "Absolutely. You can use it anytime."

Ma took him up on his offer. Once the internet was up and running, Ma used Justin's computer to log into her Hotmail account whenever she had a moment's peace, such as when Justin would be out doing repairs at one of his rental homes and you would be napping. It felt relaxing to make herself a tea and peruse emails from Ale, without the pressure of paying. She opened pictures of her siblings visiting home for the first time in decades. Ale awkwardly holding the camera towards himself with a man and a woman smiling behind him. Ma looked closer and realized it was her Kuya Onofre and Ate Fay. Older. Fatter. Kuya Onofre had salt-and-pepper hair, while Ate Fay had dyed her hair black. It hurt to know they were finally visiting while she was working abroad. She couldn't remember when she had seen them last.

On the day before Christmas Eve, Ma wanted to email everyone back home. The time difference would make the message perfectly timed with Noche Buena celebrations. The only problem was, Justin remained at the house, even during your afternoon nap time. Ma approached him cautiously as he was filling in sudoku games in the back of a newspaper. "Um . . . Justin?"

Justin put his pen down. "What's up?" he said cheerfully.

"Could I use your computer? I wanted to wish my family a happy holiday."

"Of course!" Justin accompanied Ma to the computer and booted it up, even though Ma knew how to turn it on. As the machine whirred to life, Ma smiled stiffly, hoping he would leave the room. He didn't. He slid the mouse to Ma and gestured grandly for her to sit before turning to the office closet.

Ma logged on to her Hotmail. He lingered behind her, shuffling things around on the closet shelves. "Man oh man. This place is a mess. It'll be nice to get things sorted here, eh?"

Ma turned slightly and nodded, then went back to her email.

"Yup. That will be my new year's resolution. Filing receipts as soon as I get them."

Ma opened a new email from Ale. There was a group photo in front of a kalesa. Kuya Onofre and Ate Fay stood by the donkey; Ate Marcy and a dozen children stood by the carriage in the back. Their fingers were held up in peace signs. Ma looked closely, trying to figure out whose kids were whose. And were Ging and Ellie among them? She couldn't tell. Ale must have been behind the camera again because he wasn't in the shot.

"Whoa. Is this your family?" Justin hovered by Ma's right ear to look. Ma leaned to the left. He leaned closer.

"Yes."

"So many kids. Are they yours?"

"No. They're a combination of my sister-in-law's, my older sister's and my older brother's."

"Oh, okay. I was wondering. Wow. They are so cute. Is this one your sister?" He pointed at Ate Marcy.

"No, that's my sister-in-law."

"Oh. You look alike. I thought that was your sister for sure." They did not look alike. Ma smiled anyway. Justin touched Ma's shoulder before heading back to the closet to rearrange things.

Ma typed in her message to Ale.

*Hello, my love. Thank you for these photos! The kids are so big now.* Ma wondered if she should type that. She had never seen her siblings' children. She decided to keep it anyway. *Please tell Kuya Onofre, Ate Fay and Ate Marcy I wish them a merry Christmas. When I am done here, we will save money and visit them in the States. I love you all and have a blessed season.*

It was the first week of January when the phone rang. It was the middle of the night. Ma ran to the phone in the kitchen, hoping not to wake you. Even before her eyes were fully open she knew. Like she knew when she heard the phone ring and found out Lolo had drowned when the offshore rig he was working on sank into the Persian Gulf. Because the world is round and the Philippines is one half of a globe ahead of life's tragedies, because the Philippines is ahead of Canada in the earth's rotational spin, a phone call in the middle of the night is never a good thing.

Ma picked up the receiver by the third ring. Ale was singing his words. Wailing his words? Wala na si Ate Marcy. Wala na. She had been en route back to the house after work at the bar when she was hit by a cube truck. An onlooker found her purse, which was flung to the sidewalk upon impact. The stranger used the cell inside to phone the last person she had called. Ale. Her brother. Ma covered her mouth and bit hard on her palm. She didn't want to wake you. You still had a few more hours left to sleep, and if you were awakened, you'd start the day on the wrong foot. She bit hard, her sobs muted in her throat.

"Please. Take the money." Justin stood by the coffee maker with his cup at the ready, waiting for its drips to end. He didn't understand. It wasn't so much the money. It was the time. She didn't have much time left to complete the Live-in Caregiver Program. And there had already been a few months' delay after the Meafords let her go. She just wanted this to be over and to begin the process of sponsoring Ale. And the kids? Oh no. Who was going to take care of Ging and Ellie now that their mother was gone?

Ma continued to get your bed and bath supplies ready. It was a blessing it was a foggy day for you, that you were away in your mind. Ma did not have the energy to care for you at all. On autopilot she said to Justin, "No. That's okay. I don't want to be a bother."

"You're not a bother." Justin was too impatient to wait for the coffee. He took out the carafe and replaced it with another cup so that he could pour the first round of hot liquid into his thermal mug. "She meant something to you, yes?"

"Of course." Ma searched the dish rack for a bowl. Where the heck did it go?

"Then you should go. Your family will need you there for the funeral. For the everything. I'll write you a cheque for the airfare. Just take it. You don't even need to pay me back."

Ma was beside herself. Maybe she had misjudged Justin. Yes, his growing presence in the home was a nuisance, but was it really? He was just a bit talkative. And maybe a bit too hands-on for Ma's liking. But here he was, offering to pay for my mother's way back to her homeland to properly mourn the death of her sister-in-law.

"What will you do without me?" Ma remembered how untidy you and your home were when she first arrived.

"We'll be fine. Give yourself two weeks. Really. I can handle things."

Ale did not meet Ma at the airport in Manila. Instead, his cousin Jared greeted her, explaining that the novena prayers had already started and Ale couldn't get away. The entire ride to Doña Ramos's home was a nerve-wracking one, with Jared audaciously swerving through traffic with one thumb hovering over his car horn. Ma had forgotten the chaotic nature of Manila traffic as well as the unspoken code of car horns. Jared honked when traffic was going too slow. He honked when pedestrians were crossing the street. He honked to say hello to cabbies. He honked when they finally arrived. Jared removed Ma's suitcase from the back of his Mitsubishi minivan with his muscular forearms and headed into the house. Ma had to will her hand, which was still grasping the roof handle, to unclench. Her knees were shaking as she climbed out of the van and made her way to the sound of singing inside.

Doña Ramos's home was full of Ale and Ate Marcy's relatives arranged in concentric semicircles, on the floor, on chairs, leaning on walls. An electric fan oscillated side to side across forlorn faces. Ma entered the room quietly, trying not to draw attention to herself, and found a seat on the edge of a couch beside an old man twiddling his thumbs. It was difficult to not feel the excitement of reuniting with her husband while sitting among mourners, so she clasped her hands in prayer position to hide the fact that she was searching the room for Ale. At the centre of the crowd stood a teenage girl with waist-length hair who sang a mournful Gary Valenciano song about the deceased person always being there to watch over the living. A slight teenage boy strummed the accompaniment on a guitar twice his size. Doña Ramos, now smaller and greyer, sat in her plantation chair with her rosary twirled around her fingers.

Ma spotted Ging and Ellie among the crowd, sitting on chairs meant for the dining room table. They were older now. Ellie wiped away tears with her hands, much larger than her wrists, the threat of womanhood upon her. Ging sat with his shoulders hunched and his arms limp in his lap. A faraway look. Ma wanted desperately to comfort them, but the old man beside her had fallen asleep by the second stanza of the song and was leaning on her shoulder. She craned her neck, looking again for Ale.

There was a gentle touch on her elbow. Ma stood up to meet Ale's embrace. The old man quickly came to and righted himself in his seat.

"Did you just arrive?" Ale whispered into Ma's ear. The sensation of him close to her made her heart skip a beat. She pushed aside her feelings of joy to focus on his sadness.

"Yes. I'm so sorry, Ale." The embrace quickly turned into her holding Ale up. He loosened himself from Ma's arms and stifled his sobs. A relative offered a chair for him to sit on and Ale positioned the chair towards the prayer leader, who had just begun the novena. The two-feet distance between Ale's seat and Ma at the end of the couch felt like an ocean. She couldn't help but want to reach out and hold his hand. Partly to console him, partly to prove that they were still in love, especially with everyone from his family looking at them out of the corners of their eyes.

"Lamb of God, who takes away the sins of the world," said the prayer leader, a middle-aged woman with glasses that framed her firmly shut eyes. Her palm pointed upwards, as if catching a radio signal from above.

"Grant unto them eternal rest," the crowd said in unison.

The old man beside Ma fell asleep again on her shoulder.

Nine days of prayers came and went. Each night, Ma battled jet lag on the bed while Ale stayed up and smoked cigarettes in the courtyard. Each day, Ma would wake up to the sound of a rooster somewhere in the barrio announcing the morning and wonder if her husband would continue to avoid her. Doña Ramos was gracious enough to allow relatives to shack up in the many corners of her home. The constant noise of people milling about the hallway, catching up on family gossip over cups of lukewarm Nescafé and Coffee-Mate and prepping meals became a hum that failed to cancel out Ma's anguish. It felt messy. Confusing. Enraging.

From Ma's heart to her belly button was a deep sorrow for losing Ate Marcy. Ma realized that she hadn't heard her voice over the phone in what seemed like an eternity. And the face she saw in photos was drastically changed by time, despite it being only two years since she had left. Marcy had worked so hard that it showed in her face and body.

From Ma's neck to her ears she was scheming, trying to strategize the best ways to get time alone with Ale, to confirm his love for her, to get him to look her in the eye. The worst part of it all was her anger. She could hardly admit it to herself, but it was there. What was paying for this funeral other than her remittance? What was paying for their rent? The food everyone was eating? And yet, Ale barely said a word to her. Well . . . he was barely speaking to anyone. But why was he ignoring her of all people? It infuriated Ma that he did not turn to her for comfort. He felt like a stranger.

From Ma's waist down was a hunger. A bodily hunger. Although she had to admit she did not have the body she once had on the night of that rainstorm long ago. Perhaps it was the doughy belly she had grown since she had left. She had tried to commit to an exercise regime once she moved to your home, but with Justin's random visits and your light sleeping, she had hoped the physical demands of caring for you would burn enough calories. She was mistaken.

Days later, Ale finally closed the back gate on the last guest. The last cousin (some woman who flew in from Japan without her Japanese husband and two girls, and treated the funeral like a vacation from her family) waved goodbye from her taxi van en route to the airport. Ale stood there by the gate with his hands in the pockets of his khaki shorts, his sandals kicking rocks to the other side of the fence. Ma watched. As he approached, she dared reach her hand out to him. A chance. A risk. He took her hand and held her close to him for a moment, but his arms felt wooden and empty. He released himself from her grasp well before she was ready to let go.

Ellie did not have to stand on the bed anymore to do Ma's hair. But she still needed Ma to instruct her to do a proper French braid.

"Oh no. My finger is caught here. How can I grab the part on the right if it's stuck?" Ellie said with a laugh.

"I don't know. I've always braided my own hair. I don't know how to do it from that angle." Ellie gave up and tousled Ma's mop. "It doesn't matter anyway. My hair isn't long enough to braid now."

"Why did you cut your hair, Tita MG?"

"I'm not sure. It's easier, I guess. I'm always so busy with doing things. Having it short makes things simple. No tangles. Much less shampoo. You know."

Ellie lay down on the bed, which was the bed she had shared with her mother. Ging was moved to the living room couch now that Ellie was becoming a woman. Ellie ran her hands along the sheets where her mother once slept beside her. "I met my Tita Carmen today."

"Oh yeah?" Ma turned to her and stroked Ellie's hair. Her once-wispy strands were now thick and coarse. Her scalp smelled like a teenager.

"Doña Ramos says Ging and I will have to live with her in Aklan. She's the closest relative who can care for us." Ellie rolled over again and cried into the mattress. Ma rubbed her convulsing back, the vertebrae of her spine like pebbles under her nightdress. "I wish I could stay with Tito Ale. And you. I wish you weren't away."

Ma said nothing. She continued to stroke Ellie's hair, knowing that the program would only allow her to sponsor her next of kin, and Ale's hours at the call centre would keep him from the house. She wondered if this meant Ale would have to move too. If Ate Marcy wasn't around to care for Doña Ramos, would she still allow Ale to live in the servants' quarters? Probably not. Everything was all in the air, unsettled and precarious.

When the children were asleep, Ma waited for Ale to return from the courtyard.

"Oh. You're still up?" Ale exhaled the last of his cigarette outside and closed the door quietly. Ma sat on the floor mattress hugging her knees and nodded. Ale shuffled his feet to the bathroom and Ma could hear him brushing his teeth. When he was done, he opened the bathroom door and lingered by the doorframe.

Ma looked down at her feet, then back at him, daring to hope. He shuffled back to Ma and sat beside her. A moment of silence. He turned to Ma and gave her an obligatory kiss. Then another. And another. Ma let out a small moan to feign pleasure, despite it not feeling pleasurable.

"Shhhh." Ale put his finger to her lips. Ale kissed Ma again, this time harder, as if doing so would make the kiss feel more real. It did not. He gently pushed Ma to lie down. He undid his shorts. Ma removed her panties. He entered her. Dry. He spat on his hand and stroked his penis to urge his erection forward. Ma also spat into her hand and rubbed it onto her vulva, hoping it would make it feel less painful. He entered her again. Less dry. Wet enough to finish. He moved back and forth across my mother's body with his eyes fixed on the wall behind her. He moved back and forth across my mother's body until Ma heard him hold his breath for a moment. Then he disengaged and rolled onto his back. My parents fell asleep this way. Side by side/barely touching. Relieved/confused. Hopeful/afraid.

And that was the moment.

I wish I could tell you I was gracious about it. I wasn't. When my parents were in the physical realm, we Maybe Babies were down below, down inside, abuzz with excitement about who was going to be chosen. There was this unmistakable energy inside of me. Like I knew it was going to be me. I don't know how I knew, but I did. If I had a body I would have danced because it felt like a song was being sung inside of my soul and it was full of violins and choirs and drums. I played it cool, though. I turned to the other Maybe Babies and cheerfully said things like "Let's not be too disappointed this time around" and "Don't get your heart broken if you don't get chosen" and "This is the first time she's had sex in two years, I doubt it will take!" That sort of thing. I did a horrible job of lying. So you can imagine how betrayed they all felt when I started to glow an incandescent orange. Some

194

of them wished me well. Some of them didn't say goodbye. I even heard one Maybe Baby whisper to the others that I might be like the last one and never come into being. I was much too excited to care.

Then there was this—wait, what was it? Damn it. I have to focus. See, this is what I'm talking about, Liz. The images are fading, and of course this is the part you're most likely interested in. Not about my parents' copulation, but about this in-between place where I was made, where I developed.

Okay. Let me take a breath. Maybe if I don't put pressure on myself, I'll remember. I can see why you get so upset when your memory fails. This is awfully frustrating.

There wasn't so much a bright light, but the sound of the world around me became louder. In the Deep Down Place where the Maybe Babies waited, it was the centre of the centre of Ma's body and soul, and we had to eavesdrop on her life through a thick membrane of tissue and time. I found myself in a kitchen I had never seen before, in a home I did not recognize. Several women occupied the clean and sparse space, working seamlessly as a team. No bumping into one another. No words exchanged. One woman tended to whatever was in the fryer. One woman washed dishes. Three women sat at the table making lumpia, their hands efficiently rolling each spring roll into perfectly sized portions. Lola Daning was one of them. Her hair was done in a 1940s victory roll, the pins taming her curls into its architecture. She reached her hand out to me. I looked down and realized I had hands. I had hands!

Then she said . . . she said something. Something to me. I don't remember. But it was important. Damn it. I told myself to remember and now I don't. Anyway . . . next thing I know I'm rolling lumpia with all the women. My hands were pretty good at it, if I do say so myself. They asked me how I felt. I told them I was excited to be alive one day, to take my first breath, to learn how to talk. I told them I couldn't wait to have my first taste of food, and they all laughed. A young man walked into the kitchen and the women all greeted him hello.

"Congratulations!" he said. "I hope you make it. I'll be cheering you on." I realized he was the one who was lost. And I felt bad because I remembered how jealous I was of him. But he patted me on the back and said, "No hard feelings. You have your purpose, I had mine. I'm good." I asked him what he felt his purpose was, considering the sadness Ma experienced after he died. And he told me . . . did he tell me? He did. But I don't remember. Sorry, Liz. I don't.

What I do remember is reaching for one of the spring rolls and just as I was about to take a bite, I was inside of Ma, in her womb this time. As my cells multiplied, I made some plans. I dared to plan.

I planned on riding a bike. Having a first kiss. Learning how to play an instrument. Being the first person to dance at every party. Taking my time to look at sunsets. Waking up early to look at sunrises. Finding a best friend. Even the bad stuff, I wanted so badly. The death of a pet. First heartbreak. Second heartbreak. Broken bones. Needles. Arguments. Oh! The arguments I was going to have with people! We would shout at each other. Then make up. I could not wait for my life to begin.

*

In the middle of all this dreaming and planning, I heard the phone ring. Ma had just stirred the rice and turned down the heat on the stove before it boiled over. Perfect timing. When the phone rang, Ma picked up the receiver. Ale rushed from the bathroom towards her and stopped himself. "I got it!" When she put the receiver to her ear, she heard a click. "Oh. They hung up," she said to Ale, who pivoted back to the bathroom to shave his face.

The receiver suddenly felt hot in her hand as she returned it to the cradle. She looked out at Ging and Ellie playing in the courtyard, unravelling a VHS tape they'd found on the street and tying the tape into the branches of the mango tree and the fence. The innocent play between the two children contrasted greatly with Ale's shifty face as he emerged from the bathroom. Maybe it was the way his hair was combed to the side. Or the smell of his cologne. But Ma knew.

"You won't join us for dinner?"

"No. You eat without me. Alan from work is celebrating his birthday. I told him I would buy him a beer."

Ma did not look at him as he left. She could hear the clink of the fence closing despite her ears ringing with rage. If Ma could put a microphone to her soul, she would have screamed:

*How dare you!*

*You couldn't wait two more days until I left?!*

*I've been away supporting you and our family, being treated like a slave, only to return to this broken marriage!*

*You ungrateful bastard!*

*I want to pour gasoline on your sorry face and set you alight.*

*I want to corner you with a machete and threaten you with its blade until you cry for your mother.*

*I want to cut off your dick and throw it into the gutter.*

Instead, she ate with the children and readied them for bed when it was late.

There was no drama in leaving my father. It wasn't like one of those movies my mother has watched where some white woman flees her cheating husband and gets to travel the world to find herself. Filipinas like my mother don't get the Hollywood treatment. No sassy one-liners. No breathy kisses goodbye. What I will describe may seem subdued, but I want you to try your very best to read between the lines of every gesture. From Ale's perspective, he returned home that evening to his sleeping wife, creeping about so as not to wake her. But this is what really happened . . . well . . . what I know happened from inside Ma's body.

Once the children were asleep, she found a spot in the courtyard on a folding stool by the mango tree, which Ate Marcy used to sit on when scrubbing the laundry. It was there that she could weep silently, wiping her face with one of the cotton shirts she had brought, soft enough that her face wouldn't be marked by her sorrow. She tortured herself with images of Ale bending some young, attractive woman over a hotel bed and pushing into her, revelling in pleasure with an expression she did not recognize, until it enraged her into standing and pacing along the courtyard.

Standing where a crack in the pavement split the concrete in two, Ma suddenly saw her options laid out before her.

After her last two days in Manila, Ale accompanied Ma to the airport. Despite the extra expense, Ma insisted they take a taxi instead of a jeepney. She wanted to look out the window. Young girls wearing blue school uniforms, linked at the arms while walking down the crowded street. A woman sticking her head out of the bus with a handkerchief over her mouth. Children on one corner practising dance choreography in their flip-flops. A man swatting away flies at a barbecue food stall. The traffic was surprisingly easy that day and the sun was surprisingly cool.

"Take care," Ma said, embracing Ale without finality.

My father stood back and surveyed my mother's resigned face and body. It was clear he could tell that something was different. Ma's arms were at her sides and the longing in her eyes was gone. She watched the shadow of regret cross his face, then looked away, the warmth of the Manila sun on her left cheek.

As the plane revved up its engine and accelerated down the airport runway, Ma closed her eyes. She imagined Ellie finding the note addressed to her Tita in Aklan, detailing Ma's contact information in case she needed financial support. She imagined Ale returning to the house and finding her short letter saying goodbye forever. The sound of the seatbelt alert went off and Ma opened her eyes. She looked out the window and saw her homeland was now in miniature, already a memory. Crowded clusters of concrete and glass gave way to dots of green islands, which gave way to endless ocean. Her hands opened, letting it all go into the vastness of the water. She had no idea a piece of home was inside of her, also miniature, but growing by the second.

# 8

At first, Ma thought it was jet lag. It usually took her a few days to be right side up when she returned to Canada. But this time around felt brutal. The weight of her eyelids pulling downward was unbearably heavy. While conversing with you, she'd catch herself nodding off in violent dips of the head. At one point she banged her temple on the kitchen table while you ate your breakfast.

"You've got to stop with those late nights, Jane," you said, while Ma held the soft-boiled egg in her hand and you tried your best to chip away at the shell with your crooked thumb. "You can't hold down that job and party after. You're not some spring chicken like before," you said with a chuckle, licking yolk off your fingers.

Ma thought that it was just grief over Ale. He hadn't called or emailed since she'd left the Philippines, and her complex feelings about his silent acceptance of the ending between them and the absence of any begging for her to return was overridden by this insatiable desire to rest. It was like she was too busy fantasizing about her next sleep to cry about her broken marriage. Maybe her body was trying to have her snooze through this difficult chapter in her life? Maybe? It still didn't make sense.

When you insisted on making a snowman outside because it was perfect packing snow for such a thing, she accompanied you into the cold and crisp morning. She did most of the work, rolling a small handful until it accumulated into a sizable ball. You helped her stack three of them on top of one another, put your own toque on its head and declared the job finished. And that's when Ma retched, vomiting the champorado she'd made using the cacao tablea she brought back from the Philippines. Looking at the splash of chocolate across the snowman's face, you laughed. "You're a fucking genius, Jane! You should get hungover more often."

Still, Ma didn't clue in. It wasn't until her boobs began to itch in her bra that it dawned on her. During your nap that day she patrolled the living room floor, her mind racing through the possibilities. She called Rhea.

"He cheated on you?" Rhea exclaimed. Ma could tell by her theatrical tone that she had heard of Ale's dishonesty already. The way that word spread around in her community was enraging. If only people held men accountable for their actions instead of gossiping about them, they'd be better husbands.

"You knew."

Rhea stuttered. "I . . . I didn't *know*. I heard about it but didn't believe it."

"Sure," Ma said sharply.

"Will you tell Ale? About the baby?"

"I don't know." Should she tell Ale? Maybe there was nothing to tell. In truth, she wasn't sure she would even have me. In Canada there was that *other* option, but her

Catholic upbringing made her think that it wasn't an option at all. Or was it? Who would know? She had lost one already. It wouldn't be too hard to believe that she had lost another. But if she did decide to keep me, she had about half a year left before she would earn her twenty-four months of the program. How would she be able to do this job while pregnant? And after the program was over, how could she go through the process of obtaining permanent residency status with a small baby? Where would she live? Who would hire her?

To make things worse, you started to have moments. Were they moments of clarity? Yes and no. You would suddenly look at Ma, not recognizing her, or rather realizing she was not Jane. You would size her up and down as if a stranger had entered your home, as if a stranger was washing your face clean.

"Liz. You haven't washed your mouth out since yesterday. It probably doesn't taste very good, does it?" Ma said. She tried her best to poke a toothbrush into your mouth, but you kept your lips firmly shut. Ma changed tactics. "How about this. I will leave the washroom and you can brush your teeth all by yourself. I can be on the other side of the door and you can call me if you need help. How does that sound?" Ma placed the loaded toothbrush on the counter. You threw it into the tub. A splatter of toothpaste along the pea-green porcelain.

It was always a relief when you would shift and believe Ma was Jane again, although what you said to her in confidence broke her heart.

"Listen, Jane. Have you seen her? The maid? I think she's stealing things."

Ma tried to make the face. "Stealing what?"

"All of my paperwork is gone. How can I find all of my things if she keeps shuffling them?"

Ma showed you where she had filed all the piles of paper into a banker's box stuffed into a lower cabinet in the kitchen. "See? It's divided into folders. Receipts. Magazines. Contracts. Letters. All in here. She just put it away nicely."

"But why did she have to put it away nicely if not to snoop around? You know how those people are," you said, grabbing the box.

Ma's cheeks flushed. Those people? Really? She took a deep breath to calm herself down and said, "You know, Liz. I hired her through word of mouth. I heard she's the best of the best."

Your face shifted. "How is she the best of the best?"

"She . . . she worked at the house of the . . . the president?"

"The president of what?"

Ma backpedalled. She had forgotten Canada didn't have a president. "I mean, the prime minister."

"Really? Which one?"

"The one . . . right now."

"You're kidding me." Ma hated this Canadian expression, which forced her to repeat herself.

"Really. She's the best of the best." Ma wanted so badly to scratch at her boobs but didn't want to break the illusion.

Justin barged in through the front door with his arms full. "Morning, MG! I got doughnuts from Tim Hortons. Hope you're hungry."

You snapped and looked at Ma, a sudden expression of confusion clouding your face. You clutched your banker's box and stormed into your bedroom, saying over your shoulder, "Don't touch my things, you snoop!"

Sometimes, on your suspicious days, it worked to reintroduce herself to you. As soon as she saw your face change, she would say things like "Hi, Liz. I'm MG. Jane hired me to help you." It certainly helped assuage your distrust, but it heightened your sense of entitlement.

"I've been waiting for you. You're late. You're always late. The laundry is piling up already," you said curtly one day while gobbling up your favourite chocolate pudding with a spoon. And on another day you scoffed, "Is this how fast you moved when you worked for the prime minister? I doubt it. Chop, chop."

There was one morning that was particularly challenging. You complained about a pain in your mouth and held your cheeks with every bite of that morning's breakfast.

"Can I look inside, Liz?" Ma stood up from her side of the table and stepped towards you. Already you were quite afraid and perhaps she should have seen your face changing, a shift in your perceptions. But she approached you and looked inside your mouth. A foul smell. "Oh no. That doesn't look very good," she said, touching gently a swollen part of your gum.

Out of pain? Out of fear? She wasn't sure which. But all of a sudden you clamped your mouth down. Ma managed to snap her finger back before you could bite her but did not retreat far enough to avoid you kicking her away, just above her pubic bone.

"GO AWAY! STOP POKING ME! GO AWAY!" you screamed in rounds as you writhed on the carpet. Ma held her abdomen in shock, watching you have a tantrum. She saw you bump your head on one of the legs of the dining room table but couldn't will herself to help you. All she could think about was me inside of her and whether I had just been killed.

She ran to the phone and dialed the number posted on the refrigerator. "Justin? I need to go to the hospital."

Justin drove Ma to the hospital, drove back to the house to tend to his mother and awaited word from Ma about when to pick her up. She was released three hours later.

"I'm confused. How hard did she kick you?" he asked as Ma entered the car.

"Hard enough that I was worried."

"Worried that you broke a bone?"

"No."

Justin pulled his SUV into a gas station. "One second. I need to fill up." Ma waited in the car, running her fingers around the patient identification band on her wrist. It was terrifying to think she might have lost me. It was even more terrifying to know I was still alive. The ultrasound technician had pointed to the screen, showing Ma my beating heart. Her eyes widened at the sight of me spinning in a circle. I tried to wave, but I don't think she saw me. She was too busy trying to strategize how the hell she was going to take care of me.

Through the rear-view mirror she looked at Justin inserting the nozzle into the gas tank. She had to tell him. If not now, her belly would tell the truth in a few months.

Justin did a three-point turn and drove to the car wash beside the station. "Mom's still napping. Let's get in here before Sunday when spring kicks in." He rolled down the window to enter a code from the gas receipt into the keypad by the carwash entrance. The garage's doors opened slowly, its motors roaring into action.

"I have to tell you something," Ma said as the car's wheels engaged with the carwash tracks and moved it forward.

"Whoa. Sounds serious." Justin removed his clip-on sunglasses and looked at her. "Are you leaving us? Are you quitting?" Strings of foamy multicoloured soap cascaded onto the surface of the vehicle. The chemical floral scent made bile rise in the back of Ma's throat.

"No. Not that. I'm . . . I'm pregnant." The SUV rocked side to side under the weight of blue rotating brushes, scrubbing it clean.

Justin's eyes grew two sizes larger. His smile was even larger still. "What? That's amazing!" Clear water rained down on the car, the chemical scent subsided. Justin undid his seatbelt and bear-hugged Ma. His cologne was too strong, but Ma thought twice about pulling away.

The loud sound of blowers drying the windshield forced Ma to shout, "I promise you, Justin. It won't get in the way of me taking care of your mother. I can still do my job."

The garage doors opened at the carwash exit, signifying the process was over. Justin started the engine again and drove into a parking space outside. He turned to Ma with a serious face. "What are you talking about? I don't doubt this at all. This is great news. You and your husband will have a new baby once he's sponsored here!"

Ma looked out the window. Beside them, a truck driver was reinflating his wheels. "He's not coming here."

"You're kidding me."

Ma sighed deeply before repeating, "He's not coming. He's with someone else."

"I'm sorry. Jeez, MG. I'm so sorry. That's shitty. This happened while you were away? Working? What a fucking asshole!"

Ma's eyes began to sting with the threat of tears. Ale wasn't so much a jerk. He was just another victim of time and distance. Some people make it. Others do not. It did feel good to see Justin express rage on her behalf, though.

"Will you have to go back to file for divorce, then?"

"There's no divorce in the Philippines."

"Wait . . . people don't break up?"

"People break up. It's just not legal."

"Then are you going to tell him? About the baby, I mean?" Ma shook her head. "Yeah. That sounds like a better idea. You don't want things to get too complicated. I mean . . . I know it's probably too soon to think of things positively, but maybe it was good you broke up before Ale came here, right? You don't have to deal with all that paperwork to sponsor him."

A lump swelled in Ma's throat. What was this all for, if not to be together? Now what? What does a better life in Canada mean if it's a life all alone as a single mother?

Justin took his keys out of the ignition and twirled them around his hand, catching them in his palm in a rhythmic pattern. He dropped his keys on the seat and reached out to cup Ma's cheek. Ma's face twitched at the metallic smell on his fingers. Justin took off his seatbelt and reached over to embrace Ma. It felt like the hug lasted an eternity, especially with his hand stroking the back of her head. "I'm here for you, okay?"

"Thank you." Ma patted his shoulder, hoping the embrace would end.

He finally let her go but still touched Ma's shoulder. Looking directly into her eye he said, "I have to tell you, no one, I mean no one, has ever been this amazing with my mother. Like . . . ever. We need you as much as you need us, you know? I mean . . . have the baby. Stay at the house. With the baby. Why not?"

Ma couldn't believe her ears. "Really?"

"I'm serious!"

Relief washed over Ma's body, just enough to help her ignore her discomfort around him but not enough to keep the nausea at bay. She opened the passenger-side door and vomited onto the pavement.

When did Ma see the red flag? Should she have seen it when Justin came to the house with a new crib? Was the red flag the way he took his time in my mother's room, assembling the rails and dowels into something my mother never asked for, which barely fit at the foot of her bed? Should she have drawn a boundary when he began painting the walls of the room without discussing colour choices with her? Was the red flag in his arm that he draped over my mother's shoulders after he had finished slapping on that sage green? The way he assessed his job well done, while still holding Ma at his side? Maybe it was farther back than that. His ta-dah arms. Yes. That was it. The way he outstretched his arms that looked like he was going to catch her in a hug. Catch her. Trap her.

But how does one draw boundaries with someone who is so kind? So giving? Someone whom you need to survive?

*

I had just grown tiny legs. Spinning around and dividing cells was so last month. I was ready to kick. To my mother, it felt like bubbles popping inside of her, right below her belly button and slightly to the left. She assumed it was a twitch, but when she looked down at the skin around the area it wasn't moving. The sensation was coming from inside. This was my first communication with her. A long-awaited Morse code from me to her. *I'm here!* I wanted to scream at her. *This is me! Your baby. We are going to spend a lot of time together, you and I.*

It wasn't until she was helping you out of the shower, by steadying your hands as you carefully stepped out of that pea-green tub, that Ma clued in. She bent down and towelled off your legs just as I kicked. Well . . . I kicked a few times just to get the point across. *Legs. Legs. I grew legs, Ma! Can you feel them?* I felt her palm carefully touch the abdomen above me. I couldn't wait to feel her touch directly on my skin. We were almost there. Almost.

Justin barged through the front entrance and Ma could feel a draft pass under the bathroom door. She quickly grabbed the hand towel that hung by the sink to block out the cool wind.

"You wouldn't believe the deal I got on this diaper change table!" his muffled voice said as he passed the closed door.

Ma shouted as loud as she could through the pressed wood without startling you. "Your mom is finishing her shower, just a second." She pumped lotion into your palm to get you to rub on your upper arms and torso while she tackled your lower half.

"I'm just going to leave the parts in the foyer and I'll put it together tonight," Justin continued from the living room.

Maybe he didn't hear her. Maybe he just wasn't listening. He opened the bathroom door. You were still naked. Ma was still slathering lotion on your calves. You covered yourself with your hands. Ma froze. "It's a beaut. It's got drawers and everything." Justin closed the door, ending the conversation as quickly as it began. His entrances and exits always had you both holding your breath. Both of you exhaled in unison. Ma proceeded to dress you.

"Polly," you whispered to Ma, your jaw tight. "How many times is Dad going to pretend that was an accident?" You had never referred to Ma as Polly before, and this new assigned persona made it more difficult for her to make the face that reassured you. You caught a glimpse of Ma's troubled expression. "If he comes for you again . . . call my name, okay? Scream it. Bang on the wall. I'll wake up this time. I promise."

The change table was more difficult to assemble because the family Justin had bought it from through Craigslist had lost the instructions. By nightfall, after you had gone to sleep, the bottom frame of the structure sat lopsided in the foyer next to the boot tray. Justin went to the kitchen and cracked open a bottle of Labatt beer and called it a day. From the couch, Ma heard the beer bottle cap hit the kitchen counter, and she made a mental note to put it in the garbage the next day. She would have done it then and there if she wasn't so exhausted.

"Man oh man. Once this thing has its drawers, you'll have tons of places to put diapers, clothes, you name it." Justin returned to the foyer and surveyed the half-built table. Ma nodded, wondering where in the hell it was going to fit. She didn't want to pop his bubble because popping his bubble would have been rude. Instead, she adjusted the sofa pillows to accommodate her new body's needs. Ma had thought that aches and pains were to happen after she started showing, but her feet already felt swollen and inflamed.

Justin took a sip of his beer, then turned to Ma. "You look tired." Ma smiled with half her mouth. She was much too exhausted to humour him. "Did you want a foot massage?"

"No. That's okay. I think I might go to bed. I'm very sleepy." It was indeed a long day. A morning of you having tantrums about the temperature of your tea and an afternoon of Ma reassuring you during a bout of confusion about what your middle name was.

"I can rub your feet while we watch TV. How about that?" He had his ta-dah arms outstretched, the wingspan alarmingly long, his expression needy. Ma looked at the change table in progress. He had gone through so much trouble for her over the last few weeks. The only price to pay for his generosity, it seemed, was her joy. She nodded. He sat down beside her and used the channel changer to turn on the TV. He switched it to a program where neighbours renovated each other's houses on a one-thousand-dollar budget. Ma felt his hands grab at her feet and place them on top of his lap.

"Can you believe this?" he said, kneading into the fluid collected at Ma's arches. "I don't know if I would continue a friendship with someone if they did this to my house." Ma's eyes grew heavy. It felt unnerving having Justin touch her so intimately, but she couldn't help but succumb to the sensation of compression on her heels, her toes, her Achilles tendon.

She awoke with a start, Justin's hands still massaging her feet. An infomercial about an air fryer played on the screen.

"Sorry! I fell asleep." Ma removed her feet from Justin's lap and groggily made her way to her bedroom. She was much too fatigued to even brush her teeth or get into her pyjamas. Her sheets were delightfully cold as she slipped into the bed and fell fast asleep.

I began kicking because I could hear Justin quietly turn the knob of Ma's bedroom door. She did not feel me. I kicked harder.

On Ma's shoulder she has the body memory of lying on her side. She was dreaming of biting into a polvoron candy and letting the powdery texture fill her mouth. On Ma's right breast she has the body memory of Justin's hands sliding under her shirt, the shirt she did not change because she was too sleepy to get into pyjamas, and cupping her.

Ma's eyes opened to the smell of his cologne.

"No. No." Ma tried to turn around and loosen herself from his grip.

She could feel Justin's stubble on her ear as he said, "I wanted to say good night." She could feel his erection through his pants.

"What are you doing?"

"I'm holding you."

Ma said (cried?) she said . . . yes, she said . . . she did say it . . . she said, "No. Please don't."

"You left without saying good night." He rocked into her buttocks. "Don't you want to say good night to each other?"

Ma's arms went wooden while he burrowed his face into her neck. Her eyes were fixed and frozen. *Move, move!* she screamed inside her motionless body. *Wake up, damn it! Do something!* she screamed outside her body, her soul lingering above and beside her, by the doorframe, outside the window. Screaming.

At the tip of Ma's fingers lives the memory of digging handfuls of mud, as thick as wet concrete. After Mount Pinatubo erupted, it rained, sending a deadly combo of volcanic ash and water down the mountain in unrelenting torrents of lahar. Ma dug her way to the arm of a woman who was about to be washed away by the heavy current. She dug, with her own fingers, to the woman's slippery arm and pulled her to safety. Screaming. Screaming with every scoop of her palms. Fingers. She remembered her fingers.

With those same fingers, she pried Justin's hands from around her breast. His grip was strong, but she did it, bone by bone. She wriggled free and managed to untangle herself from the bedsheets and step past the crib, that damn crib she never wanted, onto solid ground. Holding her arms out she said again, this time in a louder voice, the loudest voice she could manage, although it was higher pitched, "No. Don't!"

"What's wrong with you? Weren't we just cuddling? I just want to cuddle." His words were delivered in a way that made Ma question if she were imagining things. And yet, his body stepped forward, the wingspan of his ta-dah arms threatening to hug her again.

Ma looked at the crib, the fucking shade of green painted on the walls. If Ma could have put a microphone to her soul, she would have said . . . she would have said . . . no . . . she *did* say it. I remember she said it out loud. "NO! NO! NO!" She banged her fist on the wall that she shared with you. She banged it with every no she screamed. And right when Justin was about to step forward, right as he was about to hug her, hold her, touch her again, that's when you entered the bedroom and hit him on the back of his head with one of the wooden slats of the change table he had left in the foyer. You held your crude weapon close to your chest, its weight heavy in your arms.

Justin moaned. "What the fuck, Mom?!" He attempted to stand, holding his head in pain.

"Get out!" you shouted. "Don't touch her again!"

Justin scoffed. "Do you even know who *she* is? You can't even remember your own name, you batty old bitch!" His humiliation transformed his shouts into boyish sobs.

"GET OUT!" you roared loud enough that you coughed.

Justin stumbled towards the foyer. You followed closely, holding the wooden slat out like a threat. Ma walked behind you, shaking like a leaf. Justin continued, trying to maintain his dignity. "I'm going to kick you out of this house. I'm going to send you to the old folks' home. The worst one I can find. And I'm going to leave you there to die." He hastily stuffed his arms into his coat and stepped into his boots.

"Say anything you want." Your voice was suddenly serious and deliberate. "Tell the world you got beaten up by a couple of girls." Justin ran to his car and sped off into the dark of the night.

You dropped the wooden slat, turned and opened your arms to Ma. She ran into your embrace, choking on tears.

"Liz. I don't know what happened. I'm ... I don't know ..."

"Shhhhh ... shhhhh. Daddy won't touch you again." You held her firmly. "Did you see him run? Ha! We did it, Polly. We fucking did it."

\*

Rattled and shaken, you both set up camp on the sofa under the warmth and weight of Ma's comforter. I'm not sure if you noticed, but you held hands under the covers. It was as if you both feared that letting go would mean losing the other in a forceful current. Lahar rushing down the volcano.

You held hands as if your life depended on it. Red palms. White knuckles. You both held on through the night, nodding in and out of sleep, until the sun peeked through the backyard brush and over the river. You both held on until the blue jays began to do their daily dance, swooping back and forth across the bay window, and the cardinals chirped their mating songs from the tops of the cedars. It would have been a perfect spring day to go out for a walk, but you both were too drained and wired to move from your seats.

The only times you broke apart were for bathroom breaks (which were much more frequent these days for Ma) and for snacks and meals (which, for this day, had very little structure). Occasionally, Ma would break apart from you to open and close her hands, which were still sore from Justin's attack. When a memory of his breath on her neck or the fear of what the future held for Ma's employment and your housing flashed through her mind, Ma would return to clasping on to you under the covers, the sensation of your touch grounding her in the safety of her present.

Over corned beef and pandesal sandwiches Ma made for a second (third?) lunch, you watched Judge Julia together.

"Look at this loser, right here," you said, pointing at the

man onscreen. "If your poodle wasn't groomed right, you don't slash someone's tires for god's sake!" You shook your head and took another bite of your sandwich. Ma wiped away the sauteed onion that lingered on the side of your mouth.

By nightfall, you both had moved on to full plates of leftovers while watching some new show where an odd cross-section of people competed against each other and voted on who would leave the tropical island they were stranded on. Ma shook her head watching Americans fail miserably at building shelters for themselves and cooking over an open fire.

"I'm telling you: Stacy is going next. She has to. We all saw what she did." Ma steadied the plate of spaghetti on your lap as the host announced that Stacy was indeed voted off the island. You cheered. "See? I knew it. Serves her right." You linked arms with Ma under the covers and started channel surfing again, your crooked thumb pressing the buttons on the remote control. "I love watching TV with you, Jane." Ma made the face, assuming the persona of your chosen sister. "I hope the Rogers guy doesn't figure out we've been getting free cable this entire time. I'd hate for him to cut us off. I don't know what I'd do without the Food Network."

Ma woke up in the middle of the night to the sound of the Canadian national anthem playing on the television, followed by white noise. You were asleep on her shoulder. The duvet was littered with bits of bugle chips, your last snack of the evening. She snuck out of the blanket and was about to turn off the television when she saw a field mouse out of the corner of her eye.

"Ah!" Ma quietly squealed under her hands that tightly clamped her mouth. Looking back at you, she was grateful you didn't hear her. Your head was still slumped on the sofa cushions, the light from the television flashing across your slack jaw. She assumed that when she looked back at the mouse it would have run away. Instead, it stood there on the old, ratty carpet meeting Ma's eyes. Its feet curled in two pink fists at its chest. Ma kicked at it, hoping it would feel threatened and flee. It did not. It barely blinked. On its own time, the mouse traipsed back through a crack in the hatch.

Once Ma turned the television off, the white noise was exchanged for the sound of softly falling rain. Ma debated whether or not to wake you and tuck you into bed. She decided against it and fell asleep beside your snoring body. In the darkness outside, the pitter-patter of rain showered on the old home's roof.

The next day began with a drop of water falling directly into Ma's tear duct on her left eye. Bull's eye. Spring had begun and the roof was leaking. Ma served your breakfast on a TV table, sitting away from the various pots and pans she'd placed around the house to catch the drips dribbling from the yellowed lesions on the ceiling.

"Our things! Jane!" you said, pointing frantically at the basement. The sound of gushing water downstairs had Ma scrambling to open the hatch. Water was pouring in through the cracks of the home's foundation and through the basement window. She ran to the foyer and stepped into her wellies before descending the stairs.

"I'll come down and help you. You can't do it all yourself, Jane. I keep telling you!" Ma heard you say from upstairs.

"No, Liz. Please. Don't come down." Although, Ma could have really used the help. She waded through the calf-high muddy water, up and down the tight concrete stairs with armfuls of boxes. Anything that looked important. After more than a dozen trips, Ma's body felt weak. The initial adrenalin rush was long gone, and the smell of mould was making her nauseous.

"What an asshole," you said with your hands on your hips, surveying the boxes that were piled all over the living room. "I hope our landlord dies a horrible death. He deserves it for putting us out onto the streets."

When you were down for a nap that afternoon, Ma looked at the piece of paper with Justin's phone number on it, still pinned to the refrigerator behind a magnet. She picked at a piece of skin on her lip considering if she should call him and tell him about the roof and the basement. No. It was too soon. She didn't want to see him right now. She never wanted to see him again. And who knew what consequences were in store for her after what had happened? Maybe this was the end. Surely he was going to fire her. After a night of worry, Ma had resigned herself to a half-baked plan to relocate back to Tita Connie and Tito Remy's place to begin her search for a new job and to ask Ash to advocate for your housing. For now, what was she going to do with all of this stuff from the basement?

Ma opened one of the boxes to assess the damage. It was tightly packed with VHS tapes. One of them was labelled "PRIDE 1983." She took the tape out and slid it into the player that was sandwiched underneath the television and the DVD machine. She pressed play and turned the television's volume down to three, hoping not to wake you. The tape caught and Ma could hear the reels turning. Lines across the screen. Then an extreme close-up of a person looking in the mirror. Flock of Seagulls hairdo.

"Get that thing off of me, Liz."

From behind the camcorder was your voice. "And here we have Jane Sarah Marie Loughlin. Getting ready for the march. Putting on the lipstick she just stole from the drugstore down the street."

"Did you just make up my middle names? You're such a cunt," Jane said, removing lipstick from her teeth.

You laughed and turned the camcorder on yourself. A fringe of blond bangs framed your face. A heavy dose of eyeliner. You pursed your lips in a kiss, then turned the camcorder back to Jane.

"I'm so annoyed you bought that thing." Jane had moved on to mascara, applying it in thick coats onto her eyelashes.

"I don't know why you're going through this much prep before the march. You know we're gonna be the grannies of the bunch, don't you?"

"What the hell do you mean?"

"We're getting old now, woman."

"We're in our fifties. We're not old, you hag."

"No one is going to want to pick us up. We're old news. Even Ricky said so."

"Ricky can lick my labia."

"Ricky already licked your labia."

"Shut up and pass me a tissue. I got some mascara on my cheeks. Fuck."

A jump cut. Lines across the screen. The camcorder zoomed in, then out, on Jane sitting on a park bench. A large wet stain on her purple dress. A bright, sunny day.

"I swear to god, Liz. If you don't turn that off, I will punch. Your. Face."

"Tell me what happened. Tell the camera. So that we'll remember."

"Why do we need to remember this shitshow?" In Jane's hand was a twig that she broke off in bits as she spoke.

"So that one day people will look back on this and remember what happened."

Jane rolled her eyes and sighed heavily. "Fine. Today, we tried to join the Dyke March and someone from the crowd threw garbage at us. There. That's what happened."

"I'm sorry, hun," said your voice behind the camcorder.

"I'm sorry to you too. I wasn't the one who got called names." Jane leaned on her fist and looked away.

A moment of silence. Jane looked at the camera. Slowly, ever so slowly, a smile grew on her face. She winked. The sound of you chuckling behind the camera.

"Ice cream?"

"Maybe."

"Come on. I know you want ice cream."

"Fuck yes."

Ma looked at your bedroom door, then at her watch. Still another hour before you would wake up. She went through the tapes, one by one, quickly scanning them, pretending she was doing so to check if there was any water damage. At least that was the excuse she was prepared to give if you had woken up and found her snooping. In truth, she wanted to learn about you, know who you were before the cloud of dementia flew over your universe.

As she made her way through the tapes, she noticed that the footage became more artful. In one tape labelled "INTER-VIEWS, TAPE 1 of 3," Ma watched short clips where six different trans women put their makeup on while you asked them questions about their lives. One tape was raw footage of Jane dressed in a white nightgown and flower headdress stepping from the bank of a river to a small boulder.

"One more time."

"Again? Fucking hell, Liz."

You laughed. "One more time and I'll treat you to lunch. I promise." You made her do it four more times.

One tape had the plastic tab broken open on the side. Ma slipped it into the player. No sound other than your breathing behind the camcorder. An extreme close-up of you holding hands with Jane. You zoomed out abruptly to include a shot of Jane on her side, her eyebrow-less face smooshed into a pillow.

A small smile played on her face even though her eyes remained closed. "I'm gonna kill you, Liz. Turn that thing off."

"I love the sound of your voice."

"Jeez. Stop treating me like a museum piece, will you? I'm just dying, but I'm not dead yet. I'm trying to sleep."

"I love you, Jane Sarah Marie Loughlin."

Jane's eyes opened slightly. "You know I love you. You're my sister."

"You're *my* sister."

"Now fuck off with that camcorder."

The last tape in the box had no label and was full of disjointed footage of you accidentally pressing record when you meant to press stop. And pressing stop when you meant to press record. Lots of shots of sidewalks where you placed the camera thinking it was off.

"Oh, fucking hell, I did it again!" you said in one shot with the camera aimed at your chin. "Boris. It didn't record your interview. Sorry. Can we do it again?" There was no footage of Boris. Then there was a clip of you struggling to position the camera on a tripod. The sound of you cursing to yourself while setting up the shot. Finally, you sat in front of the camera, only the frame was tight on your nose. You reached your arm to somewhere off-camera and the lens zoomed out to reveal you from the waist up. Ma could see time working its way around the edges of your face in laugh lines and crow's feet. The furrow of your brows arched over a worried look in your eyes. Was this after the dementia started? Judging by your confused expression, most likely.

"Hello, world. Hello. My name is Liz Cahill. No. Wait." You looked off in the distance somewhere. Was it a window? Back to the camera. "Hello, Liz. It's me. Your younger self. This is what I look like. I don't want you to be scared. You have seen beautiful things. You have loved lots of people and lots of people have loved you." You grinned and shielded one side of your mouth as if you were telling a secret. "And I mean a *lot* of people." Quiet laughter, then a hard swallow. "You might not remember it all, but I gotta tell you, it was fuuuun. And you got to be you. Some people were not happy about it. Some people tried to get you down. But you kept going because you're not one to quit. You used this camera to give voice to others. There are many people who felt important, felt cared for because of you and your films. So don't be sad. You are a motherfucking miracle." Your arm reached out off-camera. Lines across the screen, then blue.

Ma heard moaning from the bedroom and knew your nap time was done. She put the tapes away.

\*

Weeks later, a knock on the door made Ma's heart thump in her chest. Justin had not returned to the house at all, and today she was convinced that it was him. Much to her surprise, Ma was still being paid, but now she received her paycheques by mail, signed by him, folded into a piece of blank white paper and placed in a plain envelope. It was a welcome change to not have them hand-delivered like before, with him barging into the house and inevitably giving Ma a bear hug immediately afterward. Still, she used the bank card she had been given for groceries and supplies nervously, expecting the cashier to tell her there was an interruption in funds. That never happened. The bills were most likely redirected as they were not in the mail anymore; however, the electricity, heat and water kept running. And yet, when she heard the knock on the door, she assumed the worst.

"Hey, MG!" Ash said, when Ma cracked the door open. At first, Ma didn't recognize them. It had been months since they had visited, though they called fairly often. They had dyed their curls a bright purple that reminded her of the ube cakes back home. On the front panel of their denim overalls was embroidered the word "TOP" in swirly calligraphy. As they entered the foyer, Ma could see the word "BOTTOM" was embroidered on their wide bum. Ash waved at you, sitting at the kitchen table, even though you were looking out the window, somewhere far away in your mind. "Happy sunshine, Liz!" You didn't respond. Ash didn't take it personally.

Unsurprisingly, they brought a paper bag full of food that complicated Ma's menu for the day. "Would you be open to me making all of us shakshuka? It's this dish my mom used to make me." Ash pulled out cans of crushed tomatoes and a small carton of organic eggs and placed them on the kitchen counter. "I've been living the vegan life, but I thought today we could celebrate."

"Celebrate what?" Ma said, smelling the bunched cilantro.

"Guess who's graduating with honours in midwifery?" Ash pointed at their chest. "This guy right here!"

Ma cheered and slapped their arm. Ash recoiled in shock. Ma had forgotten how Canadians don't hit each other on the arm when overwhelmed by happiness the way Filipinos do. They usually offer a tepid "yay!" and keep their hands to themselves. "Wow! Congrats, Ash. That's amazing."

"Speaking of midwifery . . ." Ash looked at you, sipping your tea silently, then turned to Ma with a lowered voice. "Are you . . . ?"

Ma nodded and tightened her shirt over her belly to show me off.

"How are you feeling about it all?"

Ma's eyes searched the ceiling for an answer to Ash's question. "I feel . . . scared?" This was the first time Ma had admitted this to herself, let alone anyone else. Babies were always blessings, she was taught growing up. But it felt wrong to pretend this was the case, given her precarious condition. While Ash made a mess of the kitchen, cutting onions the wrong way and stirring the sauce for no good reason, Ma tried to sit back and explain the situation. Ale was not coming to Canada. Her marriage was over. And then there were the circumstances around Justin. The ends of her fingers tingled as she told the story. It was so much more than a story, and she had been too ashamed to call Ash sooner. She slowed her breath, realizing her shoulders were up near her ears and her palms were sweaty.

"That fucking asshole." Ash tossed the wooden spoon hard enough that it sank into the food in the cast iron pan. They turned off the element and sat at Ma's feet. "I am so sorry, MG. I believe you. I believe everything you say. That was not your fault." Ma didn't know what to do with this. It made her uneasy to be held in Ash's gaze. Was it not her fault? Even just a little? She did accept his money for her airfare to the Philippines, and that foot rub. "Are you worried about what this will do to your arrangement here with Liz?"

"I am. I keep thinking he's going to punish me by . . . I don't know . . . not paying me or even firing me."

"Have you talked to him?"

"Not yet. I don't want to. I don't know what I will do if he comes here again."

"I don't think he will." Ash shook their head confidently.

"Really? Why not?"

"Do you know how humiliated he is right now? He just got beaten by his old mother. He'd rather pretend this all didn't happen. I know for a fact he needs you more than you need him." Ash went back to the stove. They fished out the spoon they'd dropped into the pan and got another one out from the drawer.

"You think so?" Deep down, Ma knew this too, but it felt nice to hear praise.

"I totally think so. It would take forever for him to find someone who is as good as you are with Liz. You know her now. You've bonded. Also, how would Justin face either one of you again, right?" They licked sauce off their fingers and added, "Do you think this might endanger your application to stay here, though?"

"I don't know," Ma said, although she had not stopped thinking about it, configuring all the horrifying possibilities in her mind.

"Well, how many more months do you have before you've completed the program?"

"I'm done by mid-August."

"And—correct me if I'm mistaken—there's a document he needs to sign that says how many hours you've observed taking care of Liz, right?"

"Yes."

"So that may be the only interaction you'll be forced to have over the next while, right?"

"I think so."

Ash got up and walked to the stovetop to serve the shak-shuka on three plates. The eggs were overdone, but Ma bit her lip. "Okay, then. How about this? When you have to get that document signed, we can schedule it so that I'll be with you."

"Oh no. That's too much trouble, Ash."

"No way. It's not any trouble at all. It's not like I'm a stranger to confronting Justin." A sly grin played on Ash's face. "Let's just say he's lucky there was a broken beer bottle in my hand and not a gun."

"What?!"

"Don't worry! I wouldn't have really used it. Like, *really, really*. I just threatened him. It was before Justin shipped her out here to this crappy place far away from her friends and chosen family. My ex and I were helping Liz pack up house, and Justin had the audacity to tell us to leave. Um . . . hello? We're helping your mother move, you ungrateful transphobic fuck. No matter how much she cared for him, no matter how hard she worked to support him, put him through college, et cetera, he has always sided with Liz's toxic-ass blood family. Words were exchanged. There was a bit of shoving. Next thing I knew I grabbed my beer bottle and smashed it against the wall to make a weapon. Like in the movies, you know?" They chuckled to themself. "It was kinda funny because when it broke, the bottom part fell off and I was left with just the neck of the bottle. What was I going to stab him with? This glass cylinder?" Ma covered her mouth to stop herself from laughing. "Anyway . . . worst thing that can happen is, I'll be called away for a birth. But I can arrange for a backup person to help you. No problem. You shouldn't have to face him alone." This made Ma nervous. She had owed Justin for his kindness before and look what happened. Maybe kindness always had its price.

After lunch (which was much too bland, but Ma felt too guilty to sprinkle salt on it and insult them), Ash headed out back and mowed the overgrown lawn. Ma placed you on a Muskoka chair that she covered with a blanket to save you from its wood splinters. She got to work, collecting twigs that would catch in the blades of the old lawn mower, and set them to the side.

"Hey, MG! Look at this," Ash called out from the edge of the backyard. Ma removed her garden gloves and waddled her way towards the river vista. "The garden shears were pretty dull, but I managed to clear this section here." They pointed to a wooden-framed terrace hidden behind overgrown vines. "I've never been down here. I could never see it. But look, here are some steps, and underneath this ivy is patio stone." They carefully tiptoed down the treads and looked out over another edge. "And here I can see steps down toward the river. Whoa! And kayaks! Holy shit! There are kayaks!"

Ash spent the good part of an hour clearing the lower patio area and steps, determined to show you. Ma wasn't so sure. Although you were silently enjoying the sunshine, Ma could tell by your eyes that you were due for a nap soon. Ash insisted, helping you on one side while Ma was on the other, letting you slowly make your way down the steps to the patio, then down a few more steps to the riverbank.

Ash turned the yellow plastic kayaks right side up. One kayak was a single. The other was a tandem. Although their bottoms had become muddy and mossy, the insides were surprisingly clean. Ash shook the two paddles and a few earwigs ran into the depths of the swampy ground. They handed one to Ma.

"What is this?" Ma knew what it was. What she meant to say was "What the hell do you expect me to do with this?"

Ash smiled. "I think we should go out. We can launch the kayaks from here." Ma shook her head. "Aw, come on! My dad and his wife had these at their cottage. They're meant for beginners. They're virtually impossible to capsize. And this river is only as deep as your hip. The water is super calm. Come on!" Ash's voice was annoyingly cheery. Ma was about to ask you what you thought, but you were already stepping into the tandem, taking a seat at the front of the boat like a duck to water. "Go in the single. I'll row Liz around like the queen she is." Ma felt her sneakers sinking into the mud. She had no choice but to participate. Ash steadied the cockpit as Ma stepped in.

"Here. Take this." Ash handed Ma a paddle, then pushed the stern until the thing began to wobble and float.

"Agh!" Ma yelped as she helplessly watched the kayak move through the reeds.

Ash tried not to laugh. "You're fine. Just hold on and I'll show you how to manoeuvre around." They stepped into the tandem and pushed off the murky shore towards Ma. "There, you see?" Ash said while showing Ma how to use her paddle. Ma didn't like the condescending tone their voice suddenly had, like they were the teacher and she, the lowly student. Her face burned with embarrassment. "Now let's use our rainbow strokes to turn the bow and head down the Rouge."

*Down the Rouge?* Ma wanted to yell, but she was suddenly surprised at how easy it was to turn.

"Great job, MG!" Ash said. Ma turned away from them to roll her eyes, although she *was* doing pretty well. Once she figured out the proper motion for paddling, it became difficult to stay behind you and Ash.

The river was indeed calm. With each cut of the blade into the water, you all drifted past turtles sunbathing on driftwood. Past herons taking flight to their secret places. Past ducks and their ducklings zipping towards the shore and magically disappearing into the mess of brambles and tree roots. Exhilaration rushed through Ma's body. I felt it too. The sun was shining on her face, through the membrane of her belly and onto my growing parts. The smell was intoxicating. A combination of grass, clay and rain. She was surprised to feel this good on a watercraft. It was the first time in a while she had not felt nauseous. I kicked her to keep going, but Ma realized she was alone. She used her sweep stroke, pushing the blade towards the hull to turn the kayak around.

"Are you oka—" Ash put a finger to their lips while Ma was mid-sentence. They pointed to the thick of green rushes. A bit of mottled brown and white peeked through the cattails. Ma cautiously paddled forward and saw a fawn wading knee-deep among the reeds. Its eyes were immense pools of black behind a fringe of thick lashes. Ma looked at Ash and shared a look of amazement. That's why neither of them saw you getting out of the cockpit and jumping into the water.

"Liz!" Ash called out as you drudged through the lily pads with your arms outstretched.

The fawn leapt through the marsh and out of sight in three graceful vaults. You shrieked, "Come back! Please! Come back!" The marsh made a tide line of mud along your summer dress. You turned to Ma with a grave look in your eyes. "Shit, Polly. When Dad finds out the dog ran away because we left the gate open, he's gonna go berserk."

After Ma and Ash jumped in after you and plodded to the nearest shoreline, all three of you made it back to the house, filthy and soaked from the chest down. It was a minor feat, making it to the bathroom without soiling the already stained carpet, but Ma managed to get you there for a much-needed hot shower. After you were dressed in dry clothing, you went down for a nap.

Ash took a closer look at the pile of boxes in the living room while they sipped on tea.

"What are these boxes?" Ash used one hand to roll up the waist of the sweatpants they had borrowed from your closet. Ma tried not to smile at how much shorter their legs were in comparison to yours.

Ma closed your bedroom door quietly, her arms full of wet, dirty clothes. "I brought them up when the basement flooded because they looked important. I'm glad I did because there are videos of when Liz was younger." Ma dumped the laundry by the closed hatch and went to one of the boxes. "See?"

"Whoa, whoa, whoa. What videos?"

"Videos. Interviews. First with Jane, then with others."

Ash leafed through the top of the pile. "This must be the raw footage. Wow. This is wild."

"Why?"

"Because Liz's work was revolutionary."

"Those interviews?"

"Yes. Her films were the first of their kind, documenting the lives of trans folks in Toronto. Like . . . there was no judgment. No trauma porn. They were just trans folks talking about . . . things. Like what their lives were like . . . or how their job interviews went." Ash pensively took the box to the couch and rifled through the bottom layers of tapes, closely scanning each label. "I remember seeing her first documentary, *Cawthra Square Blues*. There was this trans man talking about how much he loved growing cherry tomatoes on his apartment balcony. And I was like, 'Wait a minute . . . is he? Is he like me? Am I like him?' It was the first time I saw anyone like that. I can't tell you how much it meant to me. It was like those maps in malls with the arrow that says 'YOU ARE HERE,' only it was 'YOU ARE ONE OF THEM.' I swear to god, I thought I could hear angels singing." Ash was lost in thought, holding one of the VHS tapes. "Listen . . . do you think I could take these? Not to keep. But to transfer them onto DVDs maybe? That way they can be digital and last forever."

"You know how to do that?" Ma wrapped her hands around the warmth of her mug.

"Not me. This woman I have a crush on in the year below me is a bit of a cinephile. I bet she can get it done if I pay her a small fee." Ma nodded. Forever sounded better than rotting in a basement. The flood had drained to god knows where, and the possibility of it happening again hung over Ma's head each time the forecast called for rain.

Ash moved on to another box, which Ma had yet to open. Judging by the print on the cardboard, it once held wine bottles. "Coooool." Inside, Ash found a portable cassette-tape player. The faint smell of wine filled the air. "Looks like the battery acid may have leaked. Not sure it'll play again." Underneath the player were the tapes themselves. They slid the container to the side, got up and took the videotapes to the foyer. "Shit. I should get going, especially if I'm taking this box. I'm catching the GO train back downtown. I'll let you know how I get on with transferring these to DVDs. We can have a movie night if it works out!" Ash took out a rolled-up bowling jacket from their backpack and slipped it on, zipping it to their chin. The patch on its chest read "Knock 'em Down!"

"Oh and, before I forget. Did you see that there's a new midwife clinic that's opening on Kingston Road? It's just a bus ride away from here." Ashamed she hadn't even thought this far ahead, Ma was unsure if she should shrug her shoulders or shake her head. Was she a bad mother already? Before Ash rushed out the door, they said, "If you're into finding a midwife instead of an ob/gyn, I would source one right away. Some people book as soon as they find out they're pregnant."

Ma was lucky because someone else wasn't. Of course, that's not what the receptionist said on the phone. What the receptionist said was "There has been a sudden opening for one of the midwives. Can I book you in for next Tuesday?" Ma surmised that the "sudden opening" was made because someone had lost their baby. Since losing the last one, Ma shuddered each time she heard euphemisms for infant death, as if it could soften the blow. "Does eleven, one or four work?"

This was a tricky question. She would have to bring you along without a doubt. If she chose eleven, would you both be back in time for her to make lunch? One was around your nap time, so that didn't work. Four was too risky, as your naps were getting longer and less predictable, not to mention it would interfere with dinner preparation.

"Hello? Are you there?" said the receptionist.

"Eleven works," Ma replied finally. Eleven didn't really work, but she figured she would pack a lunch just in case there were delays. Make a picnic out of it.

The day of Ma's first appointment was not your best day. Not your worst, but certainly not your best. You began the day talking to yourself. Not to Ma as you usually did. To yourself. When you refused your breakfast, Ma assumed the sore in your gums was acting up again, and when she tried to take a look inside your mouth, you pushed her shoulder hard enough that she stumbled back a bit.

"Liz. Are you okay? Is there something that's bothering you?" Ma tried to reason with you as you paced the hallway. She tried her best to check your temperature, but you refused to be touched. After looking at the clock, Ma rushed to pack a light lunch, and you both made your way to the nearest bus stop. Scarborough buses are notoriously slow, but on this day, a bus had barely left the roundabout when Ma flagged the driver down. She made sure to open her jacket and showcase her small bump to elicit pity. Thankfully, it worked and they gained seats.

The clinic was the eye of the storm sitting between the constant traffic of Kingston Road on one side and a busy DriveTest site on the other. With your unsettled behaviour, not only did Ma have to encourage you to cross the bustling road, she had to convince you to pass the long lineup of people waiting for their driver's tests to start. When you two finally entered the clinic, you made a beeline for the washroom.

"Did you want any help, Liz?" Ma said before you slammed the door in her face.

The midwife didn't make any judgments about you tagging along. Just as Ma was about to explain your presence, she introduced herself. "Hi. I'm Kimberley Maylar," she said as she shook Ma's hand. Kimberley turned to shake yours as well, but you sequestered yourself in the corner, where a children's play kitchen was situated. You did not look back at her. Instead, you sat on the mini-sized chair at the mini-sized table and rocked back and forth nervously. Kimberley arranged her long braids into a loose chignon. "Are you a PSW?"

"Yes."

Kimberley turned towards you and asked, "And what is your name?"

You did not answer, so Ma answered for you. "This is Liz."

"Wonderful to meet you, Liz," Kimberley said, before turning back to Ma. "My mother was a caregiver too. That's how she came to Canada from Grenada. Oh, the stories my mother would tell!" She shook her head and directed Ma towards an L-shaped sectional covered in several squares of different-patterned fabrics. "That's why I have a lot of respect for the work women like you do." She gestured for Ma to have a seat. The sectional felt incredibly soft compared to the fuzzy red seats on the bus not too long ago. How wonderful it would be to take a nap on it. The office didn't look much like an office. It looked more like someone's living room with its dim lighting and framed posters. "MG, as part of our educational requirements as midwives, we have students who train with us to observe prenatal appointments and assist with deliveries. Would you be open to having our resident Aroos present during today's appointment?"

"Okay. Sure."

"Wonderful. Let me get her." Kimberley left the office for a moment. Ma could hear whispering outside the door, then Kimberley re-entered the office with Aroos following shyly behind. Aroos adjusted her hijab with one hand and offered a friendly wave with the other before sitting down on a stool close to a shelf full of pregnancy books.

It felt strange, unnerving even, to be observed by Kimberley's friendly face. Ma was unaccustomed to being regarded at all, other than to be given instructions. Here in this office, however, the attention was all on her. The worries about your behaviour in a public setting never fully subsided, but they certainly eased a bit.

"Aroos, can you get me my Pinard horn?"

"In the cupboard?"

"Yes. Lower shelf."

Aroos retrieved the long wooden trumpet and gave it to Kimberley, then stood by to watch the examination. "Have you felt kicking? Hiccups? Anything?" Kimberley warmed the tool with her hands.

It suddenly dawned on my mother what the ticking sensation was that she felt in the middle of the night. "Yes. Both. Lots of kicking. Lots of hiccups."

"Let's have a look, then. Could I trouble you to open up your shirt and lower your pants?" Ma exposed the small round of her belly. I could feel Kimberley's hands palpating to assess my position, then the round edge of the Pinard listening for my heartbeat. I had just grown my heart and wanted to show off. "Nice strong heartbeat."

"Really?" Ma said, buttoning her shirt back up.

"Really." Kimberley looked back at you, still keeping to yourself in the corner. "I have a friend whose husband suffered from a brain injury. There are respite programs that give caregivers like you a break."

Ma strained to pull the elastic waist of her pants over her belly and maintain a nervous smile. "No, no. I'm fine. I can manage."

"Can you, though? I'll be seeing you every month. And after twenty-eight weeks, I'll be seeing you every week. I don't mind having Liz here at all. Don't get me wrong. But certainly, you need some time for yourself. Even a few hours to get groceries, have a nap. All you need to do is drop Liz off and she can have fun doing crafts, music workshops, story-telling. All sorts of things. Doesn't hurt to ask." Ma wasn't so sure. She had asked for help before from Justin and look what happened. Both of your futures remained uncertain thanks to her accepting someone's generosity. Ma nodded just to end the conversation.

By the time you both returned to the house, you were running a high fever. Ma was finally able to take your temperature because you were too ill to fight her any longer. She quickly called the doctor listed on the fridge to arrange for a home visit. By the time Dr. Syed arrived, your constant talking to yourself had shifted to rhythmic moaning.

"Hello, Liz. It's me, Dr. Syed." He pointed to the damp sheets you'd made a tangle of and gently said, "Let's remove these, shall we?" After a quiet examination, Dr. Syed determined that you had a bad urinary tract infection. Ma didn't realize her hands were clamped over her mouth until Dr. Syed put a hand on her shoulder. "Hey. It's not your fault. These things happen with the elderly. When you pick up the antibiotics at the drugstore, be sure to get a big bottle of cranberry juice as well."

Braving the bus in rush hour traffic (no one on the bus gave her a seat), Ma hustled to fill the prescription at the drugstore and buy the cranberry juice and hustled back (again, no one gave her a seat on the bus) to the house.

"Liz?" Ma said, entering your bedroom. You were still lying on your side, with a pained expression on your face. Despite being ready for a fight, you let her spoon the apple sauce laden with liquid antibiotics into your slack mouth. You let her tenderly shut your lips to encourage you to swallow. You even sat up a bit to take a big drink of cranberry juice. Thank goodness you were so agreeable because Ma had only enough calories in her exhausted body to make her way to the kitchen and prepare sinigang soup for dinner. Not that you ate any. Perhaps it was the combination of painkillers and antibiotics, but you slept the early evening away, snoring loudly, with your face relaxed and burrowed into your pillow.

Ma ate alone that night, relishing the quiet. Eating with you wasn't difficult, but it certainly wasn't easy to watch. If you didn't like something that was served to you, you'd spit it back onto your plate. Seeing masticated food wasn't too much of a bother before she was pregnant, but these days, Ma had to stop herself from retching. It felt nice to eat alone without having to pretend she was Polly or Jane or having to convince you she was trustworthy. Ma watched the tightly packed cold rice crumble into the steaming hot broth and ate the sinigang, savouring each sour and salty spoonful. She ate so slowly that by the time she finished the soup, mais con hielo and a cup of tea, night had fallen. The broad bay window overlooking the river had turned into a giant mirror with Ma's reflection looking back at her. A pregnant woman sitting at a kitchen table, doing nothing. Maybe Kimberley was right. Maybe she did need respite.

# 9

To register for the day program, Ma needed to find your identification. During one of your naps, she waddled to the kitchen cabinets to look through the paperwork she had organized when she first arrived. While she could find magazine clippings, receipts and contracts, she could not find any ID. Ma walked to the French doors of Justin's office and held the knobs in her hand. Since he had left, she avoided going in there at all. When she finally creaked the doors open, the smell and memory of his cologne remained. Ma breathed through her mouth as she rifled through his desk drawers. Old tax returns. Printed house listings. Tenant agreements. Then, between "CONSOLIDATION LOAN" and "RESEARCH," Ma found a document that had fallen between the two folders. Its several pages were held together by a binder clip on one side, and on the other, the sheets frayed out into a V shape from its time of being misfiled. As she did her best to straighten out each leaf, she saw the details of what looked like a transaction form authorizing the cashing out of a guaranteed investment certificate in the total of ten thousand dollars. While the GIC belonged to you, Justin, with his power of attorney, had signed off on the transaction. Ten thousand dollars. Ma looked at the date on the form, then moved to the closet, still pretending to look for your identification. In truth she was now looking for something more important.

On the upper shelf there were photo albums. She instantly regretted looking through the plastic sleeves. Seeing his face was one thing (the sum of his eyes and mouth, his unkempt beard), but seeing pictures of his life, his friends, was another. There was something about seeing him out in the world, on travelling adventures, smiling with others that made Ma's jaw grow tight. Most likely he was doing the same thing now, enjoying his freedom and quickly forgetting his actions that night not so long ago. Under a group photo of him and his buddies in front of a rugged mountain range was a photo of a woman sitting on a rock. Ma looked closer. The woman was a diminutive brunette. Was she in fact diminutive? Maybe. Or was it the way she carried herself? Was it the way she sat on the rock with her chin tilted downward while her eyes looked shyly at the camera? Ma gasped when she realized the woman had lifted her skirt slightly and separated her legs enough to reveal the small bush of her vulva. In the photo, the woman's cheeks and neck were flushed. Was this the same trip with those men in the photo above? From the look of the distant mountain range behind her, most likely it was. And when did Justin take this photo? When he snuck away from his buddies, like a naughty little secret with his then girlfriend? And how much did she want this photo taken? Ma took one last look at the woman's forced smile and shut the album. There were shoeboxes. Some were full of shoes. Some were full of photo negatives.

Ma slid Justin's hanging shirts apart to give her more room to rummage down below. One tattered cardboard box sat on the closet floor under a pile of ties. Inside were his bank statements. The pile was high enough that Ma had to reach in and pull it out in its entirety to examine them. There was a deposit of ten thousand dollars, dated the day after the GIC was cashed out, into his own chequing account.

I kicked. Ma would have taken a moment to consider the implications of what she had found, but she suddenly felt the urge to pee. I designed it that way. I knew all of her best thinking during her pregnancy occurred on the toilet. She sat there with her panties at her ankles, scratching her recently popped belly button, deep in thought. Justin took money from his own mother. You. He took money from you while you stayed in this dilapidated converted cottage, with floods in the basement and mould on the walls. He stole money from you while you lived in the house overrun by mice and damp from a leaky roof. By the time Ma flushed the toilet, she had made her decision.

Before Ma returned to looking for your ID, she took both the bank statement and the GIC transaction form to her room and hid them under her mattress. She didn't know what she was doing. But she knew it was important to have evidence of Justin's wrongdoing.

Ma was painting your nails at the dining room table when the phone rang in the kitchen.

"Good morning. This is Scarborough East Connect," said

the listless woman on the other end. "Could I please speak to Mary Grace Cun ... Cun ..."

"That's me," Ma interrupted, trying to sidestep the woman's butchering of her name.

"Con-SEP-shun?"

Ma sighed. "Yes."

"Are you the caregiver of Louis Cahill?" It took a moment for Ma to remember this was Liz's dead name.

"Yes. That is her legal name, but she goes by Liz."

"Um ... ooookaaay. I'll write that down." The sound of keys clacking on the other end. "So ... wait ... are you the caregiver for Louis or Liz?"

Ma sighed. "Louis is what her identification says, but the name she has now is Liz."

"Oh. Okaaaay. So he changed his name?"

"*She* changed *her* name." More keys clacking on the other end.

"Right. Okay. We know you had registered him—I mean her—on the waiting list for the day program at Rouge Hill Seniors' Home?"

"Yes. I did." Ma looked at you, sitting at the dining room table, trying your best to open one of the bottles of nail polish. This call had to end soon, otherwise there would be red splatters all over the chairs.

"A spot is now available for the Tuesday workshops if you're interested."

"Yes, please. That would be wonderful." You had moved on to the bottle of acetone. The lid on that bottle was easy to screw off. The woman continued in the robotic fashion of someone reading from a prepared document of talking points.

"They run from ten in the morning until one in the after-noon with a small lunch served . . ."

"Great! We will be there," Ma said nervously. The phone cord was too short to walk over to you. The woman droned on.

". . . You are welcome to drop Liz off, but filling out the intake forms for your first visit may take fifteen to twenty minutes, so do arrive early on your first day . . ." Ma dropped the phone and ran to your side to catch the bottle of acet-one just before you dropped it. She quickly soaked a ball of cotton with acetone and handed the damp circle to you, then rushed to the phone. The woman was still talking.

"While participants can bring their own snacks, they will have to be shared and must be peanut-free. Do you have any questions, Miss . . . Cun . . . Cun . . ."

"Cohn-sep-SYON. Concepcion. No. I'm good. Thank you for this great news. We truly appreciate it," Ma said, twist-ing the cap on the acetone tightly closed. She sat back down beside you. "Wow, Liz. You're doing a great job." You had managed to remove the varnish from your thumb and fore-finger, with barely a trace of red in the cuticles.

"I thought I wanted to look vampy," you said as you moved on to your ring finger. "But I think I wanna try this blue for a change and look like a mermaid."


The mermaid-blue shade was still vibrant on your nails on your first visit to the day program. Ma tried to leave. That was the point of the program: to give respite to caregivers of seniors with Alzheimer's disease, acquired brain injuries and cognitive impairment. But she found herself peeking her head into the nursing home's workshop room while you sat at a group table to make collages. The facilitator, Brian, was a middle-aged man with a perfectly structured coif. He tucked his golf shirt tight around his big belly and into a pair of tailored Bermuda shorts.

"Your composition is faaaabulous," Brian said, gesturing his splayed hand over your creation. Out of the ten participants, Ma could see that about half of them had scars that ran along one side of their scalps where hair no longer grew. One woman just stared at the magazine cuttings on the table. One man leafed through the pages of an upside-down newspaper. Another emptied out the contents of her purse onto the table in a never-ending search for something.

Ma felt a tap on her shoulder. "You know we can leave, right?" Ma nodded. She was accustomed to looking up at everyone since moving to Canada, but this Black woman stood eye to eye with her. "I'm Danah. I'm the daughter of Verna, that chatterbox over there." Danah pointed to a woman talking the ear off a man to her right who was already asleep in his chair, his eyebrows hoisted high on his forehead as if to acknowledge her while he was off in dreamland.

"Hi. I'm MG."

"Who are you taking care of?"

"Liz. She's the one who Brian is talking to right now. See? Her."

Danah looked, then gave Ma a face. "She looks like she's doing pretty well."

"Yes. Brian likes her collage. She really likes cutting the

paper." Ma laughed lightly, then looked around the edge of the doorframe again.

"Then what are you doing here? Go. Relax." Ma's smile faded slightly, considering Danah's (very strong) suggestion. Danah leaned in and said, "I don't care if it's the morning. I'm going to find a restaurant that's open and can make it happy hour." She chuckled and noticed Ma's look of concern. "It was hard for me too at first. All you have to do is put one foot in front of the other and tell yourself they're going to be perfectly fine. Brian is an amazing facilitator. They all love the heck out of him. Agnes fills in sometimes, but I find her a bit too granola. It doesn't matter though. This is our time." She patted Ma's shoulder before heading out the main entrance.

Ma did what Danah said and put one foot in front of the other, even though she really didn't know where she was going to go for her free time. As she walked towards the entrance, she could see other rooms abuzz with activity. In one room, a woman dressed in a 1940s ensemble wagged her finger and stepped side to side to the tune of big band music. The seniors followed along in their chairs at half the speed. In the cafeteria, two PSWs circulated around the tables asking seniors how they liked today's chowder.

"The broth is a bit runny and the potatoes aren't as tender as I would have liked, but it'll do for now," said one elderly man loudly. One of the PSWs was a Filipina, and as Ma passed the doorframe, they exchanged glances, with both of them raising their eyebrows in recognition of the other.

Ma put one foot in front of the other until she was outside the building and she could hear the chickadees chirping to one another in a line of bushes. Until the sign for the Rouge Hill Seniors' Home was an illegible square as she walked west on Lawrence towards a nearby strip mall. Until she found herself in a discount fashion store, trying on clothes that did not fit her belly. Until she sat on a park bench eating ice cream in the sun. The park bench she first sat on faced a splash pad with dozens of children in their bathing suits jumping in and out of sprinklers. She changed places to another bench facing a skateboard park. It felt relaxing to watch the skaters' tricks and having zero responsibility for their behaviour. It felt so relaxing that she felt a tap on her shoulder.

"Ma'am? Are you alive?" Ma opened her eyes. Six skaters, all rail thin with bushy hair, stared at her.

"See? I told you she was just sleeping."

"But she's pregnant. I had to make sure, you loser."

The tallest and smelliest one peered at Ma. "Are you okay?"

Ma sat up with a jolt and brushed the crumbs from the ice cream cone off her shirt. Her face went red as she wiped a string of drool from the left side of her mouth. "Yes. Sorry. Yes." She looked at her watch and rushed back to the seniors' home to pick you up.


Each week of the respite program was another opportunity for Ma to do nothing but what pleased her. At first, she thought that she would use the time to cook and clean. That did not happen. She believed it was the fatigue of the pregnancy that was making her lazy. But that wasn't truly what was happening. Ma was actually enjoying her time alone.

It began with her first visit to the backyard, to look out at the river. While the sound of the blue jays cackling at one another and the babbling of the brook down below was peaceful, she couldn't help but stare at the kayaks. She remembered her trip with you and Ash fondly; however, she wasn't the type of person to go out on the water on her own. Was she? After thirty minutes of staring, she thought to herself, "I'll just wash them. They're dirty. They most likely haven't been washed in years. Maybe decades. They should be washed." Ma wrestled with the hose from the house and untangled the length of it until the water sprayed in an even stream over the yellow plastic of the vessels. Once they were clean, she stared at them again. All done. The sun took too long to dry them, so Ma retrieved a tea towel from the kitchen to wipe them down. Then she found herself sitting in the seat of the cockpit, her eyes moving from the bow of the boat to the river and back again. Maybe she could kayak on her own. She looked at her watch and her heart sank. It was already 12:30 p.m.

The following weeks, she wasted no time. When Ma returned to the house, she made a beeline towards the back-yard. It was intimidating at first, to launch the kayak alone without Ash to guide her and with her belly in the way. Soon enough, though, she was paddling down the Rouge with ease. Her favourite thing to do was to push the kayak through the tunnel of an uprooted tree by the shoreline or to watch the carp part ways in the water. She always had enough time to paddle until the bridge of the highway passed overhead, return to the house, and change out of her damp pants to retrieve you from the day program.

There were times when she returned to the house over-whelmed by the need to touch herself. The pregnancy hor-mones made her nipples inflamed with desire, and she'd rush to her bedroom to stroke her body into oblivion again and again until she was ready for a nap. It felt wonderful to be naked in bed, giving herself pleasure—in exactly the way she wanted—without the help of a lover. Without the presence of Ale. She surprised herself by not fantasizing about him at all. Ever. Instead, she imagined lovers fighting over her. Tangles of hands, tangles of limbs, tangles of tongues.

After one of these sessions, Ma stretched her naked body along the length of her bed, the sheets underneath her, damp with sweat. The silence between her orgasm and the need to get dressed and pick you up was suddenly interrupted by the realization that she no longer loved Ale. Did she cry? No. She did not. It surprised her that tears never came. It surprised her how easy it was to let Ale go. In fact, it scared her. The point of working tirelessly in Canada was to one day be under the same roof as Ale again and start a family, but now. Now the future was bright with possibilities, and those possibil-ities were hers and hers alone. What if her own dreams were enough to stay in Canada? And what if she allowed herself the excitement of dreaming big on her own terms? The joy in this thought sang through her body loud enough that she wanted to touch herself again, but time was not on her side.

That day, Ma returned to you, refreshed and rested. And as always, you were full of stories from the day's adventures.

One day when Ma was on her own, she headed to the strip mall, treated herself to a Jamaican beef patty at one store and then made her way to the second-hand clothing shop in search of maternity pants. She held the patty in one hand far away from the round clothes rack as she examined each pair for its waistband elasticity.

"Hoy! MG?" Tita Connie called out from the women's activewear section. "Ssssuuuut, Remy. Look, it's MG." Tito Remy emerged from the shoe section, one foot in a sneaker and the other in a cowboy boot.

"MG? How are you?"

Ma brushed the flakes of yellow pastry from her mouth and opened her arms to embrace them both. They smelled like tapa and garlic.

Tita Connie regarded Ma's belly. "Wow! Rhea told us you were expecting. Congratulations. Did you hear about her? Manny is coming soon." Tita Connie's smile shifted into a kind pout. "We haven't heard from you in so long, MG. Why haven't you visited? Rhea has been worried about you."

The tone she took with Ma dispatched a flood of guilt through her chest. Why had she lost touch with Rhea and her family? The lie she told herself was that she was busy. She had no days off. But that wasn't true, especially with the day program giving her respite. Deep down, Ma knew the reason she hadn't been in touch was that she was scared they would cross paths with you, Liz. They would see you. This embarrassed Ma, although she would never admit it. She knew Rhea and her family would ridicule her for caring for a bakla. They would have questions she could not answer. They would make jokes. And would she have the strength, the language, the knowledge to stop them from making judgments? She wasn't so sure. She wanted to protect you. She wanted to protect herself.

After exchanging stories about Tito Remy's new obses-sion with visiting the driving range and Tita Connie fishing for compliments about her new perm, Ma said, "I'd better get going to pick up Liz."

"We can come with you," Tita Connie said, rehanging her armful of yoga pants onto the women's long-skirts rack.

"Uh . . . that's okay."

"But how are you getting home?"

"By bus."

"Then we can drive you." Tita Connie hit Tito Remy's arm and he nodded in agreement. "You're pregnant. Let us drive you, ha?"

Outside the nursing home, Ma emerged with you by her side. It was pottery day, and Brian had gifted you a bag of clay to take home, which you hugged closely to your ging-ham dress.

Tita Connie and Tito Remy stood outside the main entrance and waved hello to you. As you approached closer their wave became slower and less certain. Tito Remy squinted his eyes at you and Ma's heart began pounding in her chest. She watched him do the math in his head, adding up your makeup, your Adam's apple, your jawline, and the sums not making sense to him. Inside of Ma, I kicked. *Say something,* I wanted to scream to her.

"Liz, this is my Tito Remy and Tita Connie. Tito Remy and Tita Connie, this is Liz."

Tita Connie's smile was painfully wide, but she said noth-ing. The short drive back to the house was quiet. Tito Remy stiffly kept his eyes on the road. Tita Connie occasionally turned and smiled at you both in the back seat, but each time she did so, her eyes would scan your dress and your painted nails.

"Why didn't we take the bus?" you said while innocently pinching the plastic bag full of clay.

"Because Tita Connie and Tito Remy were generous enough to give us a ride back."

"Well, isn't that nice of them?"

The car arrived at the house, but Tito Remy did not pull into the long driveway. As you exited the car and walked to the entrance, Ma stood outside Tita Connie's door. Tita Connie rolled down the window and said in a whisper, "MG. Are you safe in there? With that man?"

Ma took a breath. How long did that breath take? A minute? A second? It felt like an eternity. In that moment she considered her answer. She could have told the story about how she had been attacked and if it hadn't been for you, she would have been even more physically and emotionally damaged than she already was. She could have said that taking care of you was her employment, that she needed you to survive and to get her permanent residency status. But you were so much more than a way out. You were so much more than your actions. And she knew she meant more to you, too. She heard herself say the truth that she had never said out loud before. "Tita. Liz is my friend. Please be kind to her and do not judge." Tita thought for a second (another minute? a second? an eternity?) and placed her hand on Ma's forearm. Ma grasped hers as well and the two were linked in a silent agreement.

"Do you need a drive tomorrow?" Her words made Tito Remy do a double take.

"No, Tita," Ma replied. "It's only every Tuesday."

"Okay. We will see you next week, then." The rosary looped around their rear-view mirror jingled as they drove off down the road.

That night, Ma enjoyed an unusual burst of energy. She didn't want to waste it on cooking, so she ordered a pizza in while you made a wonderful mess of the clay on the kitchen table making what you called "boobie cookies."

"Jane. Look. It's like they're all staring back at me!" You chuckled while fashioning the nipples to your batch of two dozen breast sculptures of various sizes and shapes. "Yours are like these ones." You pointed to one pair with the nipples looking out, cockeyed and asymmetrical. "That's why we keep losing money. You try and stuff the bills down there and they keep sliding through!" You guffawed and lightly hit the back of Ma's shoulder. Ma smiled and continued to eat her favourite part of the pizza slice: the crust.

At the end of the night, she helped you get to bed despite what seemed to be a palpable excitement in the air. You hummed to yourself while brushing your teeth, while rinsing out your dentures. You sang songs while Ma helped you into your pyjamas. Ma could feel it too. What was it? Was it the weather? A perfect early summer day with the windows open and the sound of the babbling river outside? Was it the fact that I had rearranged my body inside of my mother so that the incessant sensation of needing to urinate dissipated a bit? Was it the open-heartedness of Tita Connie?

Ma tucked you into your blankets. That's when it dawned on her. Out of everyone in the entire living world, Ma was the person who knew you best. She would be the final person on this earth to know your favourite foods, where you ache after a bad night's sleep, what makes you constipated, what helps you with your nausea, what TV shows you like, what songs you like to sing. Ma would be the best and final person. She removed the covers from your right foot, to keep you from overheating, just the way you like it. Your eyes were at half-mast as Ma switched your bedside lamp off.

"Good night, Liz."

"Good night."

Ma suddenly wanted to know more about you. She walked to the pile of boxes, which had since been put in the corner, beside the bay window. The basement had dried out long ago, but Ma's curiosity had kept the boxes upstairs. She opened the wine box with the cassette player in it and looked at the selection of tapes underneath. Ash was right. The player had leaked battery acid, leaving a white crust stain on one side. Ma took the AA batteries from the television remote control and placed them in the player. She considered which tape to try first. One read "Steely Dan" and below the text was a blond woman with sunglasses. Another tape was a compilation of Daryl Hall and John Oates's best hits, but Ma didn't particularly like the moustache on the one guy and the Flock of Seagulls hair on the other. She searched for a musician she knew. A cassette tape featured two women back to back on a white background. Above their heads read "Heart" in swirly letters.

"Yes!" Ma whispered to herself. She knew Heart well. Their songs were her favourite karaoke tunes to sing back in Hong Kong when all the helpers would get together on Sundays. She slid the cassette into the player and pressed play. Blaring over the small speakers was the whine of an electric guitar and a bass-heavy riff. Ma scrambled to turn down the volume. Whoever used the player last listened to music at level ten. She managed to get it down to a five. The song was about being seduced, and that was exactly what was happening to Ma. The repetitive beat of the drums inspired Ma's shoulders to bop up and down while the woman's silken voice made her head turn in circles. It had been a long while since she had danced. Maybe years? She turned the volume up a bit. Just two notches. That's all. Shouldn't hurt. She closed her eyes to let the music bend her body into shapes she thought she had long lost. When she opened them, she saw you coming out of your bedroom.

"Liz! I'm sorry. Did I wake you?"

Without missing a beat, you screamed, "Turn it up! I can't hear it! Turn it up!" Ma smiled and did as you asked. Level ten. She placed the player on the fireplace mantel in the living room. You began marching in rhythm to the song. Breaking the cadence of your movements, you waved your arms around the room to match the flowing nature of the melody. To her surprise, you put one foot on the coffee table and started playing air guitar. You obviously knew the song like the back of your hand because your air guitar matched the licks in the recording perfectly. Ma did air drums.

When the song ended, the silence in the room drove you wild. You walked in a circle with your arms overhead and repeated over and over again, "Replay! Replay! Replay!" But when Ma tried to rewind the cassette, a horrible crunch sound was heard. She carefully opened the player and saw a brown cluster of entangled tape.

"Oh no! I'm sorry, Liz." You wilted. "I will try and fix it, okay? I promise." Wounded, you made your way back to your bed. Ma dabbed a bit of sweat from your brow with a tissue before tucking you in again. You touched Ma's hands lovingly.

"I knew that bouncer was going to fuck up our night. Give a dyke a badge and a flashlight and she thinks she has all the power."

Ma made the face. "That's okay. We got one dance in."

"Didn't we ever?" You kissed Ma's hands.

Using a pencil, Ma was able to turn the reels of the cassette to wind the tape back into place. As she returned the cassette to the box, she spied another case that read "FOR LIZ" scribbled in black marker. At the end of the letters was a heart drawn in red pen. She slipped the tape into the player and pressed play.

A song was abruptly overridden by a loud clicking sound.

"Jeez. I can't stand these things. I can never figure out if I'm supposed to press record or press record and play at the same time. Anyway. Here I am." It was Jane's voice, now barely a whisper. It sounded like she was recording it lying down. Ma ran her fingers over the buttons of the player, wondering if this exact machine was the one Jane used to record this message. "Today is a rainy day. It's been a long spring. A long, long spring. But like you said, the rain that will turn everything green is just around the corner." The sound of shifting. Blankets rubbing against the microphone. "But I'm here to tell you . . . Liz . . . I'm not gonna see that rain." Sniffles. The blowing of a nose. "Goddamn it. My nose is so chafed from all the crying. I'm gonna get to a place where I'll be all peaceful about it all. But right now, I'm going between being

255

super angry about having cancer and being super happy I have you as my best friend. You know? Right now . . . you're at the No Frills getting groceries for us. And you have no idea I'm recording this. You've always went above and beyond for everyone. Everyone. And I know you have Justin, but you've parented so many other kids. So many little kids who would have been lost if it weren't for you. We did that together, you and I." The sound of weeping. "Anyway . . . fucking hell, my nose hurts each time I blow it. What I want to tell you is this: I love you. You're my sister. So many of us have been orphaned. Lost. We've always had each other. I don't want you to ever feel lost after I'm gone, okay? I want you to be happy. Find love. Find friends. Of course I want you to be sad for a little bit. But after a minute, I want you to move on and be happy. Okay?" The sound of the door opening. "I gotta go. I love you, Liz."

Ma pressed stop. Her reflection in the bay window looked back at her. Lips tight. Jaw proud. She was determined about two things:

1. She was going to find a newer cassette tape player at the second-hand shop, and
2. She was going to stay by your side.

It was mid-August when Ma completed her hours under the Live-in Caregiver Program. It was time to see Justin. Ash was instrumental in planning how the day was going to unfold, printing out important documents for the meeting. A manila envelope containing them all was sitting on the passenger seat of the car Ash had borrowed.

"Want to sit up front so we can chat, MG?" Ash said as they helped buckle you up in the back. Ma took the paperwork off the seat and sat down. The car was littered with dirty tissues on the floor and random half-eaten snacks in all the storage compartments. After securing her seatbelt, she crossed her arms over her belly, trying to keep her elbows from touching the sticky door armrests. "Yeah. I know. You don't even have to say it." Ash shifted the gear to drive and the motor made a strange coughing sound. "Shit." The car ambled forward. They looked to the side and saw Ma's concerned face. "It's a community car. My ex-lover Rajesh is the owner, but they loan it out to anyone who needs it. I thought, today is not the day to use transit, you know? We have to strategize." They looked at you in the rear-view mirror. "Is today a foggy day, Liz?"

Ma turned to you and smiled. "Foggy but happy, right Liz?" You shrugged your shoulders and stared out the window.

Miraculously, the car was able to drive west on Kingston Road towards the swanky Beach area of Toronto. It drove until the suburban high-rises and strip malls became chic condos and charming storefronts. The car turned left into an enclave of stately homes facing the lake. It was strange, knowing the lake was the same body of water that fed into the river of your house, but the energy was certainly different. Here, people clustered along the tidy landscaped walkways to chat over Starbucks coffee while their dogs sniffed each other's bums. Couples brunched at tables set up on the sidewalk outside fancy restaurants. A farmers' market was in full swing and a dozen stalls showcased their vibrantly coloured produce. To calm her nervous energy, Ma put her hand inside her purse pocket and felt for the photo of her father, Lolo Ruben. Running her thumb over the edges of its small frame didn't dispel all her fears, but it certainly kept her grounded.

You all arrived at the address listed on the cheques Justin issued to Ma. Ash suggested the confrontation happen on a Sunday to increase the chances Justin would be home. They were right. Ash parked the beaten-up Honda behind the chunky Escalade and used the emergency brake to keep it from rolling back down the steep driveway.

Justin's home was a detached Victorian with an imposing turret at its centre. A man in the neighbouring yard pretended to clip his hedges while he stared at Ma helping you out of the car. As with all of your foggy days, you were quietly compliant and let Ma take your arm up along the manicured lawn and rock garden. Ash waited until you both were on the stoop for them to say in a whisper, "Can you believe this house?"

"This is a very fancy neighbourhood," Ma said, gawking at her surroundings.

"Yup. All of this money and he puts his own mother in a rundown shack." Ash took a breath. "Okay. You ready?"

Ma looked at Ash and realized they were wearing a rather aggressive-looking leather jacket, jeans and steel toe boots. It seemed like such a hostile change from their usual playful attire. Even their eyes had black liner, which hardened their baby face. "Yes."

The doorbell was an antique brass dial that Ash turned to make a stern bell ring inside. Silence. After cupping their face over the front window, Ash declared, "He's either hiding from us or he's not—" Ash's jaw tightened and Ma followed their gaze down to Justin, opening the gate at the side of his house. He looked slightly out of breath, holding an edge trimmer and winding its cord into a tight circle. Justin froze at the sight of all three of you at his front door.

"MG?" Justin shot a look at Ash. "And what's she doing here?"

Ash puffed out their chest. "Hello, Justin. Haven't seen you since you moved Liz away from her chosen family. And just a reminder, my pronouns are they/them, thank you very much." A contrived singsong accusatory tone coloured their delivery. There was a moment between you all, long enough to be awkward but too short to call it a standoff.

The front door swung open. An Asian woman in summer shorts and a T-shirt stood there and looked at you, Ma and Ash with a wide, unexpected smile. She quickly tied up her wet hair. "Sorry I didn't get to the door right away. I was in the shower. Can I help you?"

Justin immediately dropped the trimmer and hurried towards the door, pushing past Ash. "Hey, Denise. These are some of our tenants. I forgot we had a meeting today."

Denise gave a welcoming gesture, and you three entered the tastefully designed foyer with double-height entry and dramatic lighting fixtures. Ash and Ma couldn't help but look up at the handcrafted staircase. You seemed bothered and whispered into Ma's ear, "I can't stand the smell of him." Ma put her arm around your shoulders as you all followed Justin down a hallway with a built-in bookcase. You were right. His cologne wafted through the house, thick and strong. A stomach-curdling combination of musk and car freshener.

A set of French doors led to an office with a wide wooden desk covered in tchotchkes. In one corner a set of golf clubs leaned on a filing cabinet. Ma sat you down in one of the leather chairs, then sat down beside you. Ash stood with their arms crossed over the manila envelope.

"Is there anything I can get you three? Some water maybe? It's so hot outside." Denise looked at your face with curiosity. Perhaps she saw the resemblance between you and Justin.

Justin waved his hand. "No, no. They're fine. This won't take long."

"You sure?"

"Denise. Please."

Denise's smile faded and she left the office. Her bare feet hardly made a sound as she walked away and turned on the television in the living room.

Justin shut the doors and took a seat behind his desk. He tried his best to look confident by crossing his ankle over the opposite knee and leaning back on his chair. "If you need another place to sit, there's a chair behind the—"

"I'm fine with standing, thanks," Ash said curtly.

"Suit yourself. What are you all doing here? Why did you bring my mother to my house?"

Ash opened the manila envelope and took out one of the documents.

Justin glanced at it briefly. "What's this?"

"It's MG's Employer Declaration of Hours Worked. MG has completed her program and she needs you to sign it so that she can apply for permanent residency status."

"And what if I don't? For some strange reason, I haven't been around the house in a long while. How am I to know she's been caring for my mother?"

Ma's eyes widened. "Justin . . ."

"If only I wasn't kicked out of the house so abruptly, I may have been able to see all of your hard work, MG. But I can't sign this in good conscience."

"What are you talking about!?" Ma asked, practically breathless from the shock. "I'm the one who—"

"Who what? Thanks to *some people* who kicked me out of a home that *I own*, who knows if you actually did the job and observed those hours."

Ma looked at Ash and they nodded. She reached her hand out and Ash placed the envelope in her hands. She took out the GIC transaction form and bank statements and slid them across the desk.

"What the hell is this?"

"It's proof." Ma tried her best to cough the fear out of her words. "You cashed in her investment and deposited it into your account."

"So?" Ma looked to Ash. She wasn't prepared for his casual reaction. Justin continued with a roll of his eyes. "This proves nothing. It costs money to take care of a senior. Everybody knows that. Who's to say I didn't liquidate her investment to afford paying you?"

Ash stood tall. "Look at the third document." Justin reluctantly shuffled the pages. "According to Liz's bank statements, her pension and retirement plan already cover living expenses and MG's fees. There is no reason why you'd need to cash in an investment other than stealing.

Especially when we have proof of you depositing ten grand into your personal account immediately after." Ash tapped their fingers on the desk while Justin perused the numbers. Ma's heart pounded in her chest. My heart beat twice as fast inside of her.

Justin dramatically threw the documents back to Ash and they flew into the air for only a moment before sifting back down to the desk. "This is bullshit. Pathetic. You're trying to blackmail me into signing this?"

"We're not blackmailing you. We're here to make you stop stealing from your own mother and sign MG's form like you promised, no matter what you did to her." Ma was amazed at the sight of Ash. She had never seen them so assertive and confident before. Even their body was different. Their voice was from another world.

Justin's desk phone rang.

"Babes? Did you need me to get that? I think it's your line, right?" Denise called from the living room.

"Don't worry, I'll get it." The phone rang twice more, then stopped.

"What do you think your girlfriend—"

"My wife."

Ash sighed. "Fine, your wife. What do you think your wife would say if she knew you've placed Liz in one of your many rundown properties and used her pension and retirement funds to pay your mortgage? I mean . . . does she even know Liz is your mother?"

"Give me a break." Justin scoffed and got out of his chair.

"And what do you think she'd say if we showed her proof of you stealing money?"

"Get out of my house. Go on. Get up. Everybody out." Justin began waving his arms as if he were herding sheep.

Suddenly unsure of themself, Ash gathered the papers and put them in the envelope. You saw Ma get up and you followed suit. But instead of making her way to the door, Ma stepped to the golf club set, pulled out the putter and pointed it at Justin's head. Ash gasped and moved you to the opposite corner of the office.

"What the hell do you think you're doing?!" Justin said with his arms up. "Put that down!"

"No!"

"Put that down!"

"NO!"

The phone rang again. From down the hall Denise called out. "Hun? It's your line again. Do you need me to get it this time?"

"No, babes! That's okay," Justin called back cheerfully. The phone rang two more times, then Ma smashed it with the putter.

Everyone flinched except for you. Even Ma was scared by her own behaviour. What exactly was the plan here? She didn't know what to do next, but she saw the look of terror in Justin's eyes, so she approached him slowly, the putter in her extended arms, and pointed it at him again.

"How about I smash your head in the way Liz did that night?" The voice that came out of her mouth was unrecognizable. Ma backed Justin into the wall. He stood with his arms in surrender with an inspirational poster of a sunset beach behind him that read "Believe and Succeed."

"MG. Put that down. Come on. It was a misunderstanding."

"Then why don't I tell your wife all about this misunderstanding?" Ma growled from some place deep within her. "You. Touched. Me."

Ash appeared by Ma's shoulder and shoved the declaration piece of paper into Justin's chest. Their voice cracked. "Sign it. You know MG has done the work. Sign it."

Ma handed Justin a pen from the desk. He turned around, put the paper on the poster and tried to fill out the form. "Fuck. I need another . . . can you please get me another pen. This one is—" Ma grabbed another pen from the desk and handed it to him. Justin signed the document with shaking hands. Ash took the paper and slid it back into the envelope.

Ma looked at Justin with hardened eyes. "Justin. Your mother is a good person. She deserves better. What she does deserve is me. You will stop stealing from her and you will continue to employ me to take care of her." She placed the putter back into the golf bag, then looked at the bag itself for a moment. "I'm taking these with me. Just in case I need to use them on you again."

In the hallway, Ma waved at Denise, who was eating a salad by the television. "Nice to meet you! See you again."

"See you!" Denise waved with her mouth full of red onion rounds and spinach leaves. She looked curiously at the golf clubs that Ma carried over her shoulder but continued to smile.

Ash and Ma did not cheer until the car drove off. Well . . . they didn't cheer until the car finally started, coughed out a black cloud of smoke, then drove off.

While steering, Ash undid their seatbelt and removed their leather jacket. "Holy shit! We did it!" They tossed the jacket to the back seat over the golf clubs, which you sat beside quietly, completely unaware of what had just happened. Sweat stained the pits of Ash's Care Bear shirt and rainbow suspenders.

Ma rolled down the window. Well . . . she pressed the pane of glass while turning the hand crank and made the window lower a few inches, in a crooked angle. She yelped into the opening. "YEEEEE-HEEEE!"

On the ride home they told and retold the story, embellishing it again and again with details that didn't actually happen, making it into a tall tale of smooth moves and one-liners.

"Ash, you were amazing! Your voice! Wow. I was scared."

"Really? You think so?"

"I know so. You were really tough."

Ash was all a-titter. "Okay, but can we talk about the golf club move? Like, who are you?"

"Well . . . I couldn't pick up the chair and smash it over his head. I had to improvise."

"You were like a mobster or something!"

"Oh, come on . . . Really?"

"For real! You were all, like . . ." Ash made a horrible impression of Marlon Brando. "'I'm gonna make you an offer you can't refuse.'"

Inside my mother, I was glad I had grown eyes already because I was certainly rolling them. From my perspective, it was a clumsy confrontation led by a fake butch and a pregnant woman with a dirty communal shit-box as a getaway car. But what do I know? I'm just a baby.

The team celebrated by ordering a family meal at Happy Chicken in Scarborough.

"Is it possible to have all dark meat?" Ma said to the Filipina behind the counter.

"Yes, ate."

Ash asked Ma, "And can we maybe double the fries?" They turned to the Filipina and smiled. "I'm vegan." The Filipina smiled awkwardly and pressed a few buttons on the register.

Ash parked the car at the bottom of the hill that descended into the Rouge River marsh. You all found a perfect spot to picnic far away from the fishermen, with the perfect view of the lily pads. The sharp bite of the midday sun had moved across the sky to a more livable afternoon haze.

Ma prepared you a plate of shredded drumstick and macaroni salad, which you immediately gobbled up. She took two thighs and the coleslaw. At first, Ash nibbled on the fries, then dipped the fries in the clumpy gravy, then announced, "Fuck it, MG. You make eating this chicken look so good." They made themself a full plate of drumstick and biscuits and didn't leave a single crumb behind.

"Liz, look over there. Can you see them?" Ma pointed at a duck and her ducklings wading through the marsh in an orderly line. One duckling was left behind and tried their best to zip through the water to catch up. A faint smile played on your face. Ma started wiping your hands with a moist towelette. "We did a good job today, didn't we, Liz?"

# 10

My world turned upside down when the leaves began to turn colour. There was very little room inside my mother, and the only place I could nestle my big fat head was her pelvis. Ma was annoyed by this and for good reason. The pressure of my body sat right on her bladder, which felt much like a urinary tract infection. Each time she'd go for a pee, a tiny hot trickle would sprinkle the surface of the toilet water. As well, her legs were starting to feel like they were not screwed properly into their sockets. Like jars of mayo with the lids not properly sealed. Each time she took a step with her right foot, a sharp pain shot up her lower back.

Despite this, Kimberley affirmed that this was a victory as she palpated Ma's belly in her office. "Wonderful. Looks like the head's engaged. That's a good sign. See this?" I could feel Kimberley's thumb and middle finger grasp my rump. "This is your baby's buttocks." She positioned herself so that Aroos, her student, could see.

Aroos shifted left and right to watch the process of assessing my position. She pointed to a pointy bulge at the side of Ma's abdomen. "And look, here's their tiny fist."

Kimberley's finger ran over the top of my hand and I flinched. They all gasped. "Wow! We've got a real wiggler here."

"Definitely. Lots of kicking."

I felt Kimberley's Pinard horn press against my back to listen to my heartbeat. "Have you given any more thought to your birth plan, MG?"

"Yes," Ma lied.

Kimberley called her bluff. "So what will happen with Liz? I know she's been enjoying the day program. But who will care for her during your labour? And more importantly, do you have people in mind who will care for you? A birth partner? A doula?"

Ma did her best to shirk off the conversation. It's not that she hated planning. She hated planning this birth. If she planned for the birth, it would make this all real. Perhaps if she never discussed this with anyone, I would forever be nothing more than a bump in her belly and a figment of her imagination.

But I was becoming more and more real every day. While brushing her teeth, Ma saw a strange lump at the top of her enormous abdomen. When she touched it, she tickled my foot and I tucked them back into myself and turned slightly. The sensation of me rotating made Ma feel like she was riding an invisible roller coaster. Ma spat out her toothpaste, then vomited into the sink.

Tita Connie insisted there be a baby shower, and the only reason Ma agreed to it was that she reassured Ma that she would not have to lift a finger or plan the occasion. To make things easier for you, Tita Connie decided to host the small party in your home. This way Ma could celebrate for longer, and if you needed to nap, your bedroom was nearby.

The entire event seemed like a ridiculous idea. Ma didn't really know anyone because she barely had time to socialize. Who the hell would even come all the way to Scarborough? Ma invited Ash out of obligation really. It's not that she didn't want them there. She just didn't want these two worlds colliding: the religious Filipinos in her life and her new friend who liked to wear shirts with illustrations of unicorns humping each other. It felt like a recipe for disaster. That said, Ash was not only instrumental in Ma staying in your home, they were a calming presence in your life, and Ma knew she could count on them to help with managing you, if ever you became too anxious with all the visitors on the day.

But it wasn't you who was anxious. It was Ma. She cleaned the house even though Tita Connie insisted she would do it for her. It was the only way Ma could release the growing agitation inside of her. Surfaces were wiped clean, then wiped again. Age-old stains on the carpets were treated and blotted even though Ma knew there was no hope of removing them.

You, on the other hand, felt as right as rain. You blared your new cassette tape player in your bedroom while you applied your lipstick in the mirror.

Ma stood by the doorway and shifted from one swollen foot to the other. Over the sound of Smokey Robinson and the Miracles, Ma shouted nervously, "There will be people here, okay? New people. Don't be scared, okay?"

You calmly adjusted the shoulder pads of your midi dress. "I can't wait to give everyone a twirl!"

Still, Ma prepared for the worst. If you had an episode where you were suddenly suspicious of everyone around you, Ma would ask Ash to take a walk with you to the marsh. She even created a just-in-case picnic of sandwiches and juice boxes that was packed in a small cloth lunch bag in the fridge. If one of the Filipinos made an insensitive comment, she would steer the conversation to more pleasant, neutral ground, like the weather. Or possible baby names. Or sports. No. Not sports. Or maybe it would be best to just keep everyone in separate rooms.

The anxiety became more acute once Tita Connie was dropped off by Tito Remy and she began decorating the run-down house with streamers, banners and balloons.

"These were the only ones in green and white," Tita Connie said while standing on a stool and stringing up a large pompom to the ceiling lamp. "I told the lady I didn't know if the baby was a boy or a girl, so . . ." Ma winced from her passive-aggressive comment. Tita Connie had been perplexed by why Ma didn't want to know my gender. Yes, it was because it didn't really matter. But the less Ma knew about me the better. The entire reality of birthing a new being into this world wasn't a thought she wanted to entertain. After the loss of the last baby, it felt too optimistic to believe I was actually coming.

To make matters worse, Tito Remy returned to the house. Ma had thought he wasn't attending. But he had just gone to the grocery store to get the ice Tita Connie had forgotten to pack in her catering supplies. This was not good. Tito Remy didn't seem as open-hearted to your identity. This party was definitely going to be a disaster.

Ma was on the toilet for the millionth time that day when she heard the front door open. This was not supposed to happen. The success of the day relied on her being at the door at all times to facilitate awkward intros and point everyone to the games Tita Connie had set up for everyone to enjoy. Ma rushed to the kitchen to find Ash and Tita Connie laughing. Tita Connie was busy plugging several different slow cookers into outlets, and Ash was shredding carrots on the counter.

"MG, can you believe Tita Connie made the pancit vegan just for me?" Ash shook the shredder clean, picked up the pile of carrot shavings and put them into the frying pan along with the cabbage.

"Oh. That's nice." Ma cautiously looked through the clear lids of the slow cookers and saw that the kare-kare, kaldereta and dinuguan were already made. Even the lumpia sat in neat piles on a hot plate. An aluminum tray had skewers of pork, still uncooked. Finally finding a sense of purpose, Ma said excitedly, "I can start the barbecue outside and get these on the grill, Tita."

"Don't worry about it. Your Tito Remy already preheated the grill."

As if on cue, Tito Remy entered the kitchen from the back door, waved at Ma, then looked at Ash. Ma's cheeks turned red. "Hello. I'm Remy."

Ash smiled and shook Tito Remy's hand. "Hi, I'm Ash."

"Oh, Ash. Nice to finally meet you. Thank you for your help with our MG."

"Of course."

Tito Remy took the aluminum tray and headed outside to cook. Ash looked at Ma, pointed to Tito Remy and Tita Connie and mouthed the words "So cute!"

Ma scowled and was about to head out the back door to ensure Tito Remy would barbecue the pork until the fat was caramelized (she hated underdone pork), but she heard the front door open again. Her armpits were suddenly damp.

"Helloooooo!" sang Danah, holding a twelve-pack of off-brand soda in each arm. She put them on the foyer floor as she helped her mother Verna in. They wore matching outfits of floral blouses and capri pants. "Please excuse the beverages. I would have brought something more substantial, but Connie told me not to."

"Connie? How do you know—"

"Danah! Verna! You made it." Tita Connie took off her apron and embraced them both. "We didn't see you last week when we picked up Liz and MG at the day program. I was worried you wouldn't make it."

"I wouldn't miss this for the world," Danah said.

Ma racked her brain wondering when in the world these two would have crossed paths, since the pickups were fairly quick in nature.

"MG, can you believe it? Danah and Verna go to Blessed Sacrament too. I saw her at church and was like, 'Hold the phone . . . is that the same lady?' Remember?" Tita Connie hit Danah's arm playfully.

Danah hit her arm back. "And then I saw you at No Frills the day after!" Ma squinted at the uproarious laughter. "I just knew the universe was telling us to have coffee together, so we did."

Tita Connie waved her hand at Danah trying to remove her mother's shoes. "Don't bother. We're all heading out back to enjoy the sunshine."

Since when?

In the backyard Tita Connie shooed Ma away from the punch bowl and assured her that people could serve themselves. "Just relax, ha?"

Ma tried her best to do so even though the lawn chair she chose was uneven at the legs and tilted back and forth over the buckling patio stones.

"Hello?" said a familiar voice. Rhea and her husband, Manny, rounded the corner of the house. A bit of brush caught on Rhea's hair and she pulled her long braid free with a sheepish smile. Ma tried to get up, but Rhea waved her hand. "Don't! I'll come to you!" She couldn't resist and hoisted herself off the chair. Rhea was exactly the same armful as the last time they'd embraced. How on earth did she maintain her weight?

"You look beautiful, mare."

"I'm fat now."

"Oh, stop!" Rhea giggled, then turned to Manny. "Manny, this is MG."

Manny was even shorter than Rhea but just as cute. He pushed his frameless glasses up his nose bridge before kissing Ma on the cheek. "Congratulations."

Ma was uncertain what to do now, with all of these people from different corners of her life occupying the same space. Even with the open air of the backyard, they all felt too close to one another. Too many opportunities for the wrong thing to be said. Still, they all managed to mingle without her help. Tito Remy showed off his barbecuing skills to Ash. Manny updated Tita Connie about a job prospect at a bookkeeping company. Danah shared stories about travelling to the Dominican Republic with Rhea. You and Verna served as deejays, slipping random cassettes into the player, playing a song for thirty seconds, then switching to another. Ma tried her best to enjoy her food, but the squares of pork had gone cold with her worrying.

In the midst of all this pleasant conversation, Tita Connie stood up. "Hoy. Remy. Go to the car and get the things."

"The what?" Tito Remy said cluelessly.

"The *things*." Tita Connie gave a stern look.

Tito Remy began patting his jeans for his car keys and switched to Filipino as if Ma could not understand. Holding his newly found keys in his hand he said, "Where did you put it all?"

"Underneath," Tita Connie said in English.

"Where?"

"Under. NEATH."

Tito Remy ran . . . well . . . his arms pumped harder, but his legs were just as slow . . . to the car and returned with several gift bags. Ma scratched at her neck. The lesion was long gone, but her nails chiselled away at her skin trying to find it. The gifts were placed at her feet and everyone applauded. Danah added to the haul with a silver envelope. Rhea reached behind her lawn chair and produced a wrapped box. Ma stared at the collection for a long while, holding her breath. Why would this happen? Why would people be so generous to her? She worried how inconvenient it must have been for Tita Connie to organize this, shop for the food. How difficult it must have been for Rhea to drive here on her day off when she was still getting settled with her husband in Canada. She worried about Verna and you and how uncomfortable it must have been to meet all of these new people and have your daily schedule be turned upside down.

"Aren't you going to open them?" Ma turned to see you smiling at her. You had pressed stop on your cassette player and the silence was thick in the air. "Go on. Everybody's waiting. It's not every day a girl turns thirty you know." Everyone laughed. Laughed at you? No. Scanning the crowd, Ma saw everyone looking at her, smiling. She knew if she were to open the gifts, their love for her would become real. Their joy for her, for her new baby, would become real. I would be real.

One by one she dared to look at each present. A cloth baby carrier. Onesies. A snowsuit. Packs of diapers. A diaper bag.

"I got you a gift certificate," Danah explained as Ma opened the silver envelope. "I always say, don't buy things like strollers or cribs until you meet the kid."

Ma moved on to Rhea's wrapped box and ripped open the paisley-printed paper. Inside it was a digital camera. "Mare. This is too much."

"It's not for you. It's for me. I want all the pictures emailed to me," Rhea said jokingly.

One last bag remained. Ma removed the golden tissue paper and found a set of newborn shoes.

"It's faux leather," Ash explained as Ma thumbed the purple elephant shape stitched on the top layer of blue. Ma swallowed hard. Newborn shoes for newborn baby feet. A real baby. A live baby. A baby was going to be born and it was okay to believe it was true.

In the fog of the in-between place, I looked down and saw that my feet were all grown up. I was wearing the shoes, but they were adult size. The elephant appliqués and the booties themselves were a subdued grey. I found myself in a field of green surrounded by rolling hillside. I could feel the early-morning sun on my face. I had a face. I wanted so badly to look in the mirror, but where would I find one? I looked around.

What was that sound? I followed it. Step by step through the damp grass, the sound became clearer. Clapping. Cheering. A long table was set. Long enough to stretch to the horizon. Lola Daning was there sporting her fanciest terno, with butterfly sleeves crisp and her hair coiffed high. Lolo Ruben and the one that was lost were there, both smiling ear to ear, both wearing barong tagalog. There were faces there that I did not recognize. I knew they were people from long ago. Weathered faces. Smooth faces. Teeth. No teeth. Beaded fabrics. Multicoloured textiles. Heavy headdresses and dangling earrings. Closer to the front end of the table there were those without faces. I knew they were Maybe Babies. Even though I could not see their eyes, I knew they were wishing me well too.

I approached the table. I listened to their rhythmic clapping as I scanned the feast. All desserts.

The clapping died down after one final cheer. Everyone sat down and placed napkins on their laps. Lola Daning stroked my cheek and said, "Come. You eat now."

"What for? What are we celebrating?" I asked.

"All the things you get to do. We've all lived wonderful lives and can't wait for you to experience it." Lola Daning gestured with her arms towards the length of the table, and my ancestors all nodded in agreement. "We cannot tell you the future, but we can tell you it will be an adventure."

"Really?" I asked excitedly.

"And sometimes it will be boring. And scary. And sad. And happy. There will be times you will feel alone, but we will always be here, watching, guiding you for as long as you will listen."

"I promise I will." My ancestors laughed at this.

"You say that now, but even your mistakes will lead you in the right direction. Trust us." Lola Daning sat back and cooled herself off with the wave of her woven fan. "Okay. Enough for now. Let's eat. Your time is almost here."

I did as she said. For what felt like hours, days, we feasted, and magically, the food never ran out. I dug my fork into the perfect layers of buttercream and cashews of a Sans Rival cake. I bit through the soft circles of sponge and mango jelly in a pianono. I felt my brain freeze with every bite of halo-halo with massive scoops of ube ice cream on top. I crunched through turon fresh from the frying pan. I licked my fingers of jackfruit. I slid my fork across the tender flesh of papaya. I felt juice run down my arms to my elbows as I sucked the fibre off mango seeds. I ate and ate until I felt my stomach turn.

The crowd suddenly became quiet and looked at me with warm smiles. There was a shift. The table was empty and I was alone. The morning sun was now high above my head and I had to close my eyes from its bright light.

*

Meanwhile, in the physical realm, Ma was overwhelmed by the need to nest. With the help of Tito Remy and Tita Connie, Justin's office items were moved to the basement and his desktop computer was put in the corner of the kitchen. This made space for the crib and a second-hand toy box. Tito Remy assembled a new chest of drawers. Ma was too frustrated to fold the baby clothes, since they all came in random sizes. So she settled on hanging the larger items in the closet and tossing the smaller ones in the drawers. Tita Connie painted over the walls in a creamy yellow, which Ma selected herself.

There was a manic energy coursing through Ma's body. Like she was unstoppable. I had since moved positions and the sharp pain in her back was gone. The nausea passed and she had an appetite again. With her swollen feet back to normal, Ma would take long walks with you, even as the weather began to turn cold. You didn't complain. You'd just put on your rainboots and splash in the cold puddles or you'd collect the leaves and show Ma your finds.

One day, the energy was almost unbearable. It felt like there was nothing Ma could do to get rid of the sunshine inside of her. She felt so happy she could slap somebody.

"Let's go on an adventure!" Ma said before you all suited up in your autumn wear and headed out. The wind was picking up and the new saplings by the bus stop wavered with each gust. The bus was empty, save for the very back seats where two teenage girls brushed out their blond hair and chatted loudly about how cute their math teacher was. When their chatter turned to whispers, Ma turned her head towards them, knowing that they were most likely talking about you. Sure enough, they were. Unabashed side glances, with the occasional snicker. Although she was already sweating, Ma's face grew hotter still. She undid the nautical buttons on the front of her peacoat so that she could turn around and glare at them. This only made the girls snicker more.

"What are you looking at?"

You looked back and shook your head. "Oh great, Jane. We've made friends." Thankfully, they got off early in the ride, close to a nearby high school, but not before you both flipped them the finger. Well . . . you blew into your thumb and lifted your middle finger as if inflating it into its vulgar position. Ma playfully joined in. As the bus drove off you banged on the window and flipped them the bird one more time.

Ma thought she saw a library and pulled the bus cord to be let off.

"Stay behind the white line, please," said the driver. But Ma could barely contain herself. She thought of all the books she could borrow. A pastry cookbook? She had been wanting to try making pies. Or maybe she could borrow a romance novel to help colour her imagination during her masturbation sessions?

As they approached the library, Ma realized it was not in fact a library. It was a community centre. She would have been disappointed if it weren't for the sight of a haggard man with a flannel shirt enjoying a smoke outside. He stubbed out his cigarette on the bottom of his shoe. The combination of the tobacco and the smell of a passing diesel truck triggered Ma's memories of the Philippines. It smelled just like Manila. The man walked down a set of steps to the side of the community centre, under a sign that read "Pins and Needles." Beside the orange lettering in curvy 1970s font was the shape of toppled-over bowling pins. Ma tugged on your jacket sleeve. "Let's go!"

Downstairs in the five-pin bowling alley, you took off your raincoat and threw it onto the worn blue carpet before wandering to the snack bar. Ma pointed to the shelf of shoes. "Size six for me and size twelve for her."

"For her?" the Asian lady behind the desk said, looking suspiciously at you.

Ma leaned in and in a firm voice said, "Yes. You heard me. For *her*."

The sound of the pins being knocked over was intoxicating. The fact that she did not have to run to the back of the alley to reset the frame was even more thrilling. Even though she had not played since she was in San Marcelino, Ma was earning nothing but strikes. You clapped while she happy-danced.

You had a ton of fun mainly because Ma would cheer for you even if you rolled a ball into the gutter, even if you rolled the ball using your feet. As long as you didn't drop the ball or hurt yourself, Ma cheered for you.

At this point, Ma was even more sweaty. "Stay here. I'm going to go pee."

On the toilet, Ma wiped herself and saw that the tissue was streaked with pink. "Oh no. Oh no."

Ma walked as fast as she could to the desk. "I need your phone."

The manager held up their hand. "We don't let people use the—"

"GIVE ME THE PHONE!" Ma stepped away from the desk to show her belly. "It's an emergency."

Kimberley's voice was all smiles. "This is great news, MG. That was your bloody show. Looks like you'll be in labour soon."

"Really?"

"Really. Your due date is just three days away, so it makes sense this is happening now."

"I'm not losing my baby?" Ma's voice cracked, the image of a too-ripe mango splattered on concrete flashed through her mind.

"A bloody show is perfectly normal. If you start to get contractions, try to time them."

Ma did exactly that as you both made your way back to the house. Ma phoned Ash from the kitchen.

"How can this timing be any more perfect?" they said excitedly. "I just finished attending a birth. I'm going to have a quick sleep and make my way over."

"A sleep?!" Ma said a little too loudly.

"Yes. A sleep. I need some sleep. This last labour was forty-two hours."

"WHAT?!"

"Oh gosh. Don't worry. This labour was extraordinary. I'm sure yours will be fine. But I do need to rest first."

As Ma replaced the phone receiver in the cradle, she felt the surface of her belly tighten and a gnawing sensation turn in her pelvis. Thinking she was about to have diarrhea, she ran to the toilet and sat down. Nothing. *What the hell was that?* she wondered. *Was that a contraction?* She looked at her watch. It was one in the afternoon. Just in case, Ma found an old copy of the *Scarborough Mirror* in the kitchen. In the margins of the front page, beside an article about pee-wee hockey, she scribbled "1:07 p.m."

Throughout your nap, Ma paced the length and width of the house. The books she had borrowed from the midwives' clinic suggested walking as a way of bringing on labour. It worked. Sometimes. The gnawing at her pelvis grew in intensity as time passed, but there were some contractions that were light and short. By the time Ash arrived eight hours later, the *Scarborough Mirror* was marked in almost all the margins save for the last two pages.

"Hm. Your contractions are all over the place. Interesting." Ash put away the newspaper and helped get you to bed. They could see you were anxious and could read the energy in the room. "Nothing to worry about, Liz," Ash said while scrubbing your dentures. You stood beside them with your face forlorn and sunken. "We'll make sure she's okay." Ash exited your room once they tucked you in and whispered to Ma, "We would be so lucky if you gave birth while she was sleeping. But I doubt that will happen."

The contractions intensified until Ma was left speechless during each one, until a tiny pop was heard and boiling-hot water trickled down Ma's leg.

"Ow!" It really did burn on the way down to the carpet. "Oh no. I'm sorry. I got it all over."

"Of course you got it all over, MG. That's okay. I'll clean it up."

Another contraction. Another trickle of hot liquid. Ma

walked with her legs apart to the linen closet. "There are towels in here to wipe it up."

"MG. This isn't a mess. Your water just broke. You're fine. I'll take care of it. Really." Ash rubbed Ma's back.

Ash got on the phone with Kimberley. "Her water broke just five minutes ago. All right. One moment." They handed the phone to Ma.

Kimberley was all smiles. "Hi, MG. I'm going to stay on the phone with you until you have a contraction, okay?" One quickly came, crested until it was almost unbearable, until Ma's eyes felt like they would fall out of their sockets, then subsided. "Perfect. I will make my way over. Great job, MG."

Time was not making sense anymore. How soon was it after Ma hung up that Kimberley arrived? And what did Ash and Kimberley discuss? They looked right at Ma and said things. Lots of things. But the contractions were strong enough that Ma was making sounds she had never heard herself make before.

The room was too hot. Much too hot. She tried to remove her pants but realized she was already bottomless from when her water broke. She took off her shirt. She was buck naked now, wandering the house.

"Do you feel another one coming on?" Ash asked. Ma moaned and embraced Ash like they told her to and rocked back and forth. Slow dancing. The smell of clove on Ash's sweater made her angry. Their entire ensemble today made Ma upset. The scratchiness of the wool. The buttons on their overalls. The fact that their nails were painted. Did they paint their nails *before* coming to the house? They could have arrived earlier, but no, someone had to do their goddamn nails. The contraction ended and Ma released herself from their embrace sullenly.

Time marched on and Ma began to measure it in warm baths Kimberley drew for her, in contractions, in pee tests, in cups of raspberry-leaf tea. Did Ma watch Ash feed you breakfast? Then lunch? Then dinner? Ma looked at the clock on the stove as she walked the kitchen floor. Thirty-seven hours had passed.

Kimberley placed her Pinard on my mother's abdomen while she lay down in her bed. "Nice strong heartbeat. Whoever they are, they're quite content to stay in." Kimberley returned the long horn to her kit and smiled. "This is your first lesson in parenthood, MG. They come when they want to come. They take their own time about things."

Another bout of time passed. Kimberley's face changed. She put Ma on her bed one more time and snapped on some gloves. "Let's do an internal, okay?"

Ash held Ma's hands as Kimberley inserted her lubricated glove. I felt a finger slide around my forehead. First contact. It would have been a momentous occasion if it weren't for my screaming mother. The pain of the examination brought on another contraction.

Once it subsided, Kimberley put a hand on Ma's shoulder. "All right, MG. This isn't bad news. The baby's head is down, but the back of its cute little skull is facing your tailbone." Ma was delirious. "This explains why your contractions are all over the place. Usually the space between each one becomes less and less as time goes on. But in this case, because your baby's head is butting up against your tailbone, it doesn't make any progress."

"Will I have to get an operation?"

"We don't know yet. But for now, we will try our best to turn the baby around. We're going to help you as much as we can, all right?"

In the kitchen, Ash unfolded a small stepladder they sourced from the basement. "Thanks, Ash." Kimberley helped Ma slowly make her way to the ladder. The light was dim. Ma made a mental note to change the light bulb soon. "When you feel a contraction come on, I want you to put one foot up here." Kimberley patted the highest step, three feet off the ground.

The gnawing pain in her pelvis grew and Ma did as she was told, putting her right foot up on the ladder and enduring each contraction in a supported lunge. Ash held up Ma on her left. Kimberley on her right. In between each wave, Ma walked the house as quietly as she could, knowing you were still sleeping.

Ma watched the sun rise again. She watched Ash get you ready for the day. Feed you breakfast, lunch, dinner. You argued with Ash about things, confused about why strangers were in the house and why Jane wasn't speaking to you. Ma was much too delirious to comfort you. As she paced the house, she saw Kimberley asleep on the couch and Ash checking their email on the computer. The feeling of betrayal coursed through her body. Just seeing them look in the other direction made her furious. Every minute was focused on getting me out. How dare they think of anything else? How dare they eat? Laugh? Go to the washroom? Have any needs at all?

More time passed and it was dark and quiet. Kimberley did another internal and announced, "You just turned your baby around, MG. Congratulations." But Ma could barely hear her. By then, she was on the bed, deliriously tired. When the contractions came, Kimberley welcomed her to push. Ma was on all fours, bending her back into a curve, yelling for me to leave her.

"Don't hurt her!" you said as you emerged from your bedroom. Ash tried to usher you out.

"MG . . . I mean . . . Jane is okay. She's fine."

"Jane! Look at me. We can leave now if you want. I have a car outside!" you screamed.

"Liz," Ash tried to reason with you.

"No," Ma said weakly. "Let her stay. Liz. Come. Stay here. I'm okay. I'm okay." You knelt tearfully at the side of the bed and held one of Ma's hands as she continued to labour. At the side of her vision, she saw Aroos in the corner, readying blankets for the delivery. When did Aroos arrive? How long had she been there?

I felt Kimberley's fingers around the crown of my head. I could hear Ash's voice saying, "Push, push, push, push!" then Ma's exhale. In small increments I felt my body moving along the canal, then being sucked back in. Two steps forward, one step back until the cold air touched my scalp, until my face emerged into the world.

"Great job, MG. No more pushing. Just cough for me. Good. Did you want to catch the baby, Ash?"

"Yes, please."

Ash's fingers looped around my shoulder and gently pried me out of my mother's body until the entirety of me slipped out in one quick wave. Ash placed me onto my mother's chest. Ash was in tears. Ma was in tears. But I barely cried. I looked right at her, this woman I knew so well. This woman I have watched for ages through time, through natural disasters, through death, through heartache, through pleasure and pain. I looked right at her.

Ma laughed. "She's looking at me like she knows me!"

I did know her. Her smell. Her eyes. She ran her finger along the fuzzy down of my shoulders. She looked at the lines on my palm. The curve of my ear. She touched all of these parts of me. I was a real baby.

You watched Kimberley and Aroos weigh me. Kimberley placed me in a pouch and Aroos lifted me with the hook of a scale. Seven pounds, nine ounces.

"Did you want to hold her, Liz?" Ma said gently. You nodded, unsure about all this activity in the house. You sat at the end of the bed. Ash positioned a pillow on your lap, then placed me, tightly swaddled and asleep, into your arms.

"Well. Aren't you something?" you said through tears.

And I was. I was finally something. I was finally someone.


So here I am, Liz. And there you are, looking over the edge of my crib trying to make sense of who we are to each other. In the twilight of my memories of where I came from and the twilight of your memories of your time on Earth, I am here to tell you what I know.

When you are long gone, I cannot promise you that I will recall our time together. As I grow older, you will be but a story my mother will tell me about the woman in the picture on the mantel. She will tell me about Liz, the artist, the trailblazer. About the unlikely friend she found in you. The adventures you had together.

What I can promise you is this: there are Maybe Babies inside of me now, witnessing you, the light of you, and there are Maybe Babies inside of them that will keep your legacy alive well after your last breath.

I know you search people's faces, to confirm your ramblings, to affirm you of where you are, who you are, what is happening. I see the fear in you when people do a bad job of playing along or correcting you. But I am here to tell you that you have a place, Liz.

At that long table where I sat with my ancestors, where I feasted with all those who came before me, my Lola Daning put a hand over mine and gave me this message. She placed her words along the lines of my palms so that I would not forget, so that I would not lose them in my journey here to you.

She told me that there is a chair at the table, if you want it. It is a comfy chair, with a soft seat and armrests for your weary bones. They will reserve a place setting for you, with a plate made of the finest porcelain, framed on all sides by the finest silver cutlery. There will be a place setting reserved for you, with Polly sitting next to you on your right and Jane to your left. All three of you can enjoy a feast that never runs out, food that never goes cold. You will be welcome there, at this long table stretching out to the horizon, where you can exchange stories with my people, and never live in fear and uncertainty again.

They are waiting for you and will welcome you when you are ready.

# EPILOGUE

Ma is determined to make this baby tuxedo fit, but the buttons are about to bust over my growing belly. She goes to my bedroom closet and looks at other options. She had bought the tuxedo onesie specifically for this occasion. Should she prioritize the look or the fit? I make the decision easy for her by spitting up all over the pretend cummerbund.

"Oh no!" Ma sighs heavily and pulls a ballerina onesie off its hanger. Perfect. I love that thing. The mini tutu really shows off my thick thighs. The queers are going to love my Pride ensemble.

I'm placed into my car seat at your feet where you wait quietly in the foyer, wearing a floor-length beaded gown and a tiara. Over the last while, you've stopped waving and talking to me. Today, you still manage to give me a brief smile. I smile, too, hoping it will make you laugh. Making people laugh, or whine, or question their life's purpose is my superpower after all. No luck with you today, though. You're already in your faraway place.

"Let's take a picture before Ash gets here." Ma stands back a few feet and points the camera at us. "Dina! Dina! Look at the camera, Dina."

Oh yeah. That's my name. I'm not used to it yet and seriously doubt my mother's taste. I smile. Flash.

I can hear Ash driving in before Ma announces it. I can't stand that car. The smell of it. The sound of it. I am in tears as they buckle my car seat into place. Ma buckles you up beside me. You put your hand over mine and I calm down. The car starts and Ma says, "Okay, Dina. I'm going to play some ballet music." She changes the radio station from alternative rock to classical.

Oh great. I know what she's doing. She's trying to make me sleep. She's trying to give me a nap before we get there. Ha! No way. I'm going to stay awake, lady. I'm just going to look outside at the trees whizzing past the car window. That's right. Look at me. Staying awake. Impervious to her manipulation!

Wait. Where am I? I feel Ma buckling me into the baby carrier strapped to her torso and pulling my tutu through the leg holes. Shit. She did it again. I fell asleep. What a sneaky lady. At least she has positioned me facing out instead of facing in like a chump. I love looking out and seeing things. I'm tasked to learn most of what I need to know before the age of two, so this position is essential to my cognitive development.

We begin traversing a street crowded with people. You are being guided by Ash to our right. Somewhere close by I can hear the thumpa-thumpa of dance music. A throng of shirtless men pass us, smelling like coconut oil and sweat.

An old woman with a purple cowboy hat coos at me. She sits at her sales stand where a display of dick-shaped water bottles sparkles under the hot sun. I see an alleyway where a drag queen waits for their turn to perform. A host stands on a raised platform stage and shouts into the microphone, "Who's ready for more show?! I can't heeaaaaar youuuu!" The crowd cheers.

We turn right down a quieter street, towards a small but stately yellow-brick building. Inside, a woman with short grey hair and funky glasses greets you with her arms open wide.

"Liz! You made it. It's me. Nancy." You nod silently. There is a small look of disappointment on her face, but she shakes it off and gives a wide smile to Ash and my mother. "Are you two ready?"

Ash puts their arm around Nancy. "I've been looking forward to this since spring when you told me this was happening. I can't believe it's finally here."

"Well, everyone is upstairs waiting for you all. Did you want to take the elevator? I have the keys if you need it."

"Sure. That sounds good. Is there room for all of us?"

"Yup. Let me get the key."

The elevator doors open to a hive of activity. I kick my legs in excitement. All of these faces. Young and old. Skinny and fat. All these shades of pink, brown, black. I love smiling at the most sullen ones. I love frowning at the ones who ask me to smile. I'm not your monkey.

"Aw! Look. The baby has a tutu!" says the bartender, who is serving martinis to a short line of attendees.

Nancy moves towards the corner of the room and bangs a dessert spoon on the edge of her martini glass. A volunteer hands her a wireless microphone. "Can I get your attention, please." The room falls silent, except for me. I'm a baby. I can make noise if I want to. "Thank you so much for joining us. Today was months in the making. It is a great honour for us here at the LGBTQ archives to celebrate the work of Liz Cahill, revolutionary artist and activist in the trans community. Although her documentary work transformed the ways in which the mainstream understood our way of life, time and illness robbed us of some of her most beautiful contributions. I would like to welcome Ash Amrani to say a few words."

Ash sits you down on a chair and takes the microphone. A bit of feedback. I copy the sound of the feedback and everyone laughs. I smile. Everyone laughs harder. I'm a natural entertainer. "Good afternoon, everyone. It's my honour to welcome you to today's screening. The film you are all about to see would have been lost had it not been for the love and care that MG Concepcion gives to Liz." I hear Ma gasp. I see the crowd move their gaze towards her as Ash continues. "Liz changed many lives, mine included. Those of us who followed her illustrious career as a filmmaker knew that she was in the middle of her most ambitious project yet when her health worsened. Many of us did not even know her whereabouts, let alone the status of that project. It has been an honour to maintain a relationship with her because that meant I got to cross paths with this amazing woman, MG. If it had not been for her foresight in saving Liz's raw footage from floods in her home, we would not have been able to edit together what Liz managed to shoot. I want to also thank the arts councils who sourced Liz's original grant applications for this project so that we could better understand what her vision was for the documentary she never completed herself." Ash turned their focus to you. You were looking down at your shoes. Ash spoke through a lump in their throat. "Liz. Although it is not the full-length film you had imagined, we've been able to piece together a short offering that feels as complete, as full, as alive as our love for you." Applause.

During the screening in the adjacent auditorium, I do not look at the images projected onto the white wall. No. I suck my fist and peruse the many faces in that room, watching your life work unfold in front of their eyes. Some people hold hands with one another. Some people cry. There is lots of laughter.

Liz. Even though you are far away in your mind, I want to tell you what I see because it's important for you to know. When the lights come back on, they stand for you. They give you a standing ovation. The applause continues long enough that I take my fist out of my mouth and I manage to clap my own chubby palms together. This is for you, Liz. The first time I clap my hands is to cheer you on.

# SALAMAT

How can I write this acknowledgement page without crying?

First, I must thank the original Sulong Theatre Collective, whose work in making our theatre show, *Future Folk*, helped inspire the shape of this book. Thank you, Karen Ancheta, Aura Carcueva and Romeo Candido for that grassroots research we did together, with support from Haniely Pableo, Marie Beath Badian and Lisa Codrington.

Thank you to the countless Filipinx caregivers we interviewed during that time. I will never forget the honour of performing for you all and allowing you to see yourselves onstage. I hope this book gives you the same sense of affirmation. You matter in this world.

Thank you to Ate Ruth for sharing your stories with me. You deserve a life of rest and respect.

Thank you to Ate Pinky, whose smile and determination inspire me.

Thank you to my accountability team: Charlie Petch, Kusha Dadui and Donna-Michelle St. Bernard. You challenged me to be better and I am grateful.

Thank you to my chosen sister, Charm, whom I love and respect deeply. Thank you for being the bridge to our homeland and for correcting my awful Tagalog in the manuscript. Know that Helen is a caricature of me and I am grateful you suffer through my horrible pronunciation like MG does.

To Jennifer Mother Effin Lambert. We did it again! Thank you for this opportunity to learn from you.

To my agent, Marilyn, for her endless hustle. I don't have the teeth to do what you do.

To my family, chosen and blood: I know who I am because of the love you have given me. Let us continue to live our lives, heart first.

To Mama Nancy and Uncle Raymond, for loving me.

Thank you to my supportive hubs, Nazbah Tom. You are always the first to hear my manuscript, one day's writing at a time. I could not have done this without you.

To my ancestors: thank you for guiding my fingers along the keyboard. This is our work. I will meet you at the table one day, but for now, I will continue saying what you want me to say.